PRAISE FOR CATHERINE BYBEE

WIFE BY WEDNESDAY

"A fun and sizzling romance, great characters that trade verbal spars like fist punches, and the dream of your own royal wedding!"
—Sizzling Hot Book Reviews, 5 Stars

"A good holiday, fireside or bedtime story."
—Manic Reviews, 4½ Stars

"A great story that I hope is the start of a new series."
—The Romance Studio, 4½ Hearts

MARRIED BY MONDAY

"If I hadn't already added Ms. Catherine Bybee to my list of favorite authors, after reading this book I would have been compelled to. This is a book *nobody* should miss, because the magic it contains is awesome."
—Booked Up Reviews, 5 Stars

"Ms. Bybee writes authentic situations and expresses the good and the bad in such an equal way . . . Keeps the reader on the edge of her seat."
—Reading Between the Wines, 5 Stars

"*Married by Monday* was a refreshing read and one I couldn't possibly put down."
—The Romance Studio, 4½ Hearts

FIANCÉ BY FRIDAY

"Bybee knows exactly how to keep readers happy . . . A thrilling pursuit and enough passion to stuff in your back pocket to last for the next few lifetimes . . . The hero and heroine come to life with each flip of the page and will linger long after readers cross the finish line."

—*RT Book Reviews,* 4½ Stars, Top Pick (Hot)

"A tale full of danger and sexual tension . . . the intriguing characters add emotional depth, ensuring readers will race to the perfectly fitting finish."

—*Publishers Weekly*

"Suspense, survival, and chemistry mix in this scintillating read."

—*Booklist*

"Hot romance, a mystery assassin, British royalty, and an alpha Marine . . . this story has it all!"

—Harlequin Junkie

SINGLE BY SATURDAY

"Captures readers' hearts and keeps them glued to the pages until the fascinating finish . . . romance lovers will feel the sparks fly . . . almost instantaneously."

—*RT Book Reviews,* 4½ Stars, Top Pick

"[A] wonderfully exciting plot, lots of desire, and some sassy attitude thrown in for good measure!"

—Harlequin Junkie

TAKEN BY TUESDAY

"[Bybee] knows exactly how to get bookworms sucked into the perfect storyline; then she casts her spell upon them so they don't escape until they reach the 'Holy Cow!' ending."

—*RT Book Reviews,* 4½ Stars, Top Pick

SEDUCED BY SUNDAY

"You simply can't miss [this novel]. It contains everything a romance reader loves—clever dialogue, three-dimensional characters, and just the right amount of steam to go with that heartwarming love story."

—Brenda Novak, *New York Times* bestselling author

"Bybee hits the mark . . . providing readers with a smart, sophisticated romance between a spirited heroine and a prim hero . . . Passionate and intelligent characters [are] at the heart of this entertaining read."

—*Publishers Weekly*

TREASURED BY THURSDAY

"The Weekday Brides never disappoint and this final installment is by far Bybee's best work to date."

—*RT Book Reviews,* 4½ Stars, Top Pick

"An exquisitely written and complex story brimming with pride, passion, and pulse-pounding danger . . . Readers will gladly make time to savor this winning finale to a wonderful series."

—*Publishers Weekly,* Starred Review

"Bybee concludes her popular Weekday Brides series in a gratifying way with a passionate, troubled couple who may find a happy future if they can just survive and then learn to trust each other. A compelling and entertaining mix of sexy, complicated romance and menacing suspense."

—*Kirkus Reviews*

NOT QUITE DATING

"It's refreshing to read about a man who isn't afraid to fall in love . . . [Jack and Jessie] fit together as a couple and as a family."

—*RT Book Reviews*, 3 Stars (Hot)

"*Not Quite Dating* offers a sweet and satisfying Cinderella fantasy that will keep you smiling long after you've finished reading."

—Kathy Altman, *USA Today*, "Happy Ever After"

"The perfect rags to riches romance . . . The dialogue is inventive and witty, the characters are well drawn out. The storyline is superb and really shines . . . I highly recommend this stand out romance! Catherine Bybee is an automatic buy for me."

—Harlequin Junkie, 4½ Hearts

NOT QUITE ENOUGH

"Bybee's gift for creating unforgettable romances cannot be ignored. The third book in the Not Quite series will sweep readers away to a paradise, and they will be intrigued by the thrilling story that accompanies their literary vacation."

—*RT Book Reviews*, 4½ Stars, Top Pick

NOT QUITE FOREVER

"Full of classic Bybee humor, steamy romance, and enough plot twists and turns to keep readers entertained all the way to the very last page."
—Tracy Brogan, bestselling author of the Bell Harbor series

"Magnetic . . . The love scenes are sizzling and the multi-dimensional characters make this a page-turner. Readers will look for earlier installments and eagerly anticipate new ones."
—*Publishers Weekly*

NOT QUITE PERFECT

"This novel flows extremely well and readers will find themselves consuming the witty dialogue and strong imagery in one sitting."
—*RT Book Reviews*

"Don't let the title fool you. *Not Quite Perfect* was actually the perfect story to sweep you away and take you on a pleasant adventure. So sit back, relax, maybe pour a glass of wine, and let Catherine Bybee entertain you with Glen and Mary's playful East Coast–West Coast romance. You won't regret it for a moment."
—Harlequin Junkie, 4½ Stars

NOT QUITE CRAZY

"This fast-paced story features credible characters whose appealing relationship is built upon friendship, mutual respect, and sizzling chemistry."
—*Publishers Weekly*

"The plot is filled with twists and turns, but instead of feeling like a never-ending roller coaster, the story maintains a quiet flow. The slow buildup of a romance allows readers to get to know the main characters as individuals and makes the romantic element more organic."

—*RT Book Reviews*

DOING IT OVER

"The romance between fiercely independent Melanie and charming Wyatt heats up even as outsiders threaten to derail their newfound happiness. This novel will hook readers with its warm, inviting characters and the promise for similar future installments."

—*Publishers Weekly*

"This brand-new trilogy, Most Likely To, based on yearbook superlatives, kicks off with a novel that will encourage you to root for the incredibly likable Melanie. Her friends are hilarious and readers will swoon over Wyatt, who is charming and strong. Even Melanie's daughter, Hope, is a hoot! This romance is jam-packed with animated characters, and Bybee displays her creative writing talent wonderfully."

—*RT Book Reviews,* 4 Stars

"With a dialogue full of energy and depth, and a twisting storyline that captured my attention, I would say that *Doing It Over* was a great way to start off a new series. (And look at that gorgeous book cover!) I can't wait to visit River Bend again and see who else gets to find their HEA."

—Harlequin Junkie, 4½ Stars

STAYING FOR GOOD

"Bybee's skillfully crafted second Most Likely To contemporary (after *Doing It Over*) brings together former sweethearts who have not forgotten each other in the eleven years since high school. A cast of multidimensional characters brings the story to life and promises enticing future installments."

—*Publishers Weekly*

"Romance fans will be sure to cheer on former high school sweethearts Zoe and Luke right away in *Staying For Good*. Just wait until you see what passion, laughter, reconciliations, and mischief (can you say Vegas?) awaits readers this time around. Highly recommended."

—Harlequin Junkie, 4½ Stars

MAKING IT RIGHT

"Intense suspense heightens the scorching romance at the heart of Bybee's outstanding third Most Likely To contemporary (after *Staying For Good)*. Sizzling sensual scenes are coupled with scary suspense in this winning novel."

—*Publishers Weekly,* Starred Review

FOOL ME ONCE

"A marvelous portrait of friendship among women who have been bonded by fire."

—*Library Journal,* Best of the Year 2017

"Bybee still delivers a story that her die-hard readers will enjoy."

—*Publishers Weekly*

HALF EMPTY

"Wade and Trina here in *Half Empty* just might be one of my favorite couples Catherine Bybee has gifted us fans with so far. Captivating, engaging, lively and dreamy, I simply could not get enough of this book."
—Harlequin Junkie, 5 stars

"Part rock star romance, part romantic thriller, I really enjoyed this book."
—Romance Reader

FAKING FOREVER

"A charming contemporary with surprising depth . . . Bybee perfectly portrays a woman trying to hold out for Mr. Right despite the pressures of time. A pitch-perfect plot and a cast of sympathetic and lovable supporting characters make this book one to add to the keeper shelf."
—*Publishers Weekly*

"Catherine Bybee can do no wrong as far as I'm concerned . . . Passionate, sultry, and filled with genuine emotions that ran the gamut, *Faking Forever* was a journey of self-discovery and of a love that was truly meant to be. Highly recommended."
—Harlequin Junkie

SAY IT AGAIN

"Steamy, fast-paced, and consistently surprising, with a large cast of feisty supporting characters, this suspenseful roller-coaster ride will keep both series fans and new readers on the edge of their seats."
—*Publishers Weekly*

Home to Me

Home to Me

CREEK CANYON, BOOK TWO

CATHERINE BYBEE

 Montlake

Text copyright © 2020 Catherine Bybee
All rights reserved.

Published by Montlake, Seattle

www.apub.com

Amazon, the Amazon logo, and Montlake are trademarks of Amazon.com, Inc., or its affiliates.

ISBN-13: 9781542009850
ISBN-10: 1542009855

Cover design by Caroline Teagle Johnson

Printed in the United States of America

*To every woman who has shared their personal story
with me.
You are loved.
You are worthy.
And you are strong.
Don't let anyone treat you otherwise.*

CHAPTER ONE

Erin kept a close eye on the clay target as it left its spring, flew through the air, and shattered into tiny pieces once Parker squeezed the trigger of the shotgun.

"Every time. How do you do it?" Erin was impressed. She'd only managed to hit one clay out of ten, whereas Parker had earned her nickname, Annie Oakley, in spades.

"Practice. You just started, give yourself some time."

They were in a location well up into Angeles National Forest at a shooting range. The place was dominated by testosterone with the occasional wife or girlfriend mixed in. Erin and Parker were the only women shooting without a man at their side.

"Let's throw out a few more and move over to the pistol range. Moving targets are harder. But I really want you to get the feel of how the shotgun kicks back so you can keep control of it." Parker was giving her lessons without the bucketful of questions anyone else would ask.

Erin had moved onto Parker's property at the end of the previous summer. Parker had been desperate to rent the guesthouse after surviving a fire that almost destroyed everything her family owned. And Erin had been just as eager to set up a new life far away from the main roads and close-knit neighborhoods of any big city. She wouldn't stick out in a town the size of Santa Clarita, nor would she be surrounded by the tourists and businesspeople that overran larger Southern California cities.

Erin had expected to find solitude, and what she found instead was a spectacular friend. A friend who realized Erin was hiding from her ex, but never once pushed to find out the details. No, Parker didn't pry. She simply told Erin that when she was ready, she would listen.

Even now, while shooting targets, or missing them as in the case of Erin's terrible aim, Parker could easily ask why she had a strong desire to learn how to shoot. Parker hadn't. Not once.

She handed Erin the gun with the barrel open and ready to load. This she'd figured out. Hitting shit with it . . . not so much. Although, if anyone asked, she'd say that even loading the weapon offered a certain amount of strength she didn't know was in her.

With her safety goggles on and her ears plugged with orange earplugs, *eyes and ears* as Parker called them, Erin placed the butt of the gun into her shoulder.

"Are you forgetting something?" Parker asked.

For a second, she paused, confused. Then she smiled and cocked the gun. The sound was hauntingly satisfying. It said *Don't fuck with me* with two solid clicks.

Parker smiled. "This time I want you to lean into the gun and stare down that barrel until you feel like it's an extension of your arm. You know the clay is headed to the left so don't aim to the right at all." She moved behind the pulley. "Whenever you're ready."

Erin took a deep breath, placed her finger on the trigger. "Pull."

Parker released the spring. An orange clay shot into the sky. She saw it fly past and knew she was going to miss before even squeezing the trigger.

The blast from the gun sounded in her ear and jolted her shoulder back with one action.

The undamaged orange clay flew until it hit the back of the hill to join all of its friends. Only then did it crumble.

Parker walked up behind her. "Shift your weight to your left foot." She put a hand on Erin's shoulder and gave a slight push into the weapon. "*Lean* into it."

Back in position, she took a few more deep breaths. *I can do this.*

"Pull."

Miss.

"Pull."

Miss.

"Pull."

Hit . . . Holy crap, she hit it. Erin felt like she'd won the lottery as a huge smile erupted on her face.

She sat the gun down and gave Parker a high five.

"Quit while you're ahead?" Parker asked. "Or try a few more?"

Erin put the gun down. "Let's try something smaller."

An hour later they were driving down the long canyon road smug in their marksmanship. Parker had been right. Shooting a pistol was a lot easier than the shotgun. Each plink of the metal targets was an exclamation point. Erin couldn't stop smiling.

"That was a lot more fun than I thought it would be."

Parker kept both hands on the wheel as she traversed the canyon switchbacks. "My dad used to take me out all the time. Said that since we had guns in the house, it was imperative that I know how to shoot."

"What about Mallory and Austin?" Mallory and Austin were Parker's younger sister and brother that she took care of after the passing of their parents three years before.

"Mallory went a couple of times, but didn't like it. She knows enough to be safe. Austin shot my dad's twenty-two when he was little. Now we try and come out here a couple times a year to get some practice."

"Did you guys ever hunt?"

Parker shook her head. "No. Shooting Bambi is one thing, shooting a rattlesnake is another. I guess if I got hungry enough I could. My dad did with his brother when they were younger."

Erin sighed. "I don't think I could ever shoot anything."

"Just knowing how isn't a bad thing. Knowledge being power and all that. For me, having something more than a baseball bat in the house after my parents died was a comfort. The world is a craptastic place sometimes. You can't turn on the news without seeing that."

Erin rubbed the side of her jaw where she hid a scar with makeup every day of her life. She knew how crazy people in the world could get. "Do you think it makes you paranoid?"

"Do I think *what* makes me paranoid?"

"Having a gun in the house?" Loaded and ready for anyone who might kick down the door with a gun of their own while you're sleeping to drag you back to the abuse and suffering?

Erin shook the image from her head.

"I lock the doors in case someone tries to break in. I have a fire extinguisher in case something catches fire. I have insurance in case the sky falls . . . Do those things mean I'm paranoid?"

"Those are a little different."

"Are they? Precautions and insurance. So far no one has ever broken into my house. The fire extinguisher wouldn't have helped in a forest fire, and the insurance has been my saving grace. Having a firearm to protect my family is only a safeguard." Parker paused. "And protect you, too, if I'm not mistaken. Which is why we came out here today." Parker's observation hit a little close to the mark.

The person she was safeguarding herself against had a face and a name that she was trying desperately to bury in her past. "And this is where I change the subject."

Parker laughed. "I didn't expect anything less."

Thirty minutes later they drove onto the gated property and past a crew of plumbers digging a long path across the land. The water main to the house had been washed downstream in one of the many flash floods they'd endured during the winter following the fire. Now that spring weather was finally at an end and the hot sun that defined

Southern California was out, Parker had hired the crew to fix the pipes permanently. A long fire hose connecting water from the city to the house had kept them from having to live somewhere else while they waited for the weather to cooperate.

For Erin, the inconvenience was minimal. They'd only had a cluster of days that they'd been without any running water at all. Considering the extent of damage to the property, she counted her blessings.

Colin, Parker's boyfriend, waved at them as they drove past the workers and up to the main house.

Parker beamed.

"When is he going to pop the question?" Erin asked.

"Cabo is in two weeks. I'm guessing I might come back with a little bling on my finger."

That was Erin's thought, too. Parker and Colin had been planning their Cabo trip since Christmas. Blue water, sandy beaches . . . It sounded perfect.

Parker put the car in park and opened the door. "I'll put my stuff away and come up to help you clean the guns," Erin told her.

"No worries. I was going to do that tonight. I want to spend some time with the crew and make sure they aren't messing up the new plumbing."

Erin shook her head. Parker was more hands-on than any homeowner she'd ever known.

Colin walked up the steep drive and greeted Parker with a kiss. "How did it go?"

"I hit two clays with the shotgun." Erin pumped her fist in the air.

"Better than I could do," Colin said.

Parker leaned into his side. "What Erin isn't telling you is how she made the metal targets her bitch with the Glock."

Erin smiled with the praise. "I'm not sure about the bitch part, but I did hold my own."

"She's shy," Parker said.

"I'm not the expert, you are. Have you seen her in action?" Erin asked Colin.

"Not with a gun," he teased.

Color filled Parker's cheeks.

Erin shook her head. "And on that note, I'm going to run to the store and post office. Do you need anything?"

"We're good." Parker opened the trunk of the car and removed her gun case.

After being told she didn't need to help unload the car, Erin walked across the drive to the path leading to the guesthouse. Even though the property was fenced and gated, not locking the door wasn't an option. And within the week, the security system was going in. Yet one more safeguard Erin was adding to her arsenal for preservation.

The small one-bedroom home was perfect for her. The living room and kitchen were one big space that had come furnished. Ideal since she left her previous life with two suitcases of clothing and the SD card of pictures from a cell phone.

Everything else had been left behind.

Everything and everyone.

In her bathroom, she washed the dust from her face and gunpowder from her hands. The thought of her hands not passing TSA had her grinning.

She glanced in the mirror and took a long look at herself. "One day at a time," she said to the air. She pulled the tie out of her thick hair and brushed it back into place before twisting it on top of her head. The red was fading fast, and her natural blonde was trying to show.

She hardly recognized herself.

But that was the point, wasn't it?

New look, new name, new home . . . new everything. She'd legally changed her name, social security number . . . Nothing was as it used to be.

She heard her phone ringing from the kitchen where she'd left her purse. The sound caught her by surprise. Very few people had her number, and as of yet, the telemarketers hadn't discovered her.

Caller ID said restricted number, so instead of answering it, she let it go to voice mail. After a minute, she pressed the playback button.

A familiar female voice brought gooseflesh to her arms. *"It's me. I have an update."*

All at once, every nerve stood on end and her sympathetic nervous system moved into hyperdrive.

Erin moved to her small dinette table, pulled out a chair, and sat down before the dizziness took over and she ended up on the floor.

Renee picked up on the first ring.

"Hello, Renee."

"It's so good to hear your voice. How are you? Did you try that coconut water yet?" Renee, her advocate, attorney, and savior, asked their coded question.

"I'm fine, and yes. The coconut water was delicious."

There was no coconut water. Or beet juice, or whatever organic food Renee came up with next. Didn't matter. The answer was always *yes* if Erin was safe and not being overheard. So far, she hadn't needed to respond with a *no*. God willing, she never would.

"You sound good."

"I'm a little better every day."

"Are you eating?"

Erin considered her diet, decided to keep things positive. "I'm a good five pounds overweight."

Renee huffed. "Lying sack of shit."

They both laughed.

"I'm good. Truly." She wanted to tell her that the sunshine was doing wonders for her, but that wasn't allowed. Renee didn't know where Erin was or even the name she was using. "Tell me the news."

Renee sighed. "None of it's what you want to hear."

Erin swallowed. "Are my sister and her family okay?"

"They're fine. I wouldn't have started with chitchat if they weren't."

Erin squeezed her eyes shut, felt the familiar pain in her chest with the memories of everyone she left behind. "Spit it out."

"You're not divorced yet," she told her. "And Asshat is seeking another hearing to contest the protection order."

Erin placed her head in her hand. "This is never going to end."

CHAPTER TWO

Matt shoved two heads of romaine lettuce into a bag while Jessie fondled the tomatoes. "Dude, just toss them in a bag and let's go."

"You want them to have flavor, don't you?" Jessie was about getting it right, and Matt was all about getting it done.

"I want to get this bought before we get a call," Matt said.

His crew split up when they hit the grocery store. Dressed in their blue uniforms, the four of them turned heads wherever they went. Late morning at a grocery store, and they became the target of a lot of smiling stay-at-home moms and flirting women . . . Sometimes these women were single, oftentimes they weren't.

Nothing attracted the ladies more than a man in uniform shopping for groceries. Since his crew worked twenty-four-hour shifts, it was up to them to cook their own meals, which always meant a trip to the grocery store. There were provisions at the station for breakfast and lunch, community food that they all pitched in and bought, but dinners were up to the individual crews.

Tonight it was going to be baby back ribs, baked potatoes, salad, and whatever else they could dream up and put on the grill.

Matt moved over to the potatoes and grabbed a bag instead of picking out individual ones. He looked over at Jessie, the rookie on the crew, and tapped his watch.

Jessie picked up his pace and set the produce in the cart.

Around the corner, Captain Arwin—his first name was Anton, but none of them called him by his first name—and Tom, the engineer on their crew, had their hands full of slabs of ribs.

They would make too much and hope they had time to actually eat it while it was hot.

The captain tossed the meat in the cart. Tom added a big bottle of barbeque sauce. "We still have rub at the station, right?" he asked.

"Yeah. I checked before we left," Matt told him. They grabbed a loaf of prepared garlic bread they could bake in the oven at the last minute and added milk and cookies before heading to the register.

Matt caught a smile from a twenty-something-year-old brunette pushing a cart in the next line over.

On autopilot, he smiled back before looking away.

"Can't take you anywhere, Romeo," Tom teased. Matt was the only single guy on their crew. Even Jessie, who was only twenty-three, was married with a baby on the way.

"I think Juliet was blonde."

Tom laughed and helped stack food on the belt.

"How you boys doing today?" The lady behind the register had to be in her sixties, but even she managed a smile that said what her mouth didn't.

The captain smiled with the clerk and kept the conversation going while they stacked groceries.

The minute Matt had told his family he wanted to be a firefighter, they'd given him hell. Well, humorous hell, but hell nonetheless. *What's the deal, Matt? Dating half the women in the valley isn't good enough, you have to add a uniform and make sure you have a chance with all the others?* Grace, the baby of the family, lit into him.

"Badge Bunnies will come out of the woodwork," his father had told him. As retired law enforcement, Emmitt knew the consequences more than most.

Then there was Colin, the oldest brother. "You have to make up for the fact that I'm the good-looking son."

His brother was taller, but Matt made up for it by spending time at the gym. In truth, they both didn't do poorly in the looks department. Their parents passed on some decent genes that gave them an edge in life.

They walked away from the register with a sigh of relief. They'd managed to get what they needed without a call, and the station was only five miles away. Outside the store, their truck took up the red zone space, their own personal spot wherever they needed to go. Tom walked around to the driver's side while Matt and Jessie shoved the bags inside the rig.

"Excuse me?"

Matt turned, saw the smiling brunette from the store walking toward him. "Yes?"

"You dropped this back there." She reached out, all smiles, and handed him a small business-size card.

"I don't think I—"

The card was pushed into his hand.

"I saw it fall out of your back pocket when you were reaching for your wallet."

Matt hadn't paid for the groceries. He glanced at the card, saw a name and a phone number on it with a big smiley face.

Jessie said something under his breath with a chuckle and jumped up into the truck.

"Right, ah . . . thanks."

She actually flipped her hair over her shoulder. He hadn't seen that move since high school. "You guys be careful out there."

"We will. Thank you." Matt waved the card in the air before tucking it into his pocket. A card he intended to toss in the trash the second he arrived at the station.

The woman turned around and walked away with a look over her shoulder.

"Coming, Romeo?" the captain asked.

Matt shook his head and climbed on board.

The second he shut the door, their radios went off.

At least they got out of the store with food before the call came in. Now they could only hope it wouldn't spoil before they could get it to the station.

They all put their headsets on so they could talk over the sirens. The Captain jotted down information, and Tom hit the lights and sirens before pulling out of the parking lot.

~

In order to be a voyeur, didn't the party being watched have to be naked?

Erin stood in the parking lot, eyes glued to the fire engine, or more importantly, the men climbing in. She secretly loved seeing Matt in uniform.

Watching the man smiling at another woman, however, was another thing.

Not that Erin invited his smiles.

No. That was the opposite of what she'd done since she met the man.

But he obviously didn't reserve his attention for just her.

Erin shook her head. No . . . voyeurs ogled the naked. What she was doing was stalking. Well, not technically, since she hadn't sought Matt out.

But she knew the station he worked at and Parker had told her he was working today, so when she saw the truck she waited outside in the parking lot for him to leave. Even that wasn't stalking. It was avoiding.

Nothing illegal about avoiding.

Matt watched the woman he'd been talking to walk away and then climbed into the truck.

Erin sighed.

He hadn't seen her. Good.

She stepped out of her car and jumped when the siren on the engine filled the air.

Once again she peered over at the massive red fire truck . . . engine, or whatever they called it, and felt her heart skip a beat.

Matt was running toward something.

What, she didn't know.

She really hoped it wasn't a fire.

And nothing dangerous.

Please, Lord, nothing dangerous.

She followed the truck with her gaze as it left her view, the noise following the lights.

For Parker and Colin's sake, she told herself. She hoped Matt was safe for them.

Ignoring the flutter in her chest, Erin lifted her chin and walked into the store.

~

An hour later, back in her tiny house, she searched the internet for any breaking news in the valley and didn't find anything. After twenty minutes of looking, she tossed her phone on the couch like it had grown too hot to hold.

"You're not interested," she chided herself.

She stood, went over to her refrigerator, and pulled out a bottle of sparkling water.

When she returned to the couch, her phone looked at her.

Okay, it didn't look, but it was there and telling her to pick it up.

She twisted the cap off the water, chugged it a little too fast, and found herself with the hiccups.

After the third time her diaphragm spasmed, she gave in and picked up her phone. She opened it and searched for emergency responses for LA County firefighters.

Ten minutes later, she found an app called PulsePoint and downloaded it.

"Payday!"

Within a few minutes, she was able to pinpoint Matt's station and discovered that he hadn't been called to a fire.

The call was labeled medical. The location was far up a local canyon.

She scrolled through the app and realized that most of the calls with the county, and especially in their valley, were medical.

That was a relief.

Not that she was interested.

She shook her head and moved into the kitchen. One look into the fridge and she decided she wasn't hungry. Instead of a late lunch, she grabbed an open water bottle and headed outside with her laptop. Even though it was Saturday she decided to get a few hours of work in.

As a freelance editor in the digital publishing world, she always had work.

And she was able to read at the same time.

Winning.

CHAPTER THREE

Even though Matt's crew didn't have to roll on every medical call, the bells and whistles inside the station woke him up throughout the night. There was an accident on the interstate that forced them out of bed and on the road at one thirty in the morning. By six thirty, he'd managed five hours of broken sleep, and by *broken* it was an hour here, two hours there, and a scattering of catnaps. Still, they signed off to the next shift, and Matt left the station in time for morning rush hour.

Within half an hour he was home, dropping his clothes on the bathroom floor, and stepping into the shower. Twenty minutes after that, he'd poured himself a bowl of cereal, finished his third cup of coffee for the morning, and dialed his brother.

Colin's groggy voice picked up on the fifth ring. "You do realize it's Sunday, right?"

"Some of us work for a living," Matt told him. "You said early. And it's almost eight."

"It's seven forty-five."

"Yeah, early. I want to hit Home Depot before all the weekend warriors get there."

"Call me back in an hour," Colin told him. And without another word, his brother hung up.

"Holy shit." Matt looked at the phone. "You did not just do that," he said to himself.

He took a few more bites of his breakfast, waited exactly five minutes . . . long enough for Colin to have fallen back to sleep, and dialed him again.

He answered on the second ring. "God, you're an asshole."

"I love you, too. Home Depot at eight thirty."

Colin moaned. "Nine."

"Fine."

This time they both hung up.

Matt tapped a finger on his phone, laughing.

Ten minutes past nine and he was pushing the orange cart through the home improvement store while his brother walked beside him holding a Starbucks as if it was a lifeline.

"This place is always a zoo." Colin shook his head and followed his brother around the store.

"Smells like weekend fun to me." They stood in front of the home security section, and Matt started tossing supplies he needed into the cart. "Things have changed a bit since I installed my system."

"I never felt the need to have one before."

Matt picked up an outdoor wireless camera that needed power but that transmitted the signal wirelessly. "That's because you don't work with the public as closely as I do. There's a lot of crazy in this town."

"I like my blissful ignorance." Colin glanced at the box Matt had just put in the cart. "I wonder if this will work all the way to the gate."

Matt shook his head. "It requires a wireless signal, the gate is what, a thousand feet from the house?"

"Give or take."

Matt handed him a different box. "You'll need this one and you'll have to run a wire all the way up."

Colin turned it over. "I guess that's why Parker never bothered."

"Major pain in the ass, but if I'm not mistaken, her yard is all torn up right now with the new water main."

Colin nodded, concentrated on the box for a full thirty seconds. "Yeah." He dropped the box in the cart, looked at the wall of wires. "We're going to need a lot of wire."

Matt laughed. "What happened to blissful ignorance?"

"For me." He reached for the wire. "This is to keep her safe. I can't be there all the time."

They filled the cart and kept talking.

"I'm guessing that once you two are married you'll be moving in with her."

"That's where my head is. We haven't really talked about it in depth. I should probably get a ring on her finger and set a date first."

"Cabo?" Matt asked.

"Cabo," Colin said with a nod.

"I'm happy for you. Parker is a great lady."

"I'm a lucky man."

Matt wasn't going to argue with that. Finding a flavor for the week, the month . . . a season was easy. Finding Mrs. Forever . . . not so much.

They pushed through the checkout line, out to the parking lot, and loaded up Colin's Jeep.

"Did you bring your truck?"

Matt pointed toward his motorcycle.

"Ahh, the real reason you needed to drag my ass out of bed early on a Sunday."

"My truck is at the dealership on a recall. I won't get it back until tomorrow."

Colin climbed behind the wheel. "See you at the house."

Matt sauntered over to his bike, pulled off the helmet he'd locked to the back, and placed it over his head. It was already hot and he wasn't going far, so he'd skipped the heavy jacket and took his chances. He swung a leg over the bike and fired it up.

Warm sunshine and wind brushed against him as he made his way onto the main street that cut through town. Damn, it was good to be alive.

~

Erin heard them arrive before she saw them. She looked out the window and noticed Matt pull up close to her place while Colin drove up the driveway of the main house.

She pushed down the nerves that always surfaced when Matt was around and opened the door to greet him.

"Good morning."

He took off his helmet and placed it on the seat. "What?" he asked.

"I said good morning."

His charming smile that made his eyes sparkle in the corners hit her square in the chest. Clean-shaven, perfectly trimmed soft brown hair, and hazel eyes. Kind eyes. The type that didn't turn dark right before the anger started.

She found her thoughts twisting and took a step back.

"Good morning."

"Did you guys get everything you needed?"

"I think so."

He walked toward her and it took everything in her to not retreat. Matt spent time at the gym. At least that was her assumption based on the span of his shoulders and the way his waist tapered to his hips. His arms filled out his short-sleeved T-shirt in ways that made women want to uncover the whole package.

Some women.

Not her.

Or so she kept telling herself. The strength behind all that muscle was intimidating.

He moved closer and she found an excuse to back away. "I made coffee and a coffee cake."

Matt stopped the second she was on the move.

"Coffee cake?"

"Yeah, sugar, flour, and a drizzle of frosting." She moved toward her front door.

"You had me at coffee, but I'd love to try your cake."

The innuendo made her smile along with him.

"I didn't mean that quite the way it came out."

Yeah, actually . . . she was pretty sure he had. He'd attempted to flirt with her on a half a dozen occasions over the past six months. Each time she did what she needed to do. She ignored his attention and pretended not to notice. As beautiful a man as Matthew Hudson was, he was a man . . . and she'd sworn off his entire species for life.

"You drink your coffee black, right?"

"You remembered?"

"One of my savant qualities."

Colin yelled across the lawn. "Hey, help me with this stuff."

Matt looked at her. "I'm going to . . ." He started walking.

"Go. I'll get the coffee and cake."

Inside the small guesthouse she'd occupied for less than a year, she forced her breathing to slow and her heart rate to calm down. Just the distance helped. This place had become her safe zone. A space where nothing bad had happened with no terrifying memories to sweep her back to her past. It was where she was healing. Every day she felt stronger. And with the security system Matt and Colin were going to install, she had another tool in her box of safety. One more weapon against ever falling prey again.

"Knock, knock."

Erin looked up to see Parker standing at her front door.

"Come in."

"They're here," Parker told her.

"I know. Matt already said hello."

Parker's snicker had Erin shaking her head. "Did he now?"

"Stop it."

Her friend walked into the kitchen and picked at the coffee cake Erin was slicing up. "You know he called at the butt crack of dawn."

"That wasn't necessary."

"He likes you. He wants to get here early and he'll make excuses to stay late just to earn one more smile from you."

"Shhh." Erin looked at the open door. "He'll hear."

"Oh, please . . . they're in the garage collecting man crap."

"That's funny coming from you."

Parker licked her fingers. "I had to learn how to use all the stuff my dad has in there out of necessity. They use it for fun. There's a difference. Men buy tools they don't need because they're cool, or maybe one day they'll need it. Women are like . . . nope, if I need it, I'll borrow from the neighbors."

"We do that with dishes." Erin removed two cups from the cupboard she'd filled with multicolored cups and plates.

"I don't. Well, shovels maybe. I did buy a lot of shovels this winter."

"That's because you needed them."

Every day had a physical exercise plan mapped out for anyone who lived or came near The Sinclair Ranch. The mudflow from the canyon left a mess that required big and small equipment to clean up. And while the largest of the excavators were long gone, the drifts of mud were still piled in plenty of spaces all over the property. Picking up a shovel and using every muscle available to clean up those mud drifts had everyone canceling their gym memberships.

Erin stopped short and stared out the kitchen window. "I just thought of something."

"What's that?"

"What kind of wedding gifts are you going to ask for? You already have everything you need, times two."

20

Parker picked up one of the plates filled with coffee cake and grabbed a fork. "I haven't even thought about it."

Erin remembered her own wedding and all the gifts.

Expensive gifts.

The kind rich people gave to other rich people to show off their wealth. There wasn't one toaster or Crock-Pot in the mix. The memory of a two-foot crystal vase crashing against the wall beside her surfaced and the spatula in her hand fell to the floor.

Parker put the plate down and placed a hand on her shoulder. "You okay? You're white as a sheet."

She sucked in air slowly, pushed it out. "I'm fine."

Parker picked up the spatula and bent to the floor with a kitchen towel to clean up the mess. "You were thinking about *him*, weren't you?"

She felt the blood returning to her head. "I was remembering a wedding gift."

"Remind me not to ask for whatever you were thinking of." Parker hesitated as she stood. "Wait, you were married? I thought he was an ex-*boyfriend*."

Matt's and Colin's voices carried in from outside.

"Another time." Erin dodged the question and plated another piece of cake. She ignored Parker's slack jaw and walked out the door with a hostess smile on her face.

"A little something to get you started," Erin said to them both.

Matt reached her first and took one of the plates. He looked her in the eye and his smile fell. "You okay? You're a little pale."

"I'm fine." She handed the other plate to Colin. "Coffee?" she asked him.

"That would be great."

She slid past Parker and back inside.

"You do that entirely too well," Parker whispered to her.

"Do what?"

"Pretend nothing is wrong."

Erin forced her hands to stop shaking as she poured two cups of black coffee. "Do you want some?"

Parker was silent.

Erin looked up, found her frowning.

"Sure."

She picked up both cups and headed back outside. "Cream is in the fridge."

~

Matt took his sweet time with the coffee, cake, and conversation. He was going to milk this day for as long as he could. Colin knew it from the look in his brother's eyes.

"I picked up sensors for all the windows and the doors, a motion detector for inside, and an outside camera we can mount facing the entry."

"I bought a camera for the gate," Colin added. "That's going to take a little more work and won't be in until we dig a longer trench."

"You mean we'll be able to see who is coming and going through the gate?" Erin asked.

"It will be wired with the monitor in the main house, not down here."

She tried not to show any disappointment. It would be nice to know who was coming and going. At this point, the only people who let themselves in were those who lived there, the handful of people that mowed the lawn, cleaned the pool, and read the meter . . . the garbage company and dozens of county public works employees over the past few months. So approximately half of Santa Clarita, give or take a few.

"How do you let people in from the gate now?" Matt asked her.

"I don't."

"The control is with the house phone," Colin told him.

"So what do you do when you have company? Give them the code?"

Erin looked at Matt. "I don't have company."

"What do you mean you don't have company?"

Her confession made her sound like the poster child for introverts. "I'm new here."

That seemed to help the expression of worry on Matt's face. "All we need to do is run a landline down here," Matt suggested. "But that means you'll hear it ringing when it isn't for you."

Erin shook her head. "I don't think that's necessary."

"What about when we're in Cabo? I know Austin will be in and out, but it might give you peace of mind to know who's driving through the gate."

Parker's younger brother, Austin, was in his final months of high school and had friends over quite a bit. So she could add half of the male teenage population to the list of visitors on the property.

"I think you should just stay up at the main house while we're gone," Parker said.

"Won't that cramp Austin's style?"

It was Colin that pointed out the obvious. "He's eighteen, you staying in the main house will deter any *Animal House*-type parties."

"I don't think Austin has it in him." Parker smiled at Colin.

One glance between Colin and Matt and they both shook their heads. "It's in him," Matt said with complete confidence.

"Fine. I'll stay in the main house and keep the peace."

"He can have friends over . . . just no parties."

"I get it," Erin assured Parker. Austin was a good kid, and his friends had always been polite. She didn't think there would be any problems.

Colin pushed back from the table and stood. "Well, are we going to talk about this all day, or get it done?"

"How long do you think this is going to take?" Erin asked.

"All day," said Matt.

"A few hours," Colin said at the same time.

Matt glared at his brother. "A few hours, to all day. Depends on . . ." He looked around, considered his next words. "Stuff."

Parker silently laughed.

"Okay, well, let me know if you need any help with the . . . *stuff*."

Once Matt and Colin were out of earshot, Parker leaned over and said, "Told you he'd make excuses to stay late."

Erin rolled her eyes as if she were blowing Parker's observations off.

Hours later, when they were planning dinner, her eyes didn't roll so flippantly.

CHAPTER FOUR

Matt and Colin made a pact to finish the job before cracking open the first beer or risk not completing their task. And just to ensure the day wasn't going to end when the work was done, Matt had texted Grace, and encouraged her to invite herself over for dinner.

His baby sister didn't disappoint. She'd called Parker after noon and said she was feeling left out. Parker, being Little Miss Hostess, gave her an open invitation to come by. Sometime after three, Grace showed up with a macaroni salad and strawberries. Next thing he knew, the women were mixing up margaritas. Only then did Matt pick up the pace so he and Colin could finish the job and join the fun.

He and his brother were walking back from the gate where they'd mounted the camera, but would have to wait until the rest of the trench was dug to run the wire, when they heard someone splash in the pool.

It was four thirty and the sun had started to move past the point of scalding closer to tolerable.

"Looks like the party got started without us," Colin said as they cut through the yard.

"I hope you have an extra set of swim trunks here."

"I have ya covered," Colin told him.

Matt craned his neck in hopes of seeing Erin in a bathing suit before she noticed him looking.

"Could you be more obvious?" Colin called him out.

"Yes, but our mother taught us better."

They laughed.

"I think you might be growing on her."

Matt didn't need Colin to clarify who the *her* was.

"You think?"

"Yeah, she didn't flinch from you once today."

Matt kept his voice low as they moved closer to the girls. "I also haven't been within two feet of her since this morning."

Colin nudged his arm. "Well, you're going to have to show her how to use the system, and that requires a cell phone and monitor tutorial. And since I'm part of the labor force, and not the education department, that's on you."

Matt wiggled his eyebrows. "Go find me those swim shorts. I do my best work shirtless."

Colin patted his side with laughter and walked up the path to the main house. He yelled over the music the women had turned on to catch Parker's attention. "Need anything inside? I'm changing."

Parker stood beside a blender they'd brought outside. "More ice."

Colin gave her a thumbs-up.

The splash in the pool had come from Austin.

Grace sat on the side, dangling her feet in the water, and Erin was missing.

Matt's mouth watered in anticipation of her in a swimsuit and hoped she was inside changing.

"All finished?" Parker asked as she poured a generous amount of tequila into the blender.

"That we are. The gate is going to need more attention, but you knew that."

Parker was all smiles. "Erin is going to be so happy."

He looked around again. "Where is she?"

"Inside changing."

Yeah, baby.

"Don't look so eager. You'll scare her off," Parker chided.

Matt forced his smile to fall.

"You want one of these?" Parker lifted a half-empty glass of margarita in the air.

"Absolutely."

She used his cue to push the button, and their conversation was cut off by the noise of the blender doing its thing.

". . . c'mon, you're not that much older than I am." Austin was treading water and talking with Grace.

"You're twelve," she told him.

"I'm eighteen."

Grace rolled her eyes with a wide smile.

"What's going on here?" Matt asked.

"Austin is hitting on me," she said with a sip of her drink.

Matt's mouth fell. "He's what?"

"Dude, look at your sister. She's hot."

The adolescent misplaced remark would have spiked hair on his neck if the kid were ten years older. Instead Matt shrugged and said, "It could work. Go for it."

Grace kicked her foot in the pool, splashing him with water. "Hey!"

That's when Erin emerged from around the corner wearing a sheer cover-up that tried to hide the bathing suit underneath. It failed. It was a black one-piece. The kind models wore for magazines that weren't labeled *Playboy*.

His mouth watered.

Those long legs peeked through, and even though he couldn't see all of her, his body knew she was there. All the right parts of him took notice.

Behind him, Parker handed over a drink. "Don't stare."

Shit!

"Thanks." He took a gulp of the drink and instantly winced. The ice rushed to his brain and froze off sections he hoped he never had to use in his life. He closed his eyes and forced down a few choice words.

"Slow down there."

He shook the cold from his head.

"You okay?"

Erin's voice was as smooth as whiskey and as comforting as a warm breeze on a summer night.

"I drank it too fast." He opened his eyes to find her standing in front of him.

His brain short-circuited any and all cognitive thought.

"It's in the sinuses."

"What?"

"Here."

He watched as she placed her thumb between his eyes and started to rub. She had the most mesmerizing blue eyes with long eyelashes.

"Press your tongue to the roof of your mouth."

There were places he wanted to press his tongue, but his own mouth wasn't one of them.

He enjoyed the feel of her touch, even if it was only one digit on one place that wasn't remotely sexual.

"Better?"

"Almost," he lied just to keep her there a little longer.

"What's going on here?"

Matt heard his brother's voice before his words registered.

"Matt has a brain freeze. Erin's doing some kind of Vulcan mind trap, and this little dude is hitting on me," Grace explained from the shallow end of the pool.

There was a solid ten seconds before his brother responded. During that time, Erin moved her touch away.

"Go for it, Austin."

"For fuck's sake . . . Parker, help me out here!" Grace cried.

"Austin," Parker laughed. "Knock it off."

"Thank you."

Matt fist-bumped his brother in light of Grace's unease.

"You do realize that Parker is my sister, not my mother, and I don't have to do what she says."

"That's debatable," Parker said.

"And I'm eighteen. So I'm legal." Matt almost lost it when Austin ran a hand down his puffed-up chest, which was nothing more than a smattering of underdeveloped muscles that would need two hours of gym time a day to impress his sister.

"Quite the selling point there," Erin said. "But do you even know if Grace is into guys?"

Grace pointed her drink in Erin's direction. "Yes, exactly right. I like women, Austin. Sorry."

Matt started laughing and caught Erin hiding a grin.

Austin rolled his eyes in good humor. "Yeah, yeah . . . okay. But if you change your mind, I could use an older, wiser woman to teach me a few things."

"News flash, kid . . . no woman wants to be described as *older and wiser*," Matt said as a free tip.

"I already used *beautiful* and *sexy*, and that didn't work."

Grace pushed up from the side of the pool. "I need more alcohol for this."

Austin grabbed a pool noodle to float on, his eyes fixed on Grace.

Matt shook his head.

"Are you going in?" Colin asked him.

"Did you bring a pair of trunks?"

Colin pointed to a chair where he'd placed a couple of towels and the swim shorts.

Matt grabbed them and then looked at Erin. "Mind if I change in your place?" It was closer than walking all the way up to the main house. And besides, there was something about changing in her personal space that put a spring in his step. Even if she wasn't there. He realized that might have sounded a little warped, but in his own mind, he figured he was safe.

"Go ahead."

He walked around the pool and down the short walkway to her front door. He'd been in, out, around, and even on top of the house all day, but walking in and closing himself in her bathroom to change made him feel just about as desperate as Austin was acting in the pool.

The bathroom was full of the usual chick stuff. Lotions and potions women thought they needed but not one man could identify. Considering he could count on one hand the number of toiletries he had at any given time, he thought the entire cosmetic world and how they reached into every woman's purse and pulled out handfuls of money was this side of brilliant.

Kinda made him wish he had extra money for stock options.

He forced himself not to open her medicine cabinet and pry and instead removed his clothes and pulled on his brother's trunks. They were a little tight, but not enough to embarrass him. Matt folded his clothes and left them on the side of her bathtub. He'd have to change before leaving so he didn't see the point in taking his clothes back outside.

He used the bathroom since he was there and made sure to lower the lid just like his mother taught him. Although in his own home, and at the fire station, lid lowering wasn't needed. He gave himself kudos before exiting her space.

Colin had joined Austin in the pool, and the women were sitting under the patio enjoying the shade.

"How's the water?" he asked his brother in an effort to draw Erin's attention his way. She had her back to him talking to Parker and Grace.

"Perfect. Especially after working in the heat all day."

Matt walked around the pool and over to his drink. He moved to the middle of the women and took his glass. "You ladies going in?"

"I haven't decided yet," Grace said.

Erin finally turned his way. Her eyes landed on his chest and locked into place.

"I will." Parker's words hardly registered.

Erin was staring. Maybe the woman wasn't completely unaffected by his presence.

He pretended not to notice and turned to the side much like a peacock showing a female another angle to consider. He sipped his drink, turned, and put it down right in front of Erin. Her gaze jolted to his face as if she had been caught doing something wrong.

"What about you, Erin?"

"Excuse me?"

"The pool? Are you going in?"

"Yes . . . wait, no."

Was this her speechless? He liked it.

"Maybe."

He would take the maybe and run with it . . . later. For now, he'd give her a little distance and something to watch.

He walked over to the edge of the pool and dove in.

The rush of cool water tapped his hormones down a notch and invigorated his body as he stretched out in the water. He popped his head out with a shake.

"I know where I'm spending the rest of my summer," he announced.

"Great. Be sure to come on Sunday mornings when it needs to be cleaned," Austin teased.

He glanced over and met Erin's eyes.

When he smiled, she looked away.

"Deal."

CHAPTER FIVE

She was tipsy.

Maybe even a tad drunk. And *that* was almost unheard of. The last time she felt her head buzz was on New Year's Eve when she'd said a little too much to Parker about her past. Erin never relaxed around testosterone-filled humans. That she was doing just that with two-and-a-half men present—Austin didn't feel like a full-fledged, card-carrying man quite yet—surprised her.

Dusk had fallen, dinner was only a memory . . . yet the margaritas were still being sipped and the fire pit was smoldering.

And she was tipsy.

She put her drink down and reached for a bottle of water.

Grace was sharing stories about her childhood to everyone's enjoyment. "Our parents wouldn't allow us to have computers in our bedrooms for the longest time."

"That's your fault," Matt pointed out.

"One hundred percent," Colin agreed.

"Why?" Parker asked.

The grin that split Grace's lips spoke volumes. "You tell the story better than I do," she told Matt.

"Colin was going into high school, I was in junior high, and Perv here was in what? Fifth grade?"

"I don't remember," Grace said.

Erin smiled, loving the family interaction.

"Colin finally convinced Mom and Dad to allow a computer in his room."

"Up until then we were forced to use a central computer that our parents could police," Colin added.

Matt groaned. "It sucked. Anyway, Colin was gone . . . don't remember where, and Grace and I went into his room to watch YouTube or something."

"Only that's not what we ended up watching," Grace said.

"Am I telling the story, or not?" Matt teased.

Erin laughed.

"Go ahead." Grace sat back.

"So we click on YouTube and Gracie starts talking about a better YouTube she heard about at school. And now that our parents weren't over our shoulders, we should check it out." Matt glanced at Erin.

"There's a better YouTube?" Erin asked.

"Debatable. So Grace here types in RedTube, presses enter, and our minds were blown."

Austin immediately started laughing.

Parker and Erin just looked at each other.

"What's RedTube?" Parker asked.

Grace sat back. "I don't feel so bad anymore."

"Porn," Matt pointed out. "It's an online porn site."

"In my defense I hadn't even had *the* conversation with my mother when this happened. I didn't know an adult YouTube meant naked people." Grace was all smiles.

Erin sat forward in her chair. "So what did you guys do?"

"We watched it. For a good twenty minutes."

"Until Mom walked in," Grace said.

Colin lifted Parker's hand. "You should hear Mom tell this story."

"Was she horrified?"

Matt shook his head. "First thing out of her mouth was directed at me. 'Matthew, what are you showing your sister?'"

"Asshat pointed his finger my way so fast my head spun." Grace nudged his foot with hers.

"I threw Grace under the bus, put the bus in reverse, and backed over her again. She didn't see it coming. Screw chivalry. Besides, I knew Mom would go easy on her and I'd be banned from the internet for life."

Erin found herself laughing and completely relaxed. "What was the punishment?"

"An entire dinner conversation about sex."

"That sounds painful," Parker said with a moan.

"To hear Mom tell it, she was dying of laughter the whole time. Her favorite memory of that night was when I asked why a woman would want to put a dick in her mouth."

Erin's head fell back and her shoulders shook with laughter. "Oh my God, that's hysterical."

Parker was cry-laughing right along with her.

"What did your dad say to all this?"

"All he added was one word . . ." Matt looked at Grace and they both said it together. "Foreplay."

That had Erin laughing even harder.

Grace yawned. "You have to admit, from that day on if we had any questions . . . and I do mean any, Mom and Dad gave it to us straight up."

"I guess that's why you're such a close family," Parker said.

Erin felt her giggles fading and memories of her own family push in. Not the dark hole she wanted to think about after she'd been drinking. When Grace yawned again, Erin took the cue to suggest cleaning up. "We should probably put this stuff away."

Parker scooted forward and stood. "It is getting late."

Everyone mobilized at that point in a group effort to make quick work of the mess they'd created with their impromptu barbeque and pool party.

"We've got this," Colin told her. "Matt still needs to show you how to use your new alarm system."

"Oh, that's right." And just like that, her nerves returned. Erin pulled the cover-up closer together and turned toward Matt. "You said it was easy, right?"

"Yup. I'll show you . . ." He walked the path to her front door and opened the screen for her. Apparently the chivalry that he denied his sister in junior high wasn't gone now.

She turned the main lights on in her living room and kitchen.

The brighter it became, the less her nerves danced on her skin.

"I control it from this, right?" She pointed to a portable monitor that looked like a typical tablet.

"Yes, and the app you downloaded on your phone earlier." He walked toward the larger monitor in the kitchen, and she followed. Matt pressed a button and the screen showed the two camera angles outside her space. One was at the front door; the other showed a wider angle taking in all but the very back of the house. "I've set this as your home screen so you can see what's going on outside at any given time. If Scout runs by and makes the emergency lighting go on, you can check it out here before opening your door."

He scooted a little closer and tapped the screen again. "If you press one image, it fills the screen so you can see a bigger image. Press it twice, it goes back to the double images." He then ran through the motions of showing her how to set the alarm for when she left and disengage when she returned home. The night settings were what she was really looking forward to. The alarm would be set so if anyone tried to sneak in while she slept, it would scream and the authorities would be called. Maybe she could sleep without having to be exhausted.

"Show me how the phone works."

Twenty minutes later she'd fiddled with both monitors, setting and resetting the system until she felt like she had the hang of it.

She stared at her phone and smiled when she saw the image the camera at her door displayed. "I can't tell you what this means to me."

Matt leaned against the kitchen counter, his grin spread wide. "You're welcome."

She paused, realized she hadn't said thank you yet.

Erin reached out and said, "Thank you."

His eyes drifted to where she'd touched him. The tips of her fingers were on his forearm. How they'd landed there she couldn't say.

"You were flirting with him!"

"I wasn't. I wouldn't."

"You were all over him."

"I tripped on the carpet. All he did was keep me from falling." Her *voice trembled. The look on his face told her whatever she said wasn't sinking in.*

He took a step closer. Her feet didn't move. She knew she couldn't retreat or his punishment would be worse. She couldn't swallow, couldn't breathe.

"Who is going to catch you now?"

Erin closed her eyes and flinched.

"You're okay. Put your head between your legs." Matt's soothing voice was beside her. Her vision cleared and she was sitting on one of the two stools that lived under the kitchen counter. Matt's hand was on her back gently pushing her head down. "Just breathe."

The beat of her heart was keeping time with a speed-metal band from the eighties. Her stomach sat in her throat, and she didn't have any feeling in her fingertips.

And she was cold.

So cold.

She placed both hands over her face and pulled in a few more gulps of air to try and calm her nerves. "I'm sorry," she managed as she slowly sat up.

"It's okay."

It was far from okay. "I'm sorry," she said again. A habit she had still yet to break. Repeated apologies never stopped the fists from flying. But without them, it was always worse.

"It happens." Matt knelt in front of her so she had to look down to see his face. Compassion, understanding, and a whole lot of concern laced the piercing look in his eyes.

"I'm—"

He lifted a finger in the air. "No more apologies. I'll get you some water."

She opened her mouth to stop him, but he was already up and walking to her sink. Erin took the few moments she had while Matt opened a couple of cupboards to locate a glass and fill it with tap water.

Slow breath in . . . slow breath out.

Memories, or maybe she should call them flashbacks, slammed on her like the one she'd just had and dropped her to her knees so often that even driving was sometimes dangerous. This was the second time this had happened in front of Matt. The first, Parker had told him she had a blood sugar issue.

Matt walked around the counter and pressed the glass in her hand. "Here." She was surprised to see his fingers trembling nearly as much as hers.

"Thank you." She took a sip. "Maybe I should have some orange juice."

Matt knelt a second time, his eyes found hers and held. "Sugar isn't going to help."

She opened her mouth to argue.

He tilted his strong chin to the side as if he were telling her he was onto her lie. "Feeling better?" he asked.

"I can feel my fingers again."

She looked down at his clenched hands. When she did, he flexed his fingers and rubbed them on his knees. "Did I do something to bring that on?"

"What? No." She shook her head. "I'm not sure what happened. Maybe it was the margaritas."

Matt stood and put some distance between them. He wasn't buying her excuses. With a wide berth, he reached for her phone and handed it to her. "I need to show you one more thing."

Once she unlocked her phone, she handed it back.

He swiped here, pressed in something there, and returned it to her. It was on a contact screen where Matt had typed in his number. "Any questions, call me. If anything is bothering you, call me. If you're worried, scared, or if what just happened to you happens again and you need company . . . call me."

"Matt . . . I—"

"Call me."

Her throat felt thick.

"I'll tell the others you're tired." He headed for the door. "Unless you're up to—"

"I'd appreciate that," she interrupted him.

He opened the door to leave.

"Thank you," she said before he could walk away.

"Anytime."

CHAPTER SIX

The memory of Erin's face draining of color, her blue eyes losing focus, and the rise and fall of her chest as she gasped for air kept reoccurring in Matt's head like a boomerang photo placed on social media to capture your attention. He replayed the entire time he was alone with her to figure out what had happened to bring on her reaction. It was the second time he'd seen her completely tune out. The first had been months before, when he'd raised his arm suddenly and she'd pulled back like a hand-shy dog waiting for a blow from its owner. Parker had been there and blamed Erin's reaction on low blood sugar . . . but Matt wasn't fooled. It didn't take a rocket scientist to realize that Erin had some serious baggage from her past. A past she wasn't open about.

At first he thought she was just shy, an introvert that would just as soon be alone than with others. Only she wasn't at a loss for words in a group of people. She joined the conversation, asked questions. And if he thought long and hard about it, she was great at skirting any personal questions and changing the subject. Since most of the times he was around her, Parker was there as well . . . and women stuck together. Parker did her fair share of steering the conversation away from Erin's history.

Someone had hurt her. And since she didn't talk about a family, Matt wasn't sure if it was a parent, relative, or past boyfriend. Hand shy was hand shy, and one didn't get that way without repeated hits. Hits one couldn't avoid or escape from easily.

It pissed him off.

Matt had seen his share of the seedy side of humanity as a firefighter. The number of medical calls he assisted on over the years and the homes and other people's lives he'd walked into woke him up early to the fact that some people sucked. They abused children, women, and the elderly. And abuse came in many forms, from the physical to neglect. It gutted him to see a hurt child, and to know it was done intentionally spiked a "get even" bone he had to work hard to push down.

He was a protector. Had been since he was ten.

Matt wanted nothing more than to protect Erin. Although he felt like her immediate danger was only in her head, he still had the desire to fight her demons.

He ran the paces on his home treadmill until he racked up five miles. Then he jumped off and laid waste to the punching bag hanging from his ceiling.

The desire to push his body to the limit, and erase the image of Erin damn near doing a face-plant, fueled him.

With his workout and shower behind him, he headed into his garage and turned on his sound system. Before long, he was elbow deep in repairing the engine on his dad's lawn mower that he'd promised to get to. He'd put it off for a couple of days, but was going into a busy workweek that wouldn't give him any downtime at home. So with a country station playing some of his favorite tracks in the space, Matt enjoyed the occasional breeze that drifted in from the open garage door. Neighbors would drive by, a few would yell out his name and wave, and some of the kids would ride their bikes up and down the street. He liked his neighborhood and his single-story home. It was only him, and since his brother's place was bigger, family dinners that weren't at his parents' home were always at Colin's. Only now Matt was pretty sure that would be moved over to Parker's. It was hard to compete with all that property, complete with a pool and a yard you could host your own Woodstock in.

He was singing the lyrics to a man getting drunk on a plane after being jilted on his wedding day when he heard his name being called.

He looked up to a completely unexpected visitor. "Erin?"

"Hi." She wore capri pants and a short-sleeved shirt that danced as the wind blew against it. Her hair was pulled back at the nape of her neck, and the large-rimmed sunglasses she often wore hid her eyes. "I hope you don't mind me stopping by."

Mind? Hell no. "Of course not. Anytime." He picked up a shop towel and wiped the grease and oil from his hands. "Come in."

She stepped out of the glaring sun in his driveway and into the shade of the garage. It was then he noticed the dish in her hands. She held it with one hand and removed her sunglasses with the other. "Parker told me where you lived. I wanted to bring these by."

Matt tossed the towel to the side and reached for her offering.

"My way of saying thank you for all your help yesterday."

He looked down. "Brownies?"

"Hard to go wrong with chocolate."

"My favorite."

She smiled. "I like to bake, even in the heat."

He set the dish aside and turned down the volume on the speaker. "You didn't have to."

"I know. I wanted to." Her eyes drifted around his garage and landed on a calendar above his workbench. A swimsuit edition kind that defined his man space. He suddenly felt odd for having half-naked women wearing tiny straps of material that passed as swimwear displayed on his wall.

"Come inside. Milk will go perfect with these."

"No, that's okay—"

"I insist." Now that he had her in his space, he wanted to keep her there. And not in the garage where she stuck out like a fish on shore.

"Only for a minute. I don't want to interrupt."

He ignored her words and led her inside. Years of working in the fire department equated to him always keeping his space tidy. Leaving a mess for anyone at the station wasn't tolerated. There were times they would be called out and leave on the fly, but once they were back, picking up the place was top priority. Only in the thick of a fire were messes left. He was thankful for his clean habits now when he was showing a woman he wanted to impress his home.

His kitchen was small, but more than enough space for him. Matt pulled out a chair at the dinette set for four and offered Erin a seat. "Milk? Or I can make some coffee."

"Milk would be fine."

Matt washed his hands in the sink before pulling down two glasses and small plates for their brownies.

"Have you lived here long?" Erin asked.

"About five years. I wanted a place that had enough room for RV parking. Do you camp?"

She shook her head. "I'm fond of running water."

He brought the milk to the table where she sat with her hands in her lap. He caught her scanning the room with a slight smile on her lips.

"My RV has a fifty-gallon tank. There's always running water."

She removed the plastic wrap from the brownies that had already been cut up and placed one on each plate.

"I didn't camp as a kid and can't say I've had much of an opportunity as an adult."

Matt took the seat opposite her, remembered napkins, and jumped up to retrieve them. "Then it isn't so much you *don't* camp, it's that you haven't tried."

She laughed. "I guess you could say that."

"You should try it sometime. I drag Colin out as often as he gives me a chance. We drive to Rincon a couple times a summer."

"What's Rincon?"

"It's a stretch of beach where you can park an RV and enjoy the ocean for a couple of days." He picked up the brownie and brought it to his mouth. "Mmmm, still warm." She watched as he bit in.

He would have told her it was the best thing in the world even if it sucked, but he had a hard time not moaning once his taste buds caught up with his mouth. Decadent, mouth-watering chocolate on his tongue the consistency of melted butter. "Oh my God."

He opened his eyes to find her smiling.

"You like it?" she asked.

He took his time chewing, savoring every bit before letting it slip down his throat. "Wow. That did not come out of a box."

She offered a quick shake of the head. "No. If you're going to take the time to bake, do it properly."

The next bite hovered over his lips. "You bake properly and I'll eat properly. I'm glad you brought these here and not the station. I do not want to share."

She took a small bite of her portion and smiled. "Not bad."

They took the next bite in silence, and he washed the last of it down before reaching for another one.

"I need to make sure the first one wasn't a fluke." The second brownie met the first in the bottom of his stomach. "Nope. Just as good as the first."

Hers sat unfinished. "I'm glad you enjoy them. I really appreciate your help yesterday."

"If this is my reward for helping, let me know when you need your trash taken out, or your car fixed . . . or whatever."

She pushed her chair back. "I don't want to keep you."

"You haven't finished your brownie."

"I might have eaten one while I was cutting them up."

He struggled to find a reason to keep her there. Anything to spend more time with her. Especially while she smiled at him the way she was now. "I have to work the next couple days but I'm free on Thursday. Any chance I can convince you to join me for dinner?"

And her smile was gone. "Matt . . ."

"We don't have to call it a date. Just dinner. Or maybe lunch . . . coffee?" *Anything.*

"I don't . . . I'm not really in the right place right now."

He knew her rejection was an automatic response. And in reality it wasn't a rejection directed at him. Not an *I'm not interested in you.* More of an *I'm not ready myself.* Which was the only refusal he could actually work with.

"Another time, then?"

"Matt . . ."

He waved her off. "Don't answer now. If you get hungry and don't know where to go, I'll help you out. Consider me your 911 for emergency meals."

Now she was grinning. "Emergency meals?"

"I'm good at spider removal, too."

"That comes in handy." She stood.

He directed her through his living room and out the front door.

"This doesn't look like a bachelor pad," she said, looking around the room. "Did an old girlfriend help you decorate?"

He placed a hand on his chest and winced. "I did this myself." With help from his sister, but he wasn't going to admit that freely. "Do you want to see the rest of the place?"

"No. I need to get home. I have some work to do."

He didn't push. Instead he walked her out the door and down his driveway. She unlocked her door with a remote key and he opened it for her. "Thanks for the brownies."

"Thanks for yesterday."

She slid behind the wheel, started the car, and rolled her window down.

He leaned a hand on the hood of her car. "Remember, 911 food emergencies . . . I'm your man."

She was smiling and not saying no. "Bye, Matt."

He stood tall and stepped away as she drove off.

Back in his kitchen he realized she'd left her sunglasses behind. Which guaranteed he'd see her again soon. And the dish the brownies were delivered in. He'd milk that for two visits.

With a plan in place, he popped the remainder of her brownie between his lips and headed back to his garage.

Life was good.

~

"I can't believe I'm leaving in the morning." It was Wednesday and Parker stood over an open suitcase with a dozen outfits tossed around it. Scout placed his head in his paws at the foot of the bed as if bored with the whole process.

Erin brought a sundress out from inside the massive walk-in closet and held it up. "What about this one?"

Parker's eyes lit up as she reached for the white cotton backless sundress. "I forgot I had that." She held it up to her body and looked in the full-length mirror. "I bought it when I lived in San Diego at this cute little shop in Point Loma." She sighed as if stuck in a thought.

"You went to college there, right?"

Parker snapped out of her frozen gaze and took the dress to her suitcase. "Yes. And if I'd had my act together, I would have graduated in the time I was there. Unfortunately, I was busy buying sundresses and finding a reason to wear them."

Erin knew that Parker hadn't gotten her degree and was considering going back to college to finish now that her younger brother was graduating from high school. "Regret is a wasted emotion."

Erin's comment brought Parker's head up and eyes in direct line with hers. "You don't regret your ex?"

Just the mention of his existence made her heart rate jump. "Touché."

Parker turned back around and started rolling up the outfits she'd picked out to wear. "Since we're on the subject, do you mind telling me about this ex being a one-time husband? Or are we going to forever ignore the fact that I stumbled upon that information?"

The desire to change the subject with a distraction pulled Erin's gaze in the opposite direction. "Do you have shoes to go with that dress?"

Parker stopped packing, dipped her chin, and looked at her from across the room. "I don't know why it's a big secret. Lots of people get married too young. It's obvious you had a reason to leave the jerk, so you can't blame yourself for that."

Rooted in place, Erin stared forward and remembered the words the counselor had told her before she left everything to start a new life in California. *"It's a lot harder to be a person who doesn't have a past than one who does. When people get too close to the truth, it's almost impossible to keep it to yourself. Every person you confide in makes it easier for him to find you."*

"I can see by your face you want to talk about shoes instead," Parker said.

"Yes, please." She hated the desperation in her voice.

Parker sat on the edge of the bed and lowered her voice. "How about this. I'll tell you what I think I know, and you can confirm or deny if I'm off."

She offered a noncommittal shrug.

"You married the wrong guy, who beat you up."

Erin blinked several times but said nothing.

"He did it more than once. In fact, I'm guessing it happened a lot."
More blinking.

"I'll bet this trip to Cabo that you're scared to death he will come after you here. Which explains the security system and the double-checking the locks on the doors. And the lack of friends you have around or even a regular job that makes you leave the house every day."

Erin started rolling her index finger on the pad of her thumb and kept her lips shut.

"Anything I'm leaving out?"

She heard the screech of tires and the feel of glass against her face. "Nope. That about covers it."

Parker offered a half-baked smile. "That was a little too quick, Erin."

Instead of a lie, she told her the truth. "He's a dangerous man. If he finds me, he will kill me."

The smile on her friend's face fell. "The more people you have around you, who love you, the easier it is to protect you."

"You of all people know you can't always count on that," Erin told her. "I'm learning to protect myself."

They were both quiet for several seconds.

"I'm really sorry you live with that fear," Parker told her.

She sighed, and forced her hands to relax. "Me too. But at least it's not a daily reality any longer."

"How long were you married?" she asked.

Nope . . . not going there. "Let's play another game, okay? Truth or Dare is getting old."

Parker jumped up and nodded. "Got it. Sorry. I don't want to pry."

"You're curious. I get it. I would be, too."

She tucked the cotton dress in her suitcase. "I have a pair of brown sandals that will work with almost everything."

Shoes were a much safer subject.

Erin watched Parker walk into the closet and return with the sandals.

"Please keep this between us," she told her.

Parker stopped packing and looked her dead in the eye. "I told you I won't say anything, and I haven't. Colin flat-out asked me once what your story was, and I told him that secrets are sacred."

That was a relief. "Thank you."

Another shirt went into the suitcase. "But if I figured it out, it probably isn't going to be long before others do, too. Although I didn't see the ex-*husband* thing coming."

"No one else will either." At least she hoped. Erin scanned the clothes on the bed and started to count. "I thought you said this was a five-day trip. Six if you count your travel day."

"It is."

She started to count. "So you're going to change clothes three times a day?"

Undaunted, Parker rolled up another outfit. "I haven't taken a break in three years. I want choices."

"I bet you wear three outfits and one sundress. The rest of the time you'll be in a bathing suit or naked in bed."

Parker smiled. "Options!"

CHAPTER SEVEN

Erin stood in the driveway alongside Matt, who had been roped into driving Colin and Parker to LAX for their noon flight.

While Colin put their bags into the back of Matt's truck, Parker ran through a list of things that needed to happen, or not happen, while she was away.

"I already told Austin no parties."

"I was there. I know."

"And since you're staying in the guest room, make sure Scout goes out before you go to bed. Otherwise he's up the second the sun comes out and whines to be let outside to pee."

"Got it."

"And Mallory said she was coming over on Saturday with Jase to use the pool. They'll probably stay the night."

Yeah, Erin had already been told that, too.

"Oh, and I told Austin that if he's going to stay with friends at all while I'm away, to let you know. And if he's late coming home, to let you know . . . so you won't be startled by the gate opening and closing at all hours." That was helpful. The house alarm system told everyone inside every time the gate opened and closed. A necessary evil when the gate was five acres away from the front door.

"Great."

"Oh, and—"

Colin came up behind Parker and wrapped both arms around her. "Erin's a grown woman, she'll figure it out."

"But there's—"

Matt opened the back door of his twin-cab truck. "I think we were given less instructions in high school when Mom and Dad went to Monterey," he teased.

Colin laughed. "We still threw a party."

Matt chuckled. "And blamed Grace."

Erin shook her head. "You guys are bad." She opened her arms to Parker for a hug. "Have fun and don't worry."

"Thank you."

Erin lowered her voice so only Parker could hear. "Text me if he puts a ring on it."

That earned an extra hug before she climbed in the back seat.

Matt opened his door while Colin walked around the truck.

"You forgot your sunglasses at my house. If you're around later, I can bring them by," Matt said.

Parker rolled her window down. "Wait . . . you left sunglasses . . . at his house?"

The woman wanted to read into everything. "You gave me his address for the brownies . . . remember?"

Parker's brilliant smile at what she thought was news, fell. "Oh."

"So . . . later?" he asked.

"Whenever," she told him. "I have others."

He grinned like he'd been given an invitation.

"You guys better get going. Cabo is an international flight. You need extra time," Erin said.

Matt waved as he backed out of the driveway.

"Have fun!"

And they were gone.

Scout barked at the truck as it rolled down the driveway before running to Erin's side. "It's just you and me," she told the dog.

Austin was in school and the entire place was left to her. Then, as if to remind her she wasn't completely alone, a couple of the chickens in the rebuilt coop started to make noise. Instead of heading into the house, she took the hens' cue and went to see if she could have fresh eggs to go with her coffee.

Scout stuck right by her side.

~

". . . and don't just let yourself in. Erin needs to know who's coming in the gate."

It was Matt's turn to hear all the instructions.

"I won't."

"You know, you could have just brought over her sunglasses this morning."

The sunglasses were actually in his glove compartment, but he wasn't about to reveal that tidbit. Besides, timing was everything.

"Where is the fun in that?" Colin said for him.

"Oh." Parker was silent for about ten seconds. "Colin told you the hotel we're staying at . . . right? So if there's any problems and the cell phone isn't working down there you can call?"

Matt looked at her through his rearview mirror. "Yes, *Mom*. I know the hotel and the flight numbers and I even know the location of a pot shop that delivers *chill pills* for overanxious women."

He caught his brother trying to smother a chuckle.

"I'm pretty sure that was an insult," Parker said, her lips pressed in a thin, unamused line.

Matt busted out a laugh. "If you're only pretty sure, I'll try harder next time. We've got it, Parker. Erin's an adult. Austin is . . ." He hesitated. "Not a baby. And I'm going to be around enough to make sure Erin is okay."

Colin swiveled in the front seat to look at his girlfriend. "It's going to be fine, hon. The place will still be there when we get back."

While Matt was smiling, he glanced up again and saw a look of fear pass over Parker's face. He'd seen that look before. On the faces of people who were evacuating their homes while he and his coworkers rushed in. That's when it dawned on him. Yeah, Parker might be over-the-top controlling with all her instructions and words of caution. The reality was, she'd almost lost her house less than a year prior, and he was betting she was remembering that right about now.

"It's not fire season," Matt said quickly. "Everything is still green and the Santa Anas aren't blowing."

He noticed her blinking several times. Her lips sealed.

Colin reached into the back seat. "Is that what you're worried about?"

"It's stupid."

"It's understandable," Colin assured her.

Matt hit bumper-to-bumper traffic on the 405 and took a deep breath. "I got ya covered, Parker. Go to Cabo, get a tan, and come back relaxed."

"You okay?" Colin asked her.

"Yeah. I really need this vacation."

Matt looked over at his brother and grinned. He knew he had a ring in his luggage and a pretty elaborate plan as to how to put it on her finger. Maybe once she felt like she wasn't shouldering the whole burden, she'd relax.

He looked in the rearview mirror again.

"This traffic isn't going to make us miss our flight, is it?"

On second thought . . . he wouldn't be holding his breath.

～

Erin didn't consider herself a babysitter, and Austin certainly wasn't a baby. However, once Parker and Colin pulled away with Matt at the wheel, she found herself planning meals for the next several days and scheduling an extra trip to the grocery store to ensure she had everything she needed to feed the two of them.

Then she remembered Parker's lengthy list of instructions and how Austin would often have friends over after school. Considering he was a high school senior without parents, his friends opted for his house instead of their own, even for video games. Keeping all that in the back of her mind, she doubled the amount of food she planned on cooking just in case there was another hungry kid around.

She'd always liked to bake, but it wasn't until she'd moved into the guesthouse that she really started to enjoy cooking. That was in part because she didn't eat out very often. A fact based less on the reality that dining out was expensive and more on the need to stay hidden. As her friendship with Parker grew, she'd often cook for the two of them, or even everyone in the household on weekdays when they were all there. Mallory had only moved out a few months ago, but came over on the weekend with her live-in boyfriend, Jase. It helped that Jase was also a first cousin to Colin and Matt.

She loved the big family atmosphere along with the different personalities and laughter. An image of her sister and her family floated in her head. Their last conversation before Erin disappeared forever.

"Where will you go?" Helen, her sister, had asked.

"I can't tell you. I can't tell anyone."

"How will I know the bastard didn't get to you and you're dead?"

"My divorce attorney will keep me updated on you, and you on me." It was the best Erin could do. *"Maci Brandt no longer exists. I'm legally changing my name, passport, ID, everything."*

By now her sister was crying on the phone. Erin hadn't dared to have the conversation in person or her sister may have tried to convince her there was another way out. So she'd made the phone call minutes after she'd fled.

Hours before Desmond would realize she was gone. It was against what the experts on changing your identity and disappearing forever had told her to do, but Erin didn't have it in her to let her sister worry.

"What will I tell Dad?"

"I honestly don't care. Tell him I'm dead. Whatever is easier for you." *She'd never see the man again.*

"Maci, don't do this. There has to be an easier way."

The image of a casket, the one Desmond had shown her when he pre-paid for their funeral expenses just days after she'd been released from the hospital, flashed in her head. He'd compared the white satin of the interior to her wedding gown and suggested a young corpse would look beautiful inside of it.

His threat wasn't missed.

The man was capable of killing her and making it look like an accident.

He'd be the poor widower, and she'd be dead.

"I love you, Helen. Please don't provoke him. He's dangerous. If he thinks getting to you and your family will get to me, he'd do it just to drag me back. Please, for all our sakes, don't try and find me. Stay away from him."

"Don't go. Please, let's talk this out."

"There's nothing to talk about. I'm already gone. Now tell me you love me one last time."

"Damn you, Maci." *Her sister was hurting, she heard it in her voice.*

"Those aren't going to be your last words to me."

Helen was sobbing. "Maci . . . please."

"I love you."

"I love you, too. God, I hate him. How did this happen to you?"

A very good question.

"One more time," *Erin said.*

"I love you, Maci."

She hung up the phone, tucked it into the seat of the bus she was on, and exited at the next stop.

Maci Brandt stopped existing that day, and Erin Fleming was born.

Erin had hopped around the country for six months, made sure the last of her scars could be covered by makeup, and then settled in Parker's guesthouse. Only then did she buy a cell phone instead of using a prepaid one that couldn't be traced back to her. Only then did she heave a sigh of relief and sleep more than three hours at a time. She was up to four now, and thought that was a minor miracle. She could count on both hands the number of nights she'd slept all the way through, and each one she woke dripping in sweat with nightmares that gripped her neck so tight she couldn't breathe. What she really needed was therapy. A fact she couldn't ignore but was too afraid to pursue. Because therapy would reveal her past to a stranger, and that was the one thing she was never supposed to do.

So why was she so focused on this now?

Erin moved around Parker's kitchen, enjoying the larger space to move, and prepared what she was going to make for dinner. Austin didn't rush home from school but hadn't texted to say he wouldn't be around that night. He probably didn't expect dinner from her. He was self-sufficient, as any eighteen-year-old just a few weeks from graduation was. But that didn't stop her from planning a meal.

With her laptop in hand, she made herself comfortable on the couch with Scout at her feet and the elusive cat, Sushi, curled up and sleeping at her side. Chicken roasted in the oven and all she needed to do for dinner was the sides. For now, she opened one of her client's latest books and put her editing skills to work.

Freelance editing was not her dream job, but it paid her bills and put her degree to use. A degree she had under a name she no longer used. So far no one had asked to view the papers. Now that she had six months of editing, from developmental to copy editing, under her belt, she boasted about her clients' work instead of the reason she felt qualified to do it.

Maci Brandt had never used her degree. It was only fitting that Erin Fleming did. She'd gotten her foot in the editing door with two small digital publishing houses. That's where she learned that taking independent writers that she could vet was the right route for her. Using a new name and hiding behind her computer was a lot easier than she thought it would be. It never left her mind that Desmond could do the same thing to find her. Not that he would ever think she'd be making money editing fiction. He didn't want her to work during her marriage and had only seen her in the workforce as an intern in the company he now controlled. That internship had been in the marketing department. Nothing remotely close to what she'd wanted to do once she graduated from college.

But her father had set up the summer job that had given her the credits she needed to complete her education, and the rest—as they say—was history.

Erin had dreamt of being a scaled-down version of Lois Lane. Not that she wanted Superman, but she wanted the job of a reporter. Or at least the woman in the office writing stories for the paper or magazine on important facts people needed to know.

She let the old dream slip away. Editing other people's work was satisfying. And right now she was working on a mystery writer's manuscript. The woman used a male pen name, and wanted the public to believe she was a man so long as they bought her books. The only reason Erin knew the little secret was the phone conversations she'd had with the woman over the past two books. She had midlist successes with her traditional publisher writing romance novels, but she wanted to branch into a new genre and her publisher hadn't been too excited to back that. So she did it independently. Now on her fourth straight mystery-suspense novel, the woman pretending to be a man was growing exceedingly popular.

And for good reason.

Erin was on her first read through. The kind she did for the pleasure of it. Anytime she stopped reading, she marked the page on this pass. This was her pleasure read. A way to get a feel for the book before digging in to help the author make it better. But that read came next. For now, Erin was following the male detective around the page and through the chapters as he hunted down the bad guys. The author wrote a specific detail about a flower used in tea to murder someone without detection. So while this was the pleasure read, Erin marked the page to check the facts on that later.

Fact-checking was part of the job. The part Erin geeked out on, to be honest. Falling down the rabbit hole of fact-checking sparked her own ideas for writing fiction. Not that she ever would. But that didn't stop her from scribbling random thoughts in a journal.

Like now, she took the journal and wrote *Flower Tea Murder.*

She smiled. It had a nice ring to it.

An image popped into her mind of her ex sitting at a bistro in London, the kind he took her to when they'd first arrived there, but wouldn't within a week because of the eye swelling she couldn't hide with makeup. He sat in her fantasy holding a proper English teacup, one with a dainty motif of heather or peonies. The cup was filled with tea and served with a floating flower. In her head it was blue with a dark purple, almost black center. Much like the marks he'd leave on her when he wasn't happy.

He'd sip the tea and look at her.

His smile would fall.

Erin shook her thoughts aside. It probably wasn't a healthy habit to imagine the death of her husband . . . ex-husband.

She closed her eyes and sighed.

Soon-to-be ex-husband.

As that passage ran through her head, she reminded herself to call her attorney in the morning to determine if there was new news. The last conversation left her less than hopeful that things would be resolved anytime soon. The restraining order she'd obtained had been a miracle. After nearly a year of it being in place without any contact from the man, he had a pretty good chance of having it lifted. Not that a court order would stop him from coming after her.

Images flashed in rapid succession until she pushed her computer aside and stood. She went to the refrigerator and looked at the wine she'd put in there to chill.

No. She was alone.

Completely alone, and if he found her and she'd been drinking . . .

Erin moaned out loud and grabbed a cold water. Then, because she needed to move and be distracted, she opened the refrigerator door wider and started to remove the contents inside.

Thirty minutes later she had a long list of expired condiments she'd tossed in the trash. For all she knew, Parker didn't mind expired mustard. But cleaning out the fridge required you start fresh.

The sound of the gate opening told her Austin was home.

Much as she tried not to look out the window to assure herself that it was him, she failed and ended up walking to the bay window.

She smiled.

Just Austin.

Scout moved to the top of the back stairs, the ones that led up from the garage, with his tail wagging.

Erin moved back to the glass shelves she'd removed and was washing.

Austin entered the house like a tornado.

The door slammed. A backpack hit the floor. Scout's name was yelled from the bottom of the stairway.

The dog's thumping tail was followed by three sharp barks and the animal running down the stairs to greet his favorite human.

Erin smiled.

Austin talked to the dog as he entered the house and rounded the corner of the kitchen. "Something smells good."

"I'm making a chicken."

Austin stopped moving after one look at the kitchen. "Holy crap . . . what are you doing?"

"Cleaning out the fridge. Did you know the ketchup expired a year ago?"

Unfazed, Austin walked into the pantry and returned with a snack bag of chips. "Still tasted fine."

"I'll go to the store and replace what was bad."

He glanced in the trash can she'd pulled out and filled.

"Whatever."

She no sooner turned back to the sink to finish what she started than the phone to the house did a double ring indicating that someone was at the gate.

Austin answered the phone, muttered a few syllables, said *yeah*, and then pressed the button to open it to whoever was there.

"Dinner will be ready in a little bit, if you're going to be around. If not, I'll put aside some for later."

"I can always eat."

That made her smile.

"I made extra if your friend is staying."

By now Austin was looking at the screen of his cell phone and texting away. "Sure," he mumbled.

He walked out of the kitchen, Scout at his heels, while Erin dried off the glass shelf and put it aside.

She'd have to double her time if she was going to finish the sides for dinner.

When she heard the knock on the front door, she waited for Austin to answer it.

Only he had retreated to the back of the house to his bedroom.

Drying her hands, she moved to answer the door and was met with a face she wasn't expecting so soon.

CHAPTER EIGHT

"Matt?"

He was ear-to-ear smiling with her sunglasses covering his eyes.

They looked ridiculous on him. Unable to stop herself, Erin started to laugh.

"Are they me?" he asked as he turned to the side.

"They're not bad," she lied. "Maybe you should try them with a white frame."

He looked over the rim as if considering her suggestion. "That might work with my white seventies suit I wore at a theme party last year."

"You dressed up for a theme party?"

"You sound surprised. Isn't that what people do at parties created around a theme . . . dress up?"

Erin took two steps back and opened the door for him to come in. He handed her the glasses as he walked past.

"You really didn't have to rush these over for me."

"Considering you left them at my place a few days ago, it's safe to say I didn't rush." He walked into the kitchen and did a double take at the mess. "Spring cleaning?"

More like raw nerves getting the best of her, but cleaning was helping immensely. "You could say that," she told him.

He walked past the mess, opened the fridge, and pulled out a beer she'd returned to a clean shelf. "Do you mind?" he asked.

"I'm pretty sure that's your brother's, so, no . . . I don't mind."

Matt didn't need any more encouragement. He twisted off the top and tossed it in the trash. "It's happy hour. Want one?" he asked.

"Beer isn't really my thing."

He reopened the fridge. "There's wine in here. I'm sure Parker won't mind."

"Oh, that's mine." She stood rooted in place while Matt buzzed around the kitchen like he lived there. She'd seen his truck parked in the driveway a lot since the rain had stopped. Even though Colin hadn't officially moved in, he was there a lot and apparently his younger brother spent a lot of time with him.

He grabbed the wine and closed the refrigerator door. "You'll join me, then?"

She opened her mouth to say no and hesitated.

His eyes caught hers and he tilted his head slightly, tempting her.

Erin opened the utensil drawer she was standing beside and handed him a corkscrew.

"That's my girl." His words flowed so easily they didn't even register until she'd turned around to finish cleaning the last of the shelves.

She wasn't *his* anything, but she didn't know how to correct him without sounding pathetic, so she pretended not to have heard him instead.

"Glasses?" he asked once the cork had popped free of the bottle.

"The cupboard above the coffee maker." She added a point of her elbow to aid him in finding a wineglass.

With her drink poured, he stood beside her and waited for her to turn off the water before handing her the glass. He stopped her from taking a sip by lifting his beer in the air for a toast. "To Colin and Parker."

"That's sweet." She didn't see that coming.

They both sipped their drinks.

"I have to give my brother credit. If he hadn't had the hots for Parker, I wouldn't have met you." He put his beer down and grabbed a dish towel.

"Matt." His name was a warning.

He lifted the glass shelf and started to dry it. "You can never have too many friends, right?" he asked.

Friends? She didn't think he was talking about friends. "Right."

"Right," he agreed with her.

She watched him take the shelf to the fridge and put it back inside. "Does all this go back in?"

"You don't have to help."

"Payment for happy hour." He proceeded to put everything back in order.

All she could do was stare. Matt wasn't a small man. She was five eight and he had to be six three with shoulders that filled out every shirt she'd ever seen him in. From the back, all you could see were muscles that ran down to a narrow waist and a tight . . .

Matt turned and caught her staring.

She closed her eyes and pivoted away.

He chuckled. "Busted," he said.

"Sorry." She felt her face grow hot. She reached for her wine. How many shades of embarrassed could she turn getting caught checking out his ass? "I-I was trying to picture you in that white zoot suit."

"Ah-huh . . . sure."

Oh, this was bad. "No, really."

He walked around her, picked up his beer. "It's okay, Erin."

She dared a look at him and found his soft hazel eyes and boyish smile looking back. "I'm not used to seeing a man work in a kitchen."

"Your dad never helped your mom out?"

It was her turn to move to keep her nerves from showing. "As sexist as that sounds, the answer is no. My mother didn't know the kitchen existed, and the only experience my father had with one was to pay for it." She quickly shuffled food back inside the fridge.

"Who cooked?"

Maids.

"We got by," she said instead.

"But—"

"My parents divorced early, and after my mom left, my father hired babysitters. They cooked." *Babysitters* sounded a lot easier to swallow than *nannies.*

"What about when you were at your mom's . . . did she hire baby-sitters, too?"

Erin huffed a laugh. "I misspoke and gave my mother too much credit. I haven't seen my mother since I was seven. She abandoned us." Something she'd gotten over a long time ago. Her mother wasn't part of the equation.

"Damn, Erin . . . that sucks."

She shrugged. "It is what it is. So if I was staring—"

"You *were* staring," he interrupted her with a grin.

Squaring her shoulders and lifting her eyes to once again look at him, she said, "It *really* was because I'm not accustomed to seeing a man working in a kitchen."

"So you weren't staring at my ass for the pleasure of it."

Blink . . . blink . . .

Words failed her.

He started to laugh.

"You are so full of yourself."

That boyish smile went full wattage. "I adore the way you blush."

She brought both hands to her cheeks and tried to cool them off. "You're awful."

"I know. I should be destroyed." He turned and reached for the garbage. "I'll take this out while you construct a witty response to my teasing."

∼

Matt had many traits worth touting, but he had to admit, charming women was at the top of that list. And tonight he felt like he'd just received the Golden Ticket from the judges when it came to getting what he wanted.

He wiggled his way into happy hour, which was two drinks in before he helped Erin finish making dinner . . . which he invited himself to . . . almost like a player on first base stealing second without the pitcher seeing. He sat beside Austin so he could watch Erin as she ate.

"Are you getting excited about graduation?" Erin asked Austin.

"I can't wait to get out of that place."

"I remember that feeling. I have to tell ya, though . . . it only gets harder after high school," Matt told him.

"That's what everyone says."

"Are you going to college?" he asked.

Austin shook his head. "Trade school, I think. I'm taking the summer to figure out which one."

"Parker's okay with that?" While Parker was the sister and not the mom, she stood in as a parent for Austin and Mallory for the past three years.

"She's cool. Says that college isn't for everyone. Besides, it isn't like colleges are going anywhere if I decide to go."

"That's true," Erin said.

Matt found his attention back across the table. "Did you go to college?"

She nodded.

"Where?"

The question seemed to have caught in her head because she didn't answer right away. Finally she said, "Back east."

He found the answer strange. Most college graduates boasted their alma mater with a *Go Cougars,* or *Yeah, Huskies.*

Much as he wanted to press, he saw her thumb start to rub against her finger as she pushed food around her plate instead of eating it.

"Did you go to college?" Austin asked him.

Erin grew silent as Matt told Austin his journey to becoming a firefighter. Junior college, then time on a hotshot crew before finally landing a position in LA County Fire. It had been his dream and it had taken forever. Five years of applying and testing all over the state and even Arizona, Idaho, and Nevada. Not that he had any desire to move away from his family . . . but he was willing to go anywhere to get into the field and then bank on the ability to transfer out and back home later in life if he needed.

"I was one of the lucky ones," he finished his story. "A lot of my buddies gave up. Some went on to join the police force, some went back to school or took other labor jobs in construction."

"I don't see a person who wanted to be a firefighter working behind a desk," Erin said.

"That sounds like my personal hell."

She smiled at that.

"Mine, too," Austin said. "Which is why I think college is a waste of my time. I liked the heavy equipment that was here all winter."

Matt nodded. "Good work. Great pay. Can't be outsourced."

Austin dished up another portion of mashed potatoes. "I know, right? Can't buy that from China."

"Another great job is a lineman," Matt told him.

"What's that?"

"Working on power poles. Running lines."

Erin placed her fork down on her plate. "Oh, God . . . don't put that in his head. Parker will have a heart attack."

Matt grinned. "It's okay. I taught Colin CPR. She'll be fine."

And so the conversation circled. Austin kept things interesting with only a few comments from Erin. When they were finished, only half of the food on Erin's plate had been eaten, and he and Austin made a pretty good dent in the rest of it on the table.

"That was really delicious." Matt took his plate to the sink.

"You helped," Erin told him.

"Tossing a salad isn't really cooking."

Austin placed his plate next to Matt's and moved back into the dining room. "So are you guys dating, or what?"

Erin's plate hit the counter a little too loud. "What? No."

Her cheeks were crimson in one second. They matched her red hair, which was fading to more of a strawberry blonde. Emphasis on the strawberry. He would bet his next paycheck red was not her natural color. In the six months that he'd known her, she'd grown out her hair past her midback. Her skin was quickly bronzing with the addition of sunshine, further making him believe that the trait of red hair was not in her gene pool. "Not for my lack of trying, kid," Matt said, bringing a new shade of red to Erin's face.

She glared now, in a playful kind of way. "You do need to be destroyed."

Hearing his words tossed back at him had him wiggling his eyebrows.

Erin, on the other hand, rolled her eyes. "I guess you'll be wanting coffee, since you wheedled happy hour *and* dinner out of the evening."

"And here I thought I was being stealthy." He cleaned off his plate into the garbage can and moved to help with the dishes. "But since you offered, coffee would be great."

That earned another chuckle before she turned to put on a pot.

Ten minutes later the dishes were done, Austin had gone to his room, and Matt sat with Erin on the front porch drinking coffee while the sun went down.

"Next time I'll cook you dinner," he told her.

Erin stared at him over her cup of coffee. "I already told you I wasn't ready to date."

"I didn't say date. I said dinner." He sipped his coffee. "Oh, wait. Was this a date? I didn't realize or I would have brought flowers." Teasing took the worry out of her eyes.

"Does this work on all the ladies?" she asked.

He played dumb. "Does what work?"

"Assuming a position in someone's life."

"I don't know. I've never done this before."

"Oh, please. Your moves are very practiced and smoother than a newborn's bottom."

He put his coffee aside, purposely drinking it slowly to prolong the night. "As crazy as it sounds, I don't usually have to ask a woman out repeatedly before she says yes. Since that didn't work with you, I'm trying something different."

"Assuming a place in my life."

"Technically, I'm already in your world since it is in Parker's and Parker is in Colin's . . . and Colin—"

She stopped him with a wave of her hand. "Okay, okay."

He flashed his dimples. "So you'll go out with me."

"Oh my God. I didn't say that."

From dimples to pout. "Fine. Dinner, not dating. I'm at work tomorrow but I can do Saturday."

She put her cup down. "Matt. We are not . . . I don't have time to date."

"You need to eat."

She paused.

He was getting to her, he felt it.

"Mallory and Jase are coming over on Saturday."

"Great. I'll barbeque. And it will be 'just dinner.' Not a date." Which is what she needed to hear. The fact that he'd caught her checking out his butt earlier and that all the teasing resulted in her blushing like a woman with a crush told him all he needed to know.

Erin Fleming was into him. She just didn't want to be.

And that, Matt could work with.

CHAPTER NINE

"It's been a solid year since the protection order was in place so the judge is granting a hearing."

Just listening to Renee's words made Erin's pulse race.

"He almost killed me."

"Which I will argue on your behalf. But there was no official police report and the car accident was recorded as just that. The only reason we received the protective order in the first place was because of the stack of 'accident' reports obtained by urgent care. Since there is nothing new, and no contact between the two of you, I don't think we have much hope of keeping the order in place."

Erin stared out over the property, thankful that Scout was by her side, and blinked away tears. "That's only because he doesn't know where I am." Or so she hoped.

"I'm going to point that out. But I have to warn you, I've read his rebuttal and his attorney's statement. They're pretty convincing," Renee warned.

"He's a master at manipulation."

"Most narcissists are. Look at it this way . . . once the order is lifted, his 'reasons' for not signing the divorce documents are out of the way."

"He won't sign them."

"He will eventually."

Her gut said differently. "Do what you can, Renee."

There was silence on the line. "Do you really think the restraining order is the only thing keeping him away from you?"

No. She knew from the beginning that the order was never going to stop Desmond from coming after her. But once it was off the table, there was one less emotional security blanket she could hold on to.

"He doesn't know where you are, Maci."

"That isn't my name anymore."

Renee sighed over the line. "How are you holding up? Are you meeting new friends?"

"So they can learn about my true past?"

"You can't be a hermit. It's not healthy."

"I'm fine, Renee. Thanks for your concern." Scout lifted his head off his paws, stood, and put his head in her lap. "It's okay, Scout."

"Scout? Is that a pet?"

"A dog."

"Dogs are good. Great companions, perfect alarms for bad guys." Renee's voice was hopeful.

"When is the hearing?"

"Next Friday. I already postponed once. The judge will throw it out if we don't move forward. I'm going to fight hard. You know that, right?"

Erin ran her fingers over Scout's head, scratched behind his ears. "I know. Call me when it's over."

"I will."

They hung up, and a single tear dripped off her cheek.

What if Desmond knew where she was all along and was waiting for the restraining order to go away? What if he's been watching her all along, and the hair on the back of her neck standing at attention wasn't just her imagination. What if he showed up and hurt Parker or went after Austin?

Scout added a paw to his nose in her lap.

Erin looked down at the dog. "You're too big to be a lap dog."

A second paw jumped into her lap as Scout tried to prove her wrong.

She'd have to leave. If Desmond showed up, she'd have to leave to protect the people she was starting to care for. Because he would use them to get to her. Just like he promised to do to her sister. Which was why it was best Helen didn't have any contact with her at all.

A year ago, before she moved to Santa Clarita and found refuge in Parker's tiny guesthouse, she thought she would be running for the rest of her life. Only the past six months had given her hope that she could set down roots, at least shallow ones, and try to live a real life.

If she knew for sure Desmond wasn't looking for her.

But he was.

"If you leave me, I'll hunt you down, and I will find you. When I do, you'll know just how disappointed I am." These words were delivered in her ear as he pounded into her after a fight. Although she couldn't call what they did fighting.

He hit.

She cowered.

She looked at her hands, remembered the wrist splints, finger splints, and arm cast.

Her head started to pound and forced her to think of something else.

But first, Excedrin.

~

Matt and his crew spent much of their day driving their route and checking weed abatement on commercial and residential properties. Most of the time people greeted them with smiles and handshakes, but there was the occasional homeowner who decided it was none of the fire department's business if their weeds were three feet tall and resting against their homes.

No matter how diplomatic Matt's team was, those property own-
ers always made the biggest noise and screamed the loudest when a fire
actually blew through.

It was a part of his job he didn't enjoy in the slightest.

Putting water on fire, running into a burning building to save a
life . . . he'd take that any day over policing people's gardening habits.

May first had been the cutoff for brush clearance, so on this round
they simply gave out warnings. They already had a map of residents that
needed yearly reminders, followed by a warning, followed by a date the
city or county would take action. In cases where the homeowner didn't
comply, men were hired to do the job and a bill given to the resident.
All in an effort to keep them safe.

They were climbing back in their truck after a less than friendly
interaction when Tom started to bitch. "Well, that was fun."

"He pisses and moans every year. By July he makes an effort,"
Captain Arwin told them.

"How long have you been on this route again?" Matt asked.

"Ten years at this station. Been in the valley for almost twenty. The
only time we have less complainers is after a big fire. The fact we've
only had a few today is proof that last year's fire made an impression."

Tom shook his head. "They'll forget by next year."

Jessie climbed in last and closed the door.

"Only a couple more hours of this and we can call it a day," Arwin
said.

Matt moaned and reached for the headset as Tom started the massive truck. As he did, their radios signaled a call.

"Oh, thank God," Matt sighed.

Tom turned in his seat to look at him with the same smile on his
face.

A fire was a hell of a lot better way to spend the day than knocking
on doors. As sick as he knew that sounded, it was why they all became
firefighters to begin with.

A brush fire off the interstate in Stevenson Ranch had broken out, and since the area was dense with residential homes, dispatch was sending in half a dozen trucks.

Before they got there, the fire had consumed ten acres and was racing up a hillside toward a tract of homes. There were already crews on the south flank, and their rig was diverted to the structures that would come in contact with the flames first.

The neighborhood was like most in the Santa Clarita Valley. Lots of cars parked on the streets in front of homes. And right now many of the residents were standing in the street with their cell phones in their hands capturing the fire to post on the internet later.

For him and his crew, they were in the way.

They pulled up between the first two homes on the fire front and jumped out of the rig. Once their personal protection was covering them, from helmet to boots, they strapped respiratory devices onto their backs. The captain hustled between the homes to visualize the flames.

The speed at which he ran back told them they needed to hurry.

"Movin' fast, men. Let's go."

Matt held his fist out to the men. "Let's rock and roll."

Two fist bumps later and they were running line, connecting hoses, and rushing in.

Matt's pulse jumped and he knew it wouldn't come down until it was all over.

Damn, he loved his job.

~

Erin saw smoke billowing up across the valley. It was too far away to be concerned that it would reach her, but that didn't stop her from worrying about Matt. She opened the app on her phone to see if his station had been dispatched. When she confirmed that he had, her nerves soared even higher.

When the smoke wasn't extinguished right away, she turned on the television to the local news in hopes of some coverage. All she found was a teaser saying a team was on the way, and that there was a fire with the information Erin already had. Then it dawned on her that the media probably received a lot of their information from the same source she did.

As the fire grew, and more engines were sent in, Erin's anxiety spiked.

Camera crews finally moved on scene with coverage from the closest street they could access. Flames licked up the hillside from behind. So far it appeared that the homes were being saved, but all she saw was dense smoke and fire engines littering the streets. Firefighters all looked the same with their hats on and hoses in their hands. Much as she tried to pick Matt out of the mix, she couldn't. Once the loop of film started to repeat, she relocated from her perch on the edge of the couch and into Parker's kitchen.

She needed to move.

Do something to distract herself.

For ten minutes she gathered flour, sugar, and a smattering of baking goods from the pantry and looked in the fridge. Not finding what she needed, she doubled her steps to her house, grabbed supplies, and ran back.

Before she started, she refreshed her feed on the app and flipped through the two news channels that were covering the fire.

Erin knew Parker wasn't much of a cook, but she'd inherited all the right pans and gadgets from her mother, so the kitchen was stocked with everything Erin needed to work efficiently. With the air conditioner blowing out the heat, she slowly turned the rural home kitchen into a bakery.

By the time Austin came home from school there were dozens of cookies, a full sheet of brownies, a coffee cake, and a peach cobbler cooling on a rack.

Austin dropped his backpack with his mouth gaping open. "What the hell?"

Erin pointed to the television. "There's a fire," she said as if that was an explanation of her excessive baking.

He glanced at the TV, and then back at the counter filled with all the wrong, yet completely right, things.

"Yeah, I saw. But what does that have to do with this?"

The timer buzzed with another batch of cookies. These ones were strawberry-filled sugar cookies. "Matt."

"Matt asked for a sugar high?"

One sheet out of the oven, another one in. "Matt is on the fire."

Austin popped a cookie into his mouth, moaned. "Yeah. So?"

Erin shook her head. "Matt is working the fire. I'm ahh . . ." She looked around the kitchen and brushed a patch of hair that had fallen from the loose knot she'd secured before she started baking. "I'm baking."

Austin moved in for a brownie. "You do realize you're not making any sense." He took a bite, then looked down at the half-eaten bit. "Holy wow . . . that's amazing."

"Don't eat them all. They're for Matt."

At that moment she took a good look at the sheer number of dia-betes-inducing goodies she'd managed to bake in one afternoon.

Austin piled three more brownies in his hands. "I don't think he'll be able to eat all this."

"The station. I'll take it to the station." Yes, that's what she was doing. Baking for the team.

She glanced at the clock.

"Are you going to do this every time there's a fire that Matt is on?"

Her eyes swiveled to the stove. Darn it . . . she didn't set the timer.

"I don't know. Yes . . . maybe."

She looked inside and estimated the time left to bake, then moved to the sink to work on the dishes as she went.

The lady reporting wore a yellow coat that looked to be a fashion statement more than anything that would protect her. She described the scene with words like *ferocious* and *destructive* and then followed them up with *heroic* and *fearless*. In the end she mentioned a percentage of containment and hope that the fire would be extinguished with full containment by the morning.

"I bet it's already out," Austin said with his mouth full of chocolate.

"She said by morning."

"Step outside and tell me if you see smoke."

Instead of arguing, she opened the slider and walked to the edge to get a view.

There was smoke, but it wasn't like it had been a few hours before.

Austin came up behind her. "See."

"You think it's out?"

"I think it's almost out. They don't consider it *contained* until they've literally put a line in the dirt surrounding the fire damage."

"Seriously?"

"Yup. You'll catch up on all this by the end of the summer." He turned to walk away. "If you want to get all that stuff to Matt's station so it's there when they get back, you might wanna pack it up soon."

CHAPTER TEN

There were several cars parked in front of the fire station. She recognized Matt's truck among them. A peek through the massive doors didn't show evidence that the engines were back. Part of Erin wanted Matt to be there, so she could see that he was okay, and an equal part wanted him to be gone so she could sneak in, drop off the tiny bakery she'd created, and leave before he realized she'd done the baking. She parked her car on the street and pulled the first of her provisions from the back seat.

It wasn't until she was walking up to the front door of the station that she considered that there might not be anyone inside to let her in.

She knocked several times and stood there feeling a little silly. Finally she tried the door to see if it was unlocked.

Bingo.

She cracked the door open. "Hello?" she called out.

Noise from the back of the station caught her attention, so she crept inside. "Hello?"

With her offering in her hand, she continued past the office portion of the station and toward what she assumed was the garage. Instead of an empty space crawling with firefighters, she found a large living space alive with two women buzzing around the kitchen cooking. Much like at home, the television was on with news of the fire coverage on the screen.

"Hello," she said a third time.

Both of them turned around and smiled.

"Let me help you with that." The woman who approached her was African American, somewhere in her midforties, not that Erin could really tell, with the kindest smile and most expressive eyes Erin had ever seen.

"I hope it's okay I just let myself in." Erin handed her the bag in her hand.

"Of course. Come in." The second woman was Caucasian, a good ten years younger than the other, with short brown hair and an abundance of eyeliner. Why the eyeliner stood out, Erin wasn't quite sure.

"I have more in the car," Erin told them.

"Do you need help?"

"I can get it."

Erin stacked the trays three high and brought all the rest in at the same time.

Back inside, the women helped her unpack the food.

"I'm Tamara, Anton's wife," the older woman said. "And this is Kim, Tom's wife."

Suddenly Erin felt out of place. "I'm Erin . . . uhm, a friend of Matt's."

The introduction raised their eyebrows and broadened their smiles. "I don't think we've heard about you."

The butterflies in Erin's stomach started to flap their wings. And not the fun, tingly kind one felt right before a first kiss, but the kind that threatened to bring up breakfast if she wasn't careful. "You wouldn't. I mean, we're just friends and . . ." Her face grew hot. "We haven't known each other long."

"Don't fret, hon. We're not prying. Just wondering," Tamara said. "Did you want something to drink? Water, soda? They don't keep anything stronger here."

"No, no. I probably shouldn't stay. I was just . . ." *A nervous wreck with worry.*

77

Kim pulled a bottle of cold water from the refrigerator and handed it to Erin. "You don't have to explain it to us. We understand being a mess when the guys are out there. That's why we're here," she indicated.

That replaced her frown with a smile. "I'm sorry. I don't know either one of your husbands. This must be awful for you. I'm just a friend and . . ."

Tamara grinned. "Right. I like to say it gets easier."

Kim removed the wrap from a batch of cookies. "Do you own a bakery?"

Erin shook her head. "I bake when I'm nervous."

"Oh, boy. This was just a small fire. I wonder what it will look like with a weeklong wildfire."

She swallowed at the thought. "Do you guys cook here all the time?"

"Oh, no. This is the first real fire of the season. Kim and I like to do this for them. On bigger fires they never get back to the station and there is plenty of food at the camps. Smaller ones like this are really more about us not going crazy while they're out." Tamara nodded to Kim. "Christina was here a little bit ago, but we sent her home after we heard from the guys."

"Who's Christina?" Erin asked.

"Jessie's wife."

Kim must have read the blank stare on her face. "You'll meet them all, don't worry. Christina is very pregnant. We told her we'd call if anything changed."

The thought of meeting anyone made her jumpy. "I should probably—"

"How did you meet Matt?" Tamara asked.

"My friend is dating his brother."

"How long have you been dating?"

Erin blinked several times. "We're just friends."

Kim and Tamara exchanged glances. "Ah, huh . . . right." Kim lifted a brownie. "These are fabulous."

Not realizing she'd sat or that she'd downed half the bottle of water, Erin stood. "I really should be going."

The words no sooner left her lips than the distinctive sound of a motorized door opening caught their attention.

"Looks like they're back."

Erin lost her smile. How the heck was she going to explain her presence to Matt?

~

He was hungry, filthy, and pumped full of adrenaline.

"Looks like we're getting a hot meal after all," Tom said into their headsets as they pulled the truck up to the garage.

In the parking lot Matt noticed a couple of extra cars. He liked that sometimes the wives, and even a husband or two, would be at the station when they returned from a fire with hot food and a fresh audience to talk about the day. On long calls, his mom had been known to join the families of the firefighters and help out. It was a win-win for all of them.

The fire had been fast and furious and quickly controlled because of the lack of wind and the fact that the brush hadn't completely dried out. Crews were still out mopping it up, and he was on the list of volunteers to take the extra shift the next day. Overtime was a wonderful thing. That would mean missing out on the barbeque with Erin, but he didn't think she'd mind. In fact, it might even make her think about him a little more and perhaps be quicker to say yes to a real date.

Tom backed the truck into the station, and they all climbed out of the rig.

The captain left them to the task of hooking up the exhaust pipe and readying the truck for the next call before they dragged their dirty butts inside the station.

"Feels like we wore off the winter rust," Tom said.

Matt offered a fist bump. "Couldn't agree more. Ready for the next one." In Southern California, there was always a "next one."

One step inside the station and his senses were met with the smell of garlic and spices that put his stomach into overdrive.

He noticed the captain holding Tamara in the middle of the kitchen and Kim sliding in close to Tom as they cleared the door.

"We told Christina to go home, Jessie. You need to call her before taking your shower."

Jessie was already on his phone.

Matt turned to head to the shower when he saw her.

He blinked several times.

"Erin?"

She stood on the other side of the farm-style table behind a mound of food. Her hands nervously folded in front of her, and she shuffled her feet. "Hi."

Matt wasn't sure what he was thinking. He would reflect later, and realize he probably wasn't. His feet moved until he stood in front of her and his hand reached out. One minute she was watching him nervously, and the next he was tilting her face in his hands and his lips were reaching for hers.

The second their lips touched, the adrenaline in his system peaked in a way a fire couldn't achieve regardless of how dangerous it became.

She tasted like sunshine and spring rain all at the same time.

Erin gasped, or maybe it was him. But she didn't pull away. And when his brain caught up with his actions, he held on just a little longer. "You're here."

Her face was beet red, her eyes wide with surprise, and her gaze focused on his lips. "I was, uhm . . ."

He knew he wasn't going to stop smiling anytime soon. "Worried?"

She offered three tiny nods.

Matt moved his hands to her shoulders and saw the smudge of soot he left in his wake. He tried to smooth it off with his thumb and made it worse.

Much as he didn't want to stop touching her, he let his hand fall. "I need to shower."

She was still speechless.

"Don't leave." He was pretty sure he had to tell her that or she would.

"Uhm . . ."

"Please."

Erin brought her fingertips to her lips. "Okay."

He reached for a paper towel and handed it to Erin before walking away.

The captain and Tom followed.

He heard Tamara's voice as he walked out of the room. "Just friends, huh?"

~

Erin was numb.

She looked at the paper towel in her hand and found it just as confusing as what had happened. Matt had kissed her.

And she'd let him.

In front of his coworkers.

Kim walked up to her and laughed. "You have a little . . ." She made a swiping motion at her cheek.

"There's a bathroom over there," Tamara said, pointing.

That sounded perfect.

Erin hustled behind the bathroom door, immediately noticed the soot on her face and the gleam in her eyes. She ran the water and washed away Matt's touch. Then she stood over the sink staring at herself.

He'd kissed her.

And God help her, she'd kissed him back.

Wait, had she? She closed her eyes and recalled his kiss, the second before his lips touched hers and the fluttering inside her belly. She'd noticed the day's grime on him when he walked through the back door, and the way his eyes found hers and held. He'd reached for her without thought. As if he'd done so a hundred times and kissing her was a natural thing instead of a first-time thing.

It was glorious.

He'd kissed her with such care and softness she'd gasped and leaned closer.

Yep! She'd kissed him back.

"Oh, God." Now she needed to face him again.

Him and his entire crew.

Twenty minutes later Matt and the others were dressed in their blue uniform pants and LA County Firefighter T-shirts. They dug into the pile of food like teenage kids walking in the door after school.

"This kind of eating makes me wish for a low-key fire every day," Tom said as he dished a healthy portion of garlic mashed potatoes onto his plate.

"You just don't like to cook," Jessie told him.

Tom shrugged.

"If it makes you feel any better, we don't like to eat what you cook either," Matt roasted his friend.

Erin sat quietly watching the banter with a grin. This was the largest group of strangers she'd sat down with since moving to California. And there were only five people at the table she didn't know. Maci, the woman she was before, loved this kind of thing. But Erin . . . yeah, she wasn't comfortable in groups of people. This intimate setting was bound to move on to the *get to know you* questions. And those required well-practiced lies. Good thing there wasn't any alcohol at the table.

She'd drunk enough with Parker to realize that she sucked at keeping her secrets after a few drinks.

"There's nearly as much for dessert as there is for dinner, so leave some room," Tamara told them.

"Did you make a cobbler?" Anton asked his wife.

"No. Erin brought dessert," she told him.

Kim giggled but didn't say more.

Matt leaned over. "Did you bring brownies?"

That was an easy question. "I did."

He winced.

"What? I thought you liked them."

"Your brownies are biblical and introducing them to these guys could be dangerous."

There was such pride in his voice it was hard not to smile.

"Biblical, huh?" Jessie asked.

Matt shook his head. "No. Actually, you won't like them at all. I'll save you the trouble and take them home."

"Now I have to try them, diet or not," Tamara said.

"You don't need to lose weight . . ." Kim changed the subject, and before long the bulk of them were talking like any close family would.

Anton was the boss of this family, with Jessie being the baby. Not that any of them were old or young . . . it was just how it worked. Kim was Tom's second wife. Anton and Tamara had been married "forever" as she put it before leaning over and kissing her husband. Jessie was a newlywed with a baby on the way.

"How did you two meet?" Tamara turned the conversation on Erin and Matt.

Erin paused long enough for Matt to answer. "Through Colin. His fiancée is Erin's landlord."

"I didn't know Colin had a fiancée," Tom said.

"It's not official yet," Erin added and looked at Matt. "Unless you know something I don't know."

"I'm sure he's popped the question by now," Matt said. He turned to the others at the table. "He and Parker are in Cabo. He's putting a ring on it before the end of the weekend."

"But will she say yes?" Jessie asked.

Everyone looked at Erin.

"Yes. She will," she said.

Matt smiled.

Tamara tilted her head. "That's wonderful. This is the girl that lives at the top of Creek Canyon, right? Where all the flooding was?"

Matt nodded. "Yeah. Erin lives in her guesthouse. It's been a crazy winter for all of them."

Several sets of eyes turned to her.

"That must have been awful. First the fire, then the flooding," Kim said.

"I moved in after the fire. But Parker told me it was like living through hell," Erin told them.

Anton pushed his empty plate aside and leaned back. "The Creek Canyon fire was one of the worst we've seen here. The way it exploded out of that canyon didn't give any time for air attacks or hand crews and dozers to cut a line. I'm surprised we didn't lose more homes."

From there the men talked about the fire they were just on. How it behaved, what they did to save homes. As the conversation rolled on and on, Erin realized this was why the wives were a part of this first fire of the season. The firefighters—Matt's friends—discussed their day in a way that decompressed everyone at the table. Fire was normal to them. What would scare the average person was their daily life. Or at least it was potentially a daily part of their life. Erin learned that every wildfire they'd been called to so far that year had been contained within an hour. She also discovered that the next wildfire that caught would result in phone calls and not sit-down dinners at the station.

"Normally, if a fire goes on for any length of time, a new crew is brought here to man the station while we're out on the line." There were three shifts at the station. A, B, and C. They were B shift, which meant this crew worked together most of the time. But that didn't mean they didn't work with others at the station.

Erin had a lot to learn.

When Tamara stood up and grabbed a dish, everyone else followed.

No one stayed sitting while they cleaned up the dinner mess. Any leftovers were put in containers so the wives could take them home.

"What is all that?" Jessie indicated an entire counter piled up with foil-wrapped goodies.

"Dessert," Kim told him. "I hope you left room."

Matt turned to Erin. "How many brownies did you make?"

She blinked several times. "I like to bake."

CHAPTER ELEVEN

Matt walked Erin out of the station and to her car parked on the street. "You can park in the lot next time."

"You're assuming there's going to be a next time." The smile on her face told him she was teasing.

Yet with Erin, one could never be sure. He leaned against her car door so he could spend a few more minutes with her alone before she said goodbye. "I was surprised to see you here."

She had the most beautiful eyes. Sky blue, but not pale, wide and innocent . . . the kind he could drown in.

"I was a little shocked myself," she said.

"You do realize you made enough desserts to make us all diabetic."

That made her laugh.

He liked her laugh. Now if only he could make her look him in the eye.

"I'm sorry I'm going to miss tomorrow's barbeque."

"It's okay. It's late. I'll probably sleep in and Austin and Mallory will order pizza."

He really wanted to see those eyes looking at him. "Still sorry I'm going to miss it. I mean, unless they like anchovies. Then never mind."

Bingo. Her eyes met his with a smile that lit them up.

Then he said what he knew would result in her looking away. But with this woman, he knew instinctively that talking was to his advantage. So he channeled his little sister. "I kissed you."

Her gaze immediately dropped to her feet. "I noticed."

"You didn't pull away."

Her hands started a personal tug-of-war with the strap of her purse that hung from her shoulder. "I noticed that, too."

Matt could feel her unease just as much as he felt the cool night air reminding him it wasn't quite summer.

He took a step away from the car and opened the door for her to climb in.

Erin moved in front of him and hesitated. Her eyes drifted to his and she glanced ever so slowly at his lips. It was an invitation. But instead of acting on it, he waited.

Move in, his mind screamed. Just a fraction of an inch and he could kiss her again and make sure she felt it.

"Uhm . . . ," she started.

Then the alarm inside the fire station ripped them both out of the moment.

He rolled his head back, closed his eyes.

"What's that?"

"A call."

"But you just got back."

He laughed. Couldn't help himself. "We made it through dinner. It's a blessing, trust me." He slowly brought his hand to her cheek and leaned close. "I'll call you tomorrow."

"You don't have—"

The door to the main garage rolled up.

He had to go.

His hand dropped, and the kiss she offered would have to wait. "Drive carefully."

"Be safe."

He winked. "I always am."

~

Erin's phone vibrated on the nightstand three times in a row, pulling her from her morning fog. It didn't help that she hadn't slept well all night. She'd replayed Matt's words, his expressions, and his kiss more times than a teenager on their very first date. She was helpless. Absolutely helpless. When she wasn't tossing and turning, she was checking her phone and the app that told her when his station needed to respond to a call.

Her phone buzzed a fourth time, and Erin reached over to find out what the emergency was at seven in the morning on a Saturday.

The first text was only an image sent from Parker. A picture of what she assumed was her friend's left hand with a stunning diamond brightening up her ring finger.

The second text was an image of them standing on a beach with large rocks in the background. The sky was cloudy and they were both drenched from head to toe. Almost like they'd fallen in the water fully clothed and were pulled out and dragged in the sand. They looked awful and yet they were both smiling like they'd stopped laughing long enough to pose for the camera. With this image Parker texted. Boy do I have a story behind this picture.

The third text was from Matt. Parker said yes. And . . . Good Morning.

Erin responded to Parker first. Congratulations! I can't wait to hear all about why you both look like drowned rats.

Her next text went to Matt. Good morning to you. And yes, Parker has already sent me pictures. Your brother has good taste in rings. Although Erin was fairly certain that Parker had left pictures of rings that she liked in plain view for Colin to pick up on. Still, he delivered.

Erin put her phone down and tossed her covers back. She listened for sounds of Austin or Scout and didn't hear anything. Then again, Austin slept late on weekends from what Parker had told her.

Her phone buzzed.

OMG!!! He kissed you? Matt kissed you?

Erin blinked several times, shook her head, and blinked again.

Nope, she was reading that right.

He told you? she texted.

The screen flashed three dots for quite a while. Matt told Colin, Colin told me. Close family . . . I know, it's strange. How was it?

Wonderful . . . too wonderful. We'll talk when you're home. Enjoy your new bling.

Seriously. You're killing me, Erin. Just tell me one thing. Are you smiling right now? Parker's question caught her by surprise.

Erin lifted a hand to her cheek, felt the grin on her lips.

Yes.

Sure enough, Parker needed to have the last word. Eeekkkkk! Okay. We'll talk when I get back. Following her text were three lines of hearts of different colors, kissy lips, and flowers.

The woman was obviously happy.

She wiggled her toes in the carpet and forced herself off the bed. By the time she was in the kitchen, Scout had pushed out of Austin's bedroom and stood at the sliding door wagging his tail.

It was already in the low seventies, so she left the door open for the dog to come and go as he pleased.

Instead of coffee, she boiled water for tea. Caffeine was on the high-priority list. So was figuring out how to deal with Matt. She had no business kissing him back or letting him do it in the first place.

She wasn't even divorced yet.

Not that he knew that. And not that she considered herself married. Still.

Her phone rang as the kettle on the stove started to hum.

Speaking of hot lips. "Good morning, Matt."

"I like how you say that," he told her.

She shook her head. "You're such a flirt."

"Guilty. I started to text you again and thought I'd call since we were both obviously up."

She placed the phone on the counter and pressed the speaker option. "It sounds like you've been doing lots of early morning phone calls."

"Ohhh, I'm busted, aren't I?"

She added the boiled water to the cup that housed a tea bag. "Do you share everything with your brother?"

"The important stuff, yeah. He told me Parker said yes, and I might have told him that we kissed."

"I honestly didn't think men did that," she said.

"It was more like he told me Parker loved the ring and she thought everyone needed a little romance in their life. Parker was sitting right there, and I heard her ask how everything was at the house. You know how she micromanages everything."

"Yeah. I do."

"Right. So she asked if I had been to the house. I told them you came to the station. I think Parker screamed. You know, the kind where a woman is happy screaming."

Erin pictured the scene. "Yeah. I know."

"And then I accidentally told them I kissed you." He paused. "Then there was more screaming."

"You had me up until you *accidentally* told them we kissed. How does one *accidentally* say anything?"

"I don't know. Maybe I'm delirious from a lack of sleep last night. Are you mad?"

He hadn't slept either. And that made her smile.

"No."

"Thank God."

"But I'm a private person, Matt."

"It won't happen again."

She hesitated. "The kiss?"

"No! I mean, I hope not. I'm totally game for more kissing. I'll just keep it to myself."

The reality that she was flirting back and shamelessly leading him on hit her hard. "I'm not in a great place to guarantee more kissing."

He was silent for a second. "You didn't like it?"

"No. It was . . ." She sighed. "I'm not good at this."

"You're wrong there. I didn't sleep last night because I couldn't stop thinking about you."

She rolled her eyes. "You didn't sleep last night because you were called out of bed twice."

"Wait. How do you know that?"

She winced. Probably shouldn't have shared that. "The app."

"You're totally spying on me." There was laughter in his voice.

"It's a public app. It wasn't like I was outside the station with binoculars or anything."

"That would be creepy," he said.

"Right. So I wasn't spying."

"Curious?"

"Concerned."

"That's even better."

Erin closed her eyes. "Matt—"

"It's okay, Erin. I get it. I kissed you and you liked it enough to make you think. Which I'm totally good with. I want you thinking about me."

"You're pretty sure of yourself."

"Am I wrong?"

Oh, how she wanted to call him on his words.

Instead she said nothing.

"Exactly," he concluded. "I just want you to know that I'm thinking about you, too."

She liked the sound of that . . . much as she hated to admit it.

"Let me take you out."

"No." Her response was instant. Autopilot. "I mean. I'm not in a good place right now." The line was so practiced it started to sound stale, even to her.

After a few seconds of silence, Matt said, "Okay. I won't push."

Exactly what she wanted to hear. But why did her chest ache? "Okay."

"I'm not giving up. I just won't push." His words were so light and full of sunshine the pressure in her chest lifted instantly.

"You're something else."

"Yeah. I know. And I have to go."

"Be careful," she said.

"Erin?"

"Yeah?"

"Nothing. I just like saying your name. I'll call you later." And he hung up.

Before she could wake her brain up from the conversation, her phone buzzed.

You're something else, too.

She stared at the screen. "Oh, Erin, what are you getting yourself into?"

~

Erin stood beside the doorway by the terminal exit. She was on pickup duty at the airport. Since the place was congested as usual, she opted to park her car instead of driving in circles waiting to get a call from

Parker that they were ready at the curbside. Like anytime she went to a public place as big as LAX, she wore a ball cap and sunglasses. Blend in and not be seen. Especially in an airport.

Desmond had traveled a lot. His work demanded it. Or so he'd told her. She assumed he had several affairs he was juggling. Either way, he left town a lot, which gave her time away from him. Just thinking of him had her ducking her head closer to her chest and hiding her eyes, which were no longer safely behind sunglasses, since wearing them indoors made people look closer.

More times than she'd like, she wondered if he hit the women he kept on the side. Surely she wasn't the only one. If only he'd hit the wrong one and she managed to put him behind bars. Then maybe Erin could have kept her other life.

Much as she tried to push the thoughts from her head, the familiar noise of travelers rushing about an airport sparked many memories, most of which included him.

A man wearing a business suit moved to stand beside her and for a second, she froze. From the corner of her eye she caught a digital tablet bearing the name of a traveler. Only then did she glance over to confirm that the man bore no resemblance to her husband.

Matt didn't wear a suit. At least she'd never seen him in one.

The thought of him helped her speeding heart slow to a normal pace.

A wave of travelers walked out of the secure area of the airport and forced her to focus. She scanned the crowd, looking for the happy couple. Five minutes went by and they emerged exactly as she'd pictured them. Tan, smiling, and way too relaxed for anyone to miss how they'd spent their holiday.

Parker squealed when she saw her, ran up, and shoved her hand in Erin's face before saying hello.

The ring was even more beautiful in person. "Well done, Colin," Erin said to him before opening her arms for a hug from each of them.

"I may have taken a hint."

"Congratulations."

Parker was giddy all curled up next to Colin as they walked to baggage claim. "We have so much to do. Nora is already planning an engagement party." Nora was Colin and Matt's mom.

"Your life is about to become something you don't recognize," Erin told Colin.

"Yeah, I'm starting to sense that." The smile on his face said he didn't mind. Erin had been a bridesmaid twice before getting married, and each one of her friends had acted the same as Parker. Their fiancés were just as laid-back. She had no reason to think it would have been different for her. But Erin had been wrong.

"You could have picked us up curbside—hey, you okay?" Parker was standing in front of Erin and saying something she'd missed.

"I'm sorry, yes. What were you saying?"

Parker tilted her head. "Nothing."

The two of them stood back while Colin reached for one of their bags moving down the carousel.

"How is Matt?" Parker asked.

"That's a loaded question," Erin said.

Parker chuckled. "I can't wait to hear all about it."

Erin leaned closer, lowered her voice. "Not with Colin in the room. Those two tell more secrets than thirteen-year-old girls at summer camp."

"Girls' night."

"When is that?"

"Thursday. Colin suggested it on the plane. Said I needed wine, chocolate, estrogen, and bridal magazines."

She watched as Colin found their second bag. "He's so thoughtful."

"Yeah. I'm lucky."

Erin placed an arm over her friend's shoulders. "He's the lucky one."

Colin rolled both bags in front of them. "Are you done talking about me?"

Parker shook her head. "Not even close."

Their happiness was contagious. "Ready?" she asked.

They turned and headed for the exit, and that's when she heard it.

Her name.

"Maci?"

It was far away. A woman's voice. One that wasn't familiar. Her steps faltered, and it took everything in her not to turn around to see who called her.

"Did you trip on something?" Parker asked.

"Maci? Is that you?" Still far away and behind them. Coming from inside the baggage claim area.

She picked up her pace and wove through the mass of people exiting the airport. The light at the crosswalk was flashing the countdown with only nine seconds left. "We can make it." And without waiting, she moved into the street and expected Parker and Colin to follow.

She dug her sunglasses out of her purse even though it was dusk and hid behind them as they walked into the parking garage.

"Someone's in a hurry."

Erin listened for her name, the one she no longer used, and didn't let up on her pace. "Sooner we're on the road, the better."

"Why?" Parker asked. "Do you have a hot date? Oh my God, you do, don't you? Are you and Matt going out tonight?"

Now that they were safely in the garage, Erin dared a look behind them.

Nothing. No one followed. Maybe she'd been mistaken.

Maybe someone was calling out to another Maci.

"It's Tuesday. No one goes on a hot date on a Tuesday." Erin looked over her shoulder and popped the trunk of the car open with the remote.

"You do if your date works on Friday and Saturday."

She rounded the car and climbed behind the wheel. "Matt and I are not going out tonight."

Parker climbed in behind her, leaving the front seat for Colin.

"When *is* your date?"

"There isn't one." What was taking Colin so long? Get the luggage in already.

"What? Why?"

"You of all people know why." Erin looked in the rearview mirror and sighed when Colin closed the trunk. She dug in her purse for a ten-dollar bill.

"Erin . . . Matt isn't *him*."

Erin scanned the rearview mirror, the side mirrors. No one lurked in the garage. "We'll talk about this later."

Colin tucked into the passenger seat and closed the door. Before he could buckle up, she was backing out.

Only once they were on the freeway, which resembled more of a parking lot than a highway, did Erin ease up her death grip on the wheel.

"So . . . ," she sighed. "Did you two set a date?"

Instead of an answer, two sets of eyes just stared at her.

"What?"

CHAPTER TWELVE

A small dive bar in the center of town was the perfect place for happy hour when it included coworkers. And since Erin was with Parker and a couple of other girls having some kind of slumber party at the ranch house, Matt was entertaining Colin and a few of his work buddies. By *entertaining* he meant buying the beer and driving Colin home.

"Parker is solid, man. I couldn't be happier for you." The words came from Colin's work buddy Fabio. Outside of his long hair, he didn't look anything like the man who'd graced the covers of romance novels in the eighties.

"She's pretty special." Colin was two deep in foam-topped beer, and a third one was lined up.

Glynn bumped into Colin's shoulder. "She still slinging a gun around?"

"Only when she has to," Colin said.

"That woman belongs in Texas where she can put a rack in the back of a truck. You heard about all that, didn't you, Matt?" Fabio asked.

Matt nodded. "I've heard a few tales about Parker and her shotgun. Didn't she grab a gun on the first day you met before she walked you up the wash?" Matt asked Colin.

Colin placed a hand to his chest. "Love at first sight. I knew she was someone I had to know better."

"She'll keep you in your place," Glynn teased.

Lots of male laughter and a few sly remarks about long legs and curves. None of which went too far in light of the fact that Colin was now engaged to the woman. A certain amount of respect came with the title. The truth was, Parker had gained the respect of all the men on Colin's crew because she never simply sat back and watched them work. Her hands were just as dirty and her back ached just as much as theirs at the end of the day. Matt knew. Mainly because Colin bitched to him about it constantly. Much as Colin wanted to be the one coming to the rescue all the time, Parker never waited for him and just did things herself.

Matt had to admit his own admiration for the woman. "She's going to make a fine Hudson," he told his brother.

Colin's expression softened. "Wow. I didn't really think about that. Parker Hudson."

"Mrs. Parker Hudson," Glynn added.

Matt raised his glass. "To one less bachelor in the neighborhood."

A toast and cheers were followed by a couple of burps.

~

". . . so there we were, fighting to get off the small boat Colin had chartered to take us out to Lovers' Beach. Colin was already off the boat and standing beside the ladder to help me down when up comes this rogue wave. The boat goes one way, I fly back. Colin tries to catch me and we both end up on our backs in the water with another wave crashing on the shore. We were laughing so hard we couldn't stand up. Try limping onshore in a sundress that's plastered to your legs."

"That's crazy. If the weather was so bad, why bother?"

"Because Colin had a plan. And besides, the clouds hadn't been there the whole day so the skipper, or captain . . . whatever you call the boat guy, he kept saying, 'No problem. I get you there.'"

"He wanted your money," Erin told her.

Grace kept nodding her head while Jennifer, a friend of Parker's, refilled their wineglasses.

"So we're on the beach and suddenly Colin starts tapping his pockets in a weird game of head, shoulders, knees, and toes, and then he turns and runs back into the water."

Erin's jaw slacked. "He dropped the ring."

Parker's smile grew. "Yes."

"Oh my God!" Jennifer took her place on the sofa.

"How did you find it?"

"Wait, so he starts yelling, 'It's in a black box, it's in a black box!' and I'm like, 'Holy shit,' so now we're both back in the water searching the sand for a little black box. I just kept thinking, *It's gone.* I mean, the Sea of Cortez is super turbulent and the waves are merciless."

Erin picked up Parker's left hand. "You obviously found it, what happened?"

"Wait, I'm not there yet. We had to have been out there for thirty minutes, running back and forth, sifting through sand. Eventually other people on the beach saw us and asked us what we were doing. They joined the search. Finally I just turned to Colin and told him it was hopeless. He told me he wanted the moment to be perfect. I told him that bad weather and water brought us together and we shouldn't let it kick us again."

Grace sighed. "That's so beautiful."

Parker was beaming now. "So your brother gets down on one knee, in the water, and grabs my hand. I could tell he'd practiced his speech, but he kept messing it up, cuz he kept repeating himself. It didn't help that the waves kept blowing up around us. But it didn't matter. He told me he'd replace the ring the second we were home. Even buy something from a street vendor in town to hold me over. Then he asked me to marry him. I was crying. He was crying. It was so damn perfect." Her eyes were misty with her memory.

Erin brushed away a tear.

"You still didn't tell us how you found the ring," Jennifer reminded her.

"Oh," Parker laughed. "We got back on the boat and the skipper, who had stayed in the boat the whole time, turned and handed Colin a little black box and asked if it was his."

Grace started laughing first, then they all caught the giggles.

"It was in the boat the whole time?" Jennifer asked.

"Yup. So then I made Colin get back out of the boat so we could take a picture, with the ring, on Lovers' Beach. And that is why we looked like something the cat dragged in."

"You both look incredibly happy," Erin said.

Jennifer looked at the picture that Parker had printed out. "You guys look like the sea swallowed you, then puked you back up."

"It was crazy. I'll never forget it."

"I bet my brother had a heart attack. That ring wasn't cheap," Grace said.

Parker looked at her hand. "You know what the ring cost?"

Grace looked at her like she was missing a screw. "I was with him when he bought it."

Parker's jaw dropped. "And you didn't tell me?"

"No way."

Erin rolled her eyes. "Your family is all about oversharing."

Grace turned to her with an inquisitive eye. "What makes you say that?"

Erin kept silent a beat too long, and Parker chimed in. "Erin's miffed because Matt told Colin that he kissed her."

"What?" Grace nearly screamed her question.

"Oh, please. Are you suggesting this is news to you?" Erin asked.

Jennifer waved her hand in the air. "I'm sorry. Is this a thing? Matt is your other brother, right? The firefighter?"

Parker, Grace, and Erin all nodded, helping Jennifer catch up.

"It *is* news." Grace turned to Parker. "Why didn't you tell me?"

She waved her new ring in the air. "Little distracted."

"When did this kiss happen?"

Oh, no. Erin felt the spotlight turn on her. Time to put the wine down and replace it with water, she chided herself. "Friday."

Parker leaned forward, rested her elbows in her lap. "You told me I'd get the details later. Well, it's later, missy. Spill."

She needed to defuse this, stat. "It really wasn't a big deal."

Grace practically threw herself back on the couch with a dramatic roll of her eyes. "Oh, please. Matt has been crushin' on you since Christmas. Don't tell us it wasn't a big deal."

"Since Christmas? I only saw him once before then."

"So?"

The news that Matt had been instantly attracted to her did all kinds of fun things to her belly.

Jennifer kicked her feet under her and dug a hand in a bag of chips. "Oh, this is good stuff."

The three of them looked at her. Parker and Grace laughed.

Jennifer glanced at Erin. "I've been married forever. This crush, first kiss, and engagement stuff is better than a smutty novel."

Erin unfolded from the couch to make good on replacing her wine with water. "It wasn't a . . . it was just a kiss."

Parker jumped up and headed her off when Erin reached for a water bottle. "Oh, no. I've been waiting to hear about this kiss since Cabo so just keep drinking the truth serum and sing, little canary."

Erin let Parker push her back to the couch and accepted the wine Grace thrust into her hand.

"Okay, okay . . ." She took a sip of courage and continued. "The day Matt took you to the airport, he came back to return my sunglasses."

"The ones you left at his house after you brought him brownies?" Grace asked.

"You guys really do know everything about each other," Erin said.

Grace shrugged. "He said if you kissed as good as you baked, he was in trouble."

Erin felt her face warming with all the attention.

"Baking for a man is like foreplay," Jennifer added.

Parker giggled. Grace joined her.

The wine was having quite the effect on this crowd.

Grace waved her hand in the air. "Anyway, you made him a chocolate aphrodisiac, and he made up an excuse to come see you knowing no one was at the house."

"Austin was here. We weren't alone."

Grace frowned. "Bummer."

"Doesn't matter. He didn't kiss me that night. It was the next day."

Parker squinted her eyes. "I thought he was working."

Erin knew this slightly drunk group of women was going to have fun with what she said next. So instead of pulling the bandage off slowly, she did it fast.

"There was a fire, and I was worried. So I baked. And when I ran out of sugar and flour, I took everything over to the fire station thinking he'd get it when they got back. Only there were other women there. Two of the wives of the guys he works with. I was just going to drop the stuff and leave, but then Matt and his crew showed up. He saw me. I think he was surprised. He marched up to me as if he'd done so in the past and just kissed me. And that's all there is to it." Her entire disjointed monologue was said to her wineglass.

"What did you do?" Jennifer asked.

Somehow it was easier to look at Jennifer. Probably because Erin didn't know the woman that well. "I stood there." Then she closed her eyes. "And kissed him back."

Parker screamed first, followed by Grace.

"It was only one kiss and in front of a bunch of strangers."

"It's the start of something good," Parker told her.

Erin tilted her head. "I'm not ready to start anything. Good or otherwise."

Grace stopped laughing and asked one simple question. "Why?"

Erin glanced up at Parker, who had also stopped laughing and kept her lips shut.

Keep it simple and as close to the truth without giving anything away. She put the wine down, determined to not take one more sip. "I'm coming off a bad relationship and I'm not ready to date."

Her excuse didn't pass with Grace. "The best part about getting out of a bad one is finding a good one. I'm biased, but Matt's one of the good ones," Grace told her.

"I'm sure he is. This is about me. I'm not ready."

Grace lowered her chin and stared at her. "But you kissed him back."

Parker laughed. "She didn't say her libido wasn't ready, she said *she* wasn't ready. I totally get it. Sometimes these things take time. If I had met Colin right after my parents died, I don't know if I would have been all that receptive."

Erin wanted to hug her.

"I get it. But I'm not giving up hope. Maybe your libido will tell your brain what to do."

"I'm not a guy. I try not to think with that part of my anatomy."

Erin's comment had them all laughing again.

And thankfully, Parker changed the subject to wedding dresses.

Without a doubt, Erin knew she'd dodged a bullet with the entire conversation.

And she owed Parker a batch of brownies.

CHAPTER THIRTEEN

Erin opened her laptop and clicked into her client's manuscript she'd promised to have the first round of edits on within a week. Her calendar was booked through the month, which worked really well for her bank account, but didn't leave a whole lot of room to mess around. She scheduled herself so tight on purpose. Being super busy with work was supposed to keep her focused on books and not what her soon-to-be ex-husband was doing.

Yet there she sat early in the morning after talking with the women the night before and drinking enough to leave her mouth pasty in the morning, thinking about him. Well, her thoughts were focused on Renee and what she was doing. What the judge was saying.

And there was nothing Erin could do or say to keep the restraining order in place.

She read the first page of the manuscript five times and still couldn't tell you what was going on in the story. Giving up, she shut the laptop down and walked into her small kitchen. The compulsive need to move was crawling up the back of her neck. She opened several cupboards and realized that she hadn't replaced most of her provisions after her last baking frenzy that resulted in baking a storefront number of goodies she left with Matt.

Cleaning.

Yeah, cleaning would burn some energy and kill some time while she waited for Renee's call.

Erin opened the cupboard under the sink to grab a few supplies. But seeing the mess that had started to accumulate in the small space, she decided to pull everything out and scrub that surface first.

She turned on a satellite radio station in hopes of distraction. Once everything was relocated on the kitchen floor, Erin filled the sink with hot water and proceeded to scrub the inside of the cabinet while concentrating on the words to the song playing on the radio. So when her phone rang, she jumped up, catching the back of her head on the bottom of the sink. For a second she saw stars, followed by a wave of nausea. She'd hit her scar, the one hidden by her hair but had yet to flatten out and not catch on her brush every day.

Her phone rang a second time and she used more caution climbing out from under the sink. "Hello?" She didn't take the time to look at who the caller was. She had one hand on the phone and the other one reaching to the back of her head.

"It's me." It was Renee. She sounded off.

Erin sat with her back resting on the cabinets.

"It's not good, is it?"

"There's lots to talk about, but I want to know how you liked the butter cookie recipe I sent you."

Their code. "It was great."

"Are you sitting down?"

Erin looked at the floor around her. "Yeah."

"The judge lifted the protection order. I'm sorry."

Air caught in the back of her throat. "I guess we knew that was coming."

"I tried. Desmond's arrogance was in his eyes, but I think he's been taking acting lessons."

Did she really want to hear this? Much as she wanted to just hang up and put this past her, Erin knew she had to collect all the knowledge she could on her husband's actions in order to stay one step ahead of him. Or twenty, if that was possible.

"What happened?"

Renee sighed. "He stood beside his attorney and let him do most of the talking. I honestly didn't think he was going to talk on his own behalf, but then he asked to be sworn in. He gave quite a performance. He stood in front of that judge and told him the reason you'd asked for the order was prompted by the results of your head injury after the accident. His attorney asked about the physician documentation about your amnesia right after you were taken to the hospital. He went on to plea that once you started to recover, it was obvious that your memory didn't completely return."

"So he repeated everything he did the first time."

"Yeah, only this time he managed to bring up tears for the judge. Said that he loved you dearly and couldn't bear the thought that you were out in the world alone thinking he'd tried to harm you. Said you needed psychological help. It took everything in me not to laugh."

Erin could actually picture Desmond's pretend tears that went along with his bullshit story. She'd seen it many times while he stood beside her in emergency rooms and clinics.

"What happened next?"

"I countered, of course. Asked him to explain the multitude of injury reports from the past. He kept the same story only this time said several doctors had suggested that mental illness might have played a role. I objected. He then talked about the medication you took after each trip to the hospital. Since that was in the original documentation, I couldn't object. He said that every time you hurt yourself the doctors gave you more painkillers—"

"I took only a fraction of those pills."

"Nothing we can prove," Renee told her.

Erin's head started to really pound.

"He suggested Munchausen syndrome."

"What the hell is that?" Erin cried.

"A condition where someone intentionally hurts themselves, or fakes illness, for the attention and medication."

She wanted to throw up. "So now Desmond is a doctor?"

"Actually, there was one file where an ER doctor mentioned it in his documentation. I don't think Desmond's attorney caught it the first time."

"So let me see if I have all this straight. I'm mentally ill, hurt myself for attention and drugs, and Desmond is the victim here."

Renee released a long-suffering breath. "That's the picture he painted."

"This is ridiculous."

"I'm sorry. For what it's worth, I don't think the judge bought everything he tried to sell. What the judge did do was look at the past year, saw there was no contact between you both and that the divorce should act as another means to stay away from each other. Since Desmond was never brought up on spousal abuse charges and lacked any police reports, he dismissed the protection order."

She was quiet for several seconds.

"We knew this would eventually happen, Maci," Renee said.

"I know."

"You're going to be all right."

Erin felt the tears well behind her eyes. "Okay." She was numb.

"I'm going to reach out to his attorney before I leave the office today and get a finger on the pulse of where we are in the divorce. My guess is I won't hear anything until Monday."

"Okay."

"Try not to think about this. He doesn't know where you are, and if he so much as peeked his head into your life, I would drag him back in front of this judge so fast he'd have whiplash." Renee was trying to lighten the mood. But what she failed to understand was that if Desmond showed up in her life, she wouldn't be around to press charges.

"Okay."

"I'm calling you on Monday."

Erin hung up and dropped her phone on the floor beside her. Her legs, which she'd curled up to her chest, fell in front of her and knocked down three of the bottles of cleaning supplies.

Slowly, the tears started to fall and her breathing increased to short, staccato pants. That son of a bitch. *You always win.*

"You always win," she said out loud as she kicked one foot. Her toe caught a plastic cleaner bottle and sent it skidding across the kitchen.

She kicked a second bottle. "Asshole," she yelled.

Her head was pounding, tears were streaming, and she yelled and kicked at the bottles until they were broken and spilling their contents all over the place.

"How dare you!"

Big blubbery sobs over the injustice of it all kept coming.

The pounding in her head became an actual noise that came from her front door.

"Erin?" It was Matt, and he was yelling her name. "Open the door."

"I'm okay." She looked at the mess she'd made and tried to get to her feet and instantly regretted it. Her heartbeat raced in her ears.

"Open the door, Erin." He wiggled the lock, his voice frantic.

She slipped in the mess on the floor, caught her fall with her right hand, and pain spiked up her arm.

Matt started pounding again.

She forced herself off the floor and opened the door. Tension sat in his jawline, and his eyes were sharp as a bird of prey looking from above. "Jesus!" He pulled her to his side as he wrapped his gaze around the room. "Where is he?"

"What?"

"You were yelling at someone. Where are they?"

"There's no one—"

Matt wasn't listening. He let her go and ran into her room only to return and duck into the bathroom.

"Matt, no one is here."

He was back at her side in three strong strides. His hands reached for her face . . . his thumbs wiped at the tears in her eyes. When he brushed her hair back he blew out another round of expletives. "Damn it, Erin. You're bleeding."

"What?" She reached for the back of her head and pulled her hand away. Indeed her fingertips were slick with blood. So many memories rushed forward and that's what made her knees go weak.

Matt caught her and walked her over to her sofa.

"I hit my head under the sink," she explained.

He moved quickly into her bathroom. The sound of a faucet turning on followed.

Her head spun. Emotions . . . it was adrenaline dumping in her system and emotions that were getting the best of her.

When Matt returned to the room, he positioned himself so he could look at her head.

"I'm sure it's nothing. I barely feel—ouch!"

He dabbed the wet washcloth against whatever was open back there and made her jump.

"You hit it pretty good." He kept dabbing and moving her hair out of the way. She felt his fingers following the length of her scar. "Looks like you opened an old wound."

"Do I need stitches?"

He pressed the towel against her head. "I think so."

"Darn it."

"Do you have any bandages?"

"There's a first aid kit in my linen closet."

He took her hand, brought it up to the back of her head. "Hold this."

She knew the drill. Reached up with her right hand, winced, and used her left.

He returned and replaced the cloth with a bandage, and by now they had both appeared to have caught their breath.

"What happened? Who were you yelling at?"

She turned her head—yeah, that didn't feel good—and waved at the kitchen. "I was cleaning under the sink. My phone rang, startling me. I moved too fast, hit my head. That's it."

Matt blinked several times and the owl quality in his eyes bore deep. "You're upset."

"I hit my head. It hurts."

"Are you nauseous?"

"A little," she confessed.

"Did you pass out?" His questions sounded like that of any first responder.

"No."

"Did you slip on the floor?"

"Yes. Twisted my wrist."

His gaze narrowed. "Why does it look like a toddler went crazy with the Windex?"

She glanced at the massacre on aisle five on her kitchen floor. "The phone call. It was bad news. I might have taken it out on the closest inanimate objects within reach."

Her answer gained a partial smile from Matt's lips. "You were yelling."

"It was upsetting news, Matt." *Keep it simple and keep it private.*

"Wanna share?"

A small shake of her head.

His expression told her he wasn't surprised. But he didn't press. "Okay. Let's get you to the emergency room and get you checked out."

"I'm sure a simple urgent care will—"

"I know the people in the ER. I'll make sure you get in and out fast."

~

Holding your cool when all you want to do is explode takes some serious fucking effort. And right now, Matt was exercising all kinds of patience.

Erin was not only nauseated, she was light-headed. She blamed it on not eating. Once he positioned her in his truck, he hightailed it across town to the local hospital. Even though he wasn't a paramedic, he had assisted on enough runs to know many of the veteran staff of the ER.

It was still early enough that the place wasn't wall-to-wall people.

He parked just outside the ambulance bay and used the code to go through the back door.

"We can go through the normal entry," Erin told him.

"It's okay. They know me here."

Several people turned to watch them walk in. Four staff members were in direct sight. Sadly, he didn't know any of them. Except one. "Dr. Brown."

"Hey . . ." From the look on Dr. Brown's face, he knew he wasn't placing him.

"Matt Hudson. I come in with 123 quite a bit."

Recognition followed with a nod. "Right, right." Dr. Brown's hand shot out to shake his. "I don't think I've seen you since that nasty one up in Castaic."

Matt remembered. Way too many cars thinking they were on a ride at the county fair on the interstate resulted in lots of casualties. "That was a hell of a night."

Dr. Brown nodded, smiled, and looked at Erin. "What happened?"

"My friend here. She hit her head. Nauseous, dizzy—"

"I'm feeling better now."

Matt looked at Erin briefly, turned to Dr. Brown. "Stubborn. One-inch laceration."

"Any LOC?" the doctor asked.

Matt started to shake his head when Erin said, "I didn't lose consciousness."

Dr. Brown narrowed his eyes. "Are you in the medical field?"

"No," she told him. "I just know what LOC means."

"Let's get you looked at." Dr. Brown turned to one of the nurses. "Lisa. Can you get her in a room, triage her?"

Lisa was short, thirtyish, and all smiles. "Twelve is open."

"Great."

Matt stood back long enough to watch Erin walk with the nurse into the room. He lowered his voice once Erin was out of earshot. "So, ah . . . Erin's really stubborn. I get the feeling she doesn't like hospitals or answering truthfully." Matt felt himself stretching the truth a little himself. But he really wanted to make sure she was a hundred percent okay, and that would require more than a stitch and a tetanus shot.

"You think she passed out and isn't telling you?"

"I wouldn't put it past her." Matt felt a little devious, which should have left him infused with guilt. But since Erin was insanely quiet on the way to the hospital, he justified his actions and smiled as he walked into room twelve.

Erin sat on the edge of a gurney and the nurse was taking her vital signs and asking questions. Did she have any known allergies or medical problems . . . asthma, diabetes . . . ? Erin said no to everything.

"What about tetanus? When was your last booster?" Lisa asked.

"February of last year."

Lisa didn't blink an eye, but Matt found himself categorizing the date in his head. Most of the time, when people are asked about their tetanus vaccination, they have to think and round to the nearest decade. Or they remember the time they fell off their motorcycle and needed stitches.

Matt took a chair to the side of the gurney and kept quiet.

Lisa pulled off the automatic blood pressure cuff, wrapped it up, and tucked it behind the gurney. "Dr. Brown will be with you in a few minutes. I'll tell clerical staff you're here so they can generate a chart."

"Thank you," Matt and Erin both said as Lisa left the bedside.

Erin rubbed the palms of her hands against her thighs and looked around the room. "This feels like overkill," she said.

"Being in the ER?"

"Yeah."

"Maybe," he told her. "But I'll feel better knowing you're taken care of."

She grinned. "Is this part of your hero complex?"

"I didn't realize I had one," he teased.

He noticed her thumbs rubbing against her forefingers, both of them in time with each other. Instead of pretending he didn't see her nervous action, he grabbed both of her hands. "Let me go out on a limb here and suggest that you don't like hospitals."

"Does anybody?"

She had a point.

Before he could say more, Dr. Brown came in and they both straightened their spines.

"Let's see what we have," he said with ease.

"I'm sure I just need a couple stitches. Or staples," Erin told him.

Lisa walked into the room with a handful of gauze, saline, and all the things a doctor needed to sew together skin.

Dr. Brown put on a pair of gloves and patted the back of the gurney. "Why don't you lie on your side."

Erin released Matt's hands and sat back. Tension and probably pain washed over her features when Dr. Brown touched the cut.

"What happened back here?"

Erin took a second to answer. "Car accident." She looked at Matt.

"How long ago?"

"Last year."

"This is a pretty impressive scar. Did you have any head trauma? Internal bleeding?"

She blinked several times and stared at Matt as if she were afraid to answer the question in front of him.

Much as he wanted to know the answer, and had many more questions that went with it, he found himself volunteering to leave the room. He took her hand. "Do you want me to wait outside?"

Relief flashed. "Would you?"

"Of course." He kissed the back of her hand and walked outside the room.

But he didn't go far.

He pulled out his phone and pretended to find entertainment in his e-mail while he listened to as much as he could hear.

"Tell me about the accident." Matt heard Dr. Brown's voice.

"It was bad. I woke up in the hospital and didn't remember much of anything for a few days. I was told there was swelling in my brain but it went away without surgery." Matt digested the words.

"Complete amnesia, or just to the event?"

"Event," Erin said.

"Sounds like you were lucky."

Matt heard Erin's nervous laugh. "I suppose."

"You hit a portion of the scar."

"Yeah, brushing my hair can prove interesting sometimes."

There was noise inside the room. "I'm just going to check a few more things," Dr. Brown said.

Matt found himself shuffling from one foot to the other, wondering what was happening behind the curtain.

"Are you still nauseous?"

"Not really. I'm nervous."

"Is it us? Or do you have a history of anxiety?"

"I've never been diagnosed with anxiety issues. If that's what you're asking," Erin told him.

"Let me look in your eyes." There was silence. "Follow the light with your eyes but keep your head straight."

He listened while the doctor completed his assessment. "Tell you what," Dr. Brown finally said. "I'm going to order a CT of your head."

"Okay."

"Now let me look at your hand."

Matt smiled and took several steps away from the door.

When the doctor left the room, Matt walked past him, smiled, and returned to Erin's side.

The nurse was cleaning up the bandages and tools they'd used to sew Erin up. "Can I come back in?" he asked.

"Yes." Erin grinned and sat up. "He wants to take pictures of my head and wrist."

Matt played innocent. "Oh?"

"A precaution."

"Sounds reasonable. Are you feeling better?"

"Tender, but okay."

"I can ask the doctor for pain medication if you need some," Lisa said before she walked out of the room.

"No. I'll take something when I get home."

"You sure? We have better stuff here."

Erin shook her head. "I'm sure."

Her thumb was doing the rubbing thing again when they were alone. Matt was starting to think he was the reason she was jumpy. "Do I make you nervous?"

She glanced at her hands and then put them under her legs. "It's the smell. Antiseptic and latex, mixed with whatever might be happening out there."

"And memories," he said.

"Those, too."

He took the liberty of placing his hand on her knee. "I'm a good listener. If you ever want to talk about it."

Those beautiful eyes of hers softened and her shoulders relaxed. "If you were a tiny bit of a jerk, it would be so easy to push you away."

Matt batted his eyelashes as if he were a lost puppy looking for scraps at the dinner table. "My mom says I'm a good catch."

Her core shook as she started to laugh.

CHAPTER FOURTEEN

Matt talked her out of her hospital jitters with stories of entertaining medical runs he and his crew ended up responding to. Like the man who managed to climb onto the roof of the mall with a guitar, stripped naked, and started to perform.

Erin pictured the scene that Matt laid in front of her and found herself laughing.

"There were three engines and a dozen black-and-whites on scene. We didn't know if he was mentally ill or suicidal, or just trying to make his fifteen minutes of fame happen. The thing that kept us guessing was the fact he could carry a tune."

"He was good?"

Matt was grinning. "*America's Got Talent* good. But every time someone would try and talk to him or threaten to take him down, he would step closer to the edge. We thought we had a jumper."

"What happened?"

"It was a standoff for two hours. That part of the mall was temporarily closed until the man finally sat down and waited for someone to get him."

Erin found herself feeling sorry for the stranger. "That's so sad. All that talent and not stable."

Matt shook his head. "Oh, no . . . don't feel sorry for the dude. He was the decoy. Not a crazy bone in his naked body. While he was distracting the police and half the fire stations in town, his cohorts were making off with everything they could grab from a jewelry store inside the mall."

"What?"

"It was a big story around here for a long time."

Dr. Brown walked into the room with a laptop. "Your CT report is back."

Erin couldn't read the man's expression, but he wasn't overly jovial or instantly putting her at ease. "And?"

He placed the computer on a rolling table and opened it up to show her. "Do you want Matt to leave the room?" he asked.

Unlike when she was talking about the accident, she didn't feel the need for him to leave. "No, it's okay if he stays."

Dr. Brown flashed a partial smile and clicked into the images.

Matt moved closer and reached for her left hand.

"It doesn't look like you took on any damage from today. Outside of the cut and what I'm sure will be a decent headache for a couple days. Soft tissue injury to your wrist that will feel better with an ace wrap and an anti-inflammatory."

Erin felt a *but* coming. "So, I'm fine, then."

Dr. Brown scanned through several pictures until he had one of the bone structures of her face. He started pointing. "When I asked about this car accident, you didn't tell me about your other facial fractures. Left orbital and your nose. I'm guessing these happened at a different time, yes?"

Matt leaned forward as if trying to see what the doctor was seeing.

Erin didn't need to look. Maybe she should have had Matt leave the room. "Yes. I didn't mention it because those had happened long before the car accident." She felt Matt squeeze her hand.

"Old arm fracture?" He pointed to the picture on the screen where bone had grown in a bump.

Dr. Brown looked at her in silence when she didn't add more.

118

"I've been accident-prone."

"The two most likely 'accidents' that cause facial fractures are vehicles and fists. Was there a second car accident?"

He closed the laptop and took a deep breath. She'd seen the look on several doctors' faces in the past. Unlike any other time, when Dr. Brown shifted his eyes to Matt, Erin immediately understood the conclusion he was jumping toward.

"They're old fractures, Dr. Brown. I got rid of my problem car long before I moved to this city and met anyone here."

Matt closed her hand in both of his. She could feel him physically shaking.

"Glad to hear that. You need to follow up with your primary doctor in five to seven days to take the sutures out." He turned to Matt. "If she has any neuro symptoms, vomiting, dizzy and lethargic . . . anything, I want you to get her back here," he told Matt.

"You got it."

"You know your way around an engine of a car, don't you, Matt?"

Matt let her go long enough to stand. "You bet I do."

"Good." Dr. Brown looked at her, his eyes filled with compassion. "You said you're new here. Do you have a doctor in town?"

"No."

"We will give you a couple referrals."

She smiled, accepted his hand when he reached out to shake hers. "Thank you."

"Lisa will come in with your discharge papers. Matt, can I talk to you outside?"

Erin released a long breath while Matt and the doctor left the room.

She hung her head and closed her eyes. Matt heard too much, learned too much.

The nurse walked in and went through the motions of closing the glass door that shut off the sounds from outside the room. "You okay?" she asked.

Erin faked a well-practiced smile. "I'm fine."

Lisa sat down beside her with a handful of paperwork. She repeated what the doctor had told her about following up and precautions. In addition to names of clinical physicians, the nurse handed her a list of local therapists and abuse centers. "Dr. Brown thought you might want these."

She wanted to cry.

How many times had someone handed her a packet of information, or slipped her a phone number of someone who could help? How many times? Each time they'd pulled Desmond away and each time he smiled for the doctor, expressed concern for her misfortune, and then walked her out of the doctor's office, clinic, or hospital only to take the paperwork away from her and burn it while she was forced to watch.

She blinked away tears that threatened.

Erin handed the hotline information back and kept the list of therapists. "I no longer need this," she told the nurse. "But it might help that I talk to someone."

It was as if the nurse was holding her breath. "Good, cuz I really don't want to hate on your boyfriend."

"Oh, no . . . Matt's not . . . he didn't." This wasn't good. "Please don't think that for a second—"

Lisa lifted her hand in the air. "It's okay. He seems like he cares, but you can't always tell."

For the next five minutes Erin did everything in her power to repeal any judgment on Matt. Ten minutes later they were back in his truck with the air conditioner blasting. It was only May, but the Santa Clarita Valley was pushing triple digits, and even if it wasn't hot outside, the temperature in the truck was unbearable.

Matt sat behind the wheel; both his hands gripped the thing as if he were choking the air out of an enemy.

She owed him an explanation. "Did you have plans today?" she asked.

He tried to smile, but it was strangled at best. "I was going to surprise this girl I'm trying to date and see if she might like to take a hike with me. But that plan changed."

So that was what he was doing at her house long before lunch.

"How about a walk on the beach? It will be cooler there and the doctor said to avoid anything strenuous."

He reached across the seat and grasped her hand. Somehow handholding was becoming a norm with him. And Erin had to admit she liked it.

Matt looked over his shoulder and put the car in reverse. A few miles from the hospital they jumped on the freeway.

Erin took a deep breath. "I owe you an explanation."

He pushed his lips together. "Much as I don't want to stop the flow of what I hope is information, I'm going to ask that you wait until we see the coast. Because if you're going to say what I think you're going to say, I don't want to be driving when I hear it. I won't live with myself if we're in an accident when I'm behind the wheel."

There was no way to stop the tears behind her eyes. "Okay."

He switched lanes and turned onto the highway that would take them to Ventura. Only then did he place his hand over hers, pick it up, and kiss the back of it.

～

There were plenty of places along the shore in Ventura where a couple could walk on the beach, swim in the ocean, or sit on a stone wall under the shade of a palm tree. That was where Matt took them. With the Pacific in front of them, and the temperature a good twenty degrees lower than it was at home, he occupied the space beside Erin and waited for her to talk.

After ten minutes of staring at the ocean, Matt was starting to believe that Erin wasn't going to tell him anything.

"Would it make it easier if I told you what I've already figured out?" he asked.

Like a guppy, she opened and closed her mouth several times. Finally she placed both of her hands alongside her and locked her elbows straight. "The problem is I'm not supposed to tell anyone anything ever."

"Is that what *he* told you?"

She blinked. "Yes. But that's not why I'm silent. Not anymore."

"Someone hurt you," he started for her.

Slowly, she nodded. "You can't tell anyone. Not your brother, your parents. No one, Matt. And if there's a detail I can't deliver, you just have to let it be. Okay?"

She fidgeted and then settled herself. "We met when I was an intern. My senior year of college."

"Where?"

She shook her head. "Where doesn't matter. He was older, charismatic. I was young and naive. He had clout and prestige, well respected in his . . . with his circle of friends and business associates." Erin closed her eyes. "I mistook his assertiveness as confidence and considered it an attraction. The first time he hit me we were on a trip."

Matt felt his palms tighten and his forearms flex.

"He accused me of flirting with the bartender. Convinced me that I was. I was shocked, confused. Before we flew home he convinced me it wouldn't happen again. But kept telling me that I had provoked it and needed to make sure I didn't attract other men. I had the bruise on my cheek and I felt guilty." Her chest rose and fell with a harsh, bitter laugh.

Matt wanted to reach out for her, but her posture was closed off. Like she needed to say this without any contact at all.

"He hit you more than once."

"I lost count. The second time he gave me an *I'm sorry* gift. The third he whisked us away to an island. I realize now it was to hide me. Sunglasses only did so good of a job."

The blood inside Matt's veins was surging like an overflowing waterfall hitting against the rocks. "Why didn't you leave?" He never really understood why people stuck with their abusers.

"It wasn't that simple. He isolated me. His slow manipulation of my every move was so cunning I had no idea what had happened to my life until I looked in the mirror one day and didn't recognize myself. None of the people I had been friends with before were around. When he broke my nose he flew us to Europe and told everyone I wanted a nose job. He took my passport to keep me from leaving. And when I did threaten to leave, he threatened to hurt my si—" Erin stumbled on her words.

Matt was fairly certain she was going to say *sister*.

"That he would hurt people I cared about. He proved every time that he could break me and no one else would know about it."

"Except the doctors. Surely one of the doctors said something."

For a brief second, she glanced at him, her eyes soft. "Yes." Erin reached for her face. "I could have lost my left eye. It was awful for so long. I was in the hospital for several days. The doctors knew. The nurses knew. They asked me point-blank, almost like Dr. Brown did today. I was so embarrassed. So humiliated that I'd let this happen."

Matt couldn't take it anymore. He reached out and clasped her hand. "It wasn't your fault."

"I let him do it. I never fought back, not once." There were unshed tears in her eyes. "By then he was just ugly, all the time. He didn't even need alcohol to swing a fist. Have you ever been hit in the face, Matt?"

"Not as an adult." He and Colin had their share of childhood roughhousing that might be considered fighting, but those shots were never meant to do any damage.

"It hurts. The shock that it happened is almost as bad as the physical pain."

"How did you finally get out?"

A breeze drifted from off the ocean and blew her hair back. All Matt wanted to do was pull her into his arms and assure her she was safe.

"He wanted a son."

The thought brought bile to Matt's throat.

"I told him I wasn't ready. My needs didn't play into what he wanted our life to be, so he flushed my birth control pills down the toilet and forced . . ."

Matt grunted. How any man could do what Erin was describing . . . But the last thing she needed was Matt showing signs of violence. Yet he knew, if the man was there right now, Matt wouldn't hold back.

"I was petrified that I'd get pregnant. Now suddenly it wasn't just about me."

"Did you?"

"No. I found a doctor in a different town and had her put in an IUD. Only I didn't take into account that De—" Erin flinched. "That *he* would monitor my periods. The thing about the IUD is it often stops them. So when he told me I was late he thought I was pregnant."

"He found out."

She nodded. "I told him I couldn't have a child if he was going to abuse them the way he hit me. He was outraged. How dare I call him an abuser when I was the one causing the issues. I made the mistake of telling him I wanted to leave."

Matt realized he was squeezing her hand too tightly and loosened up. Hearing her past was like watching a train wreck but not being able to tear your eyes away. You knew it was going to end badly, but you kept watching anyway. "What happened, sweetheart?"

She pointed to the back of her head. "We were driving. He was enraged. He told me if I didn't have his children, then I was better off dead." Erin was staring at the ocean now, her words a short staccato as she listed facts. "There was a red light. No one was in front of us. He was screaming. I huddled next to the door. He didn't slow down.

That's when he reached over, unbuckled my seatbelt, and crossed the intersection."

Every cell in Matt's body turned stone cold. "Fuck."

Erin was blinking away tears. "When I woke up in the hospital he was at my bedside and I didn't remember a thing. Within a week my memory came back, and when it did he was right there to tell me that he'd proved he could kill me if he wanted to."

Matt released her hand, placed his arm over her shoulder, and pulled her into his side. She softly cried in his arms as he let her story sink in.

"You got away, Erin."

"I did. But at a cost."

"What do you mean?"

"He's still out there. Holding on. Maintaining his innocence."

"I don't understand. How is he holding on? You're not with him anymore."

She moaned. "I shouldn't have said that."

Matt moved away long enough to look in her eyes. "Erin, you don't have to be careful with your words around me. This conversation is locked in a vault. Unless you point *him* out to me. In that case . . ."

She offered a pathetic smile.

"When I left I hired an attorney, filed a restraining order against him . . ." Erin looked at her hands in her lap. ". . . and filed for divorce."

Of course. That's why it wasn't as simple as walking away. She'd been married to him. "Wait . . . are you still married?"

Tears started to flow again. "He won't sign the papers. This morning when I did this"—she pointed to the back of her head—"I learned that the restraining order was lifted."

"Oh, damn."

"He doesn't know where I am. At least I don't think he knows where I am."

"To stay that way you keep all of this a secret."

She nodded. "The less people that know anything the better. Parker knows my ex hit me. She doesn't know the details."

A lot of things were starting to line up. "That's why you work from home."

"Yeah."

"And why you don't socialize a lot."

"It has to be that way," she said. "My own family doesn't know where I am. If they did, he would find a way to hurt them to get to me." She started to tremble.

"Hey." He placed both hands on her arms and made her look at him. "I'm honored you trusted me with this."

"I think you figured most of it out after today."

He agreed. "The first time you flinched when I lifted my arm, I knew. Colin and I talked about it. If it makes you feel better, every time I ask if Parker has said anything, he's told me no. Said he didn't know a woman that was better at keeping a secret."

That left a smile. "I was told that even with the best of intentions, sometimes things are said, and that's when the abuser learns things. My attorney doesn't know where I am."

"You're kidding."

"No."

"Are you even from Washington?"

When she didn't answer, he retracted the question. "Never mind. It doesn't matter. You're here. You're safe. You have an alarmed house and a landlord that will shoot first and ask questions later." He paused and pushed her hair behind her ear. "It all makes so much sense now."

She brushed away what looked like the last of her tears and sighed. "The only person I've told all that to is my attorney. Well, and the people who helped me get away."

He noticed her shoulders relax. "How does it feel?"

"Liberating."

"Your secrets are safe with me. I want you to call anytime you feel the need to murder all your cleaning supplies."

There it was. A little laugh as she lowered her forehead to his shoulder.

He took the moment to wrap her in his arms. He kissed the top of her head since it was the only part of her available to him.

"Matt?"

"Yes?"

"I'm starving."

For some reason, her words eased the tension and made him laugh.

CHAPTER FIFTEEN

Matt had turned an unused back room in his house into a personal gym. He couldn't stand the meat markets that people went to in the name of fitness. And the places that screamed testosterone were filled with an equal amount of hard bodies that hadn't touched a carb in a decade. He didn't relate to either side of the spectrum, so a home gym solved his problem.

Right now, his workout space gave him every tool needed to push himself into exhaustion.

He'd taken Erin to an early dinner in Ventura and held her hand while they walked on the beach. She told him that being an accomplished liar about her personal life had become second nature. She didn't like that her truths required others to lie for her.

Keeping her secrets would be easy enough except when it came to his family. They were close, and secrets were hard to keep around them.

Grace was the worst at pushing if she felt there was something to learn.

His mom was downright cunning in learning the truth. It was like the woman laced your coffee with truth serum, and before your first spoonful of cereal she had every detail.

Dad would sit back and wait you out. Once in a while he'd play the guilt card. "You don't think my opinion is valuable?"

And hell, Colin was the one Matt went to and told everything to. In his defense, he didn't spill to the rest of their family.

This time, he had to keep the vault shut. He'd promised Erin.

The woman had every reason to believe her ex, and Matt would continue to refer to the man as her *ex* even if his signature wasn't on the divorce papers yet. He was capable of killing Erin just to prove he could.

The images that she'd painted for him were horrific.

With music pumping, Matt pulled off his shirt, put on a pair of boxing gloves, and slowly started to work his upper body. He didn't have a face to picture, but that didn't stop him from jabbing the punching bag hanging from a special hook in his ceiling. What he wouldn't do to have five minutes with the man responsible.

"Who?" He jabbed with his right fist.

"Hits?" He crossed with his left.

"Women?" Left, right, left, left.

He chanted with every punch.

Put a dent in his bag for every tear Erin had shed.

He imagined the face of a man he hoped he'd never meet, broke his pretend face, and blackened his nonexistent eye.

"Fucking coward!" He punched the bag again and again.

When he was done, there wasn't any strength left in his arms, his back screamed in protest of the workout, and someone clapped behind him.

Matt swiveled around and drew his hands to his face.

"Colin."

"That was impressive." His brother crossed the room and patted the punching bag. Once he stopped it from swinging he looked at Matt.

"How long were you standing there?"

"Long enough to know that you're pissed at someone and I'm glad it's not me." He crossed to the radio and turned it off.

Matt wrestled the gloves off his hands and tossed them to the side. He reached for a bottle of water and sat on one of his workout benches.

"You want to talk about it?" Colin asked.

"No." His denial was too fast.

"This is about Erin, isn't it?"

Fucking vault.

Matt stayed silent. He wasn't a liar. It wasn't in him.

He kept silent.

"You know I won't say anything," Colin told him.

Matt guzzled the bottle of water, wiped his mouth with the back of his arm. "And I promised to do the same."

Colin nodded a few times. "I'll grab the beer. You hit the shower."

Ten minutes later they sat on Matt's back patio. "I'm surprised you're here. I thought you'd be at Parker's tonight." It was Saturday. A full day since Matt had been challenged to keep Erin's secrets. In that time he'd mowed his lawn, washed the truck and his RV, and fixed the timing chain on his dirt bike.

"I'll see her later. She said Erin wanted to talk to her."

"Oh?" Matt looked at him.

"She didn't say why. I was going to suggest you come to my place for happy hour but realized it had been a while since I've been here."

Matt sipped his beer. "It's going to be strange when you move for good."

Colin placed his heels on an adjacent chair. "I'm renting out the house."

"Really?"

"Yeah. Parker and I talked about it. The income will pay for the mortgage, insurance, and taxes with a little extra. I suggested selling, but she thought it might be wise to hold on to it until after her brother was old enough to actually collect his inheritance from the sale of her place." When Parker's parents passed away, they'd put a stipulation in their will that any money from the sale of the family home be held in trust until each of them had turned twenty-two. So while Parker was in the clear and her sister, Mallory, was nearly there, Austin still had four years to go.

"That's a big decision."

"The house?" Colin asked.

"Yeah."

"Not really. It's a house. Sure, Parker's place isn't really hers or mine, but leaving it doesn't feel right." The Sinclair Ranch was ten acres of prime real estate with everything you could want. The downside was the home had been kissed by a wildfire and the barns had burned to the ground, and the following winter washed away a lot of what was left with the most rain Southern California had seen in seven years. But hey, it had a pool and a guesthouse.

It had Erin.

"Have you guys talked about keeping Erin there?"

Colin turned to him. "Did she suggest she wanted to leave?"

"No. Not to me. I think she's happy." Secluded and alarmed with people close by who could be there for her. "I feel better knowing she has people around."

"Is that supposed to mean something?"

"I work long days. I don't like the thought of her being alone."

Colin stayed quiet.

Matt joined him in the silence.

They both took a drink from their bottles.

"Any chance your desire for Erin to have someone around has anything to do with the imaginary face you put on your punching bag?"

Matt sat his drink aside.

Vault.

And then there was Erin's safety.

"It's a pretty isolated property. You can never be too careful."

131

Colin's legs dropped off the chair. "Damn, Matt. Do I need to worry here?"

He shook his head. "If there was anything imminent, I'd have to break my vow to keep my mouth shut. I would never put a promise in front of anyone's safety."

"If it changes?"

"I'll let you know. For now, it would be nice to know when you're not going to be around so I can make an excuse to be there." Because if Dickface, or whatever the ex's name was, was staying away because of a restraining order, he might decide to pay a visit. "How soon will the gate camera be up and running?"

"Running cable this week."

"Need help?"

"I'm never going to say no to free labor."

Colin's feet went back up on the adjacent chair.

"Thanks for not prying, brother. I want Erin to trust me, and screwing that up so soon wouldn't bode well for anything lasting."

"Does that mean things are progressing?"

He watched the condensation on his beer drip down the side of the bottle. "Man, I really hope so. We had dinner, but it wasn't quite a date. She keeps saying she's not ready for the whole dating deal, but sometimes when she looks at me I get the feeling she's not even convincing herself with that story."

"We've all noticed the attraction, and if she's revealing secrets to you, then there's something there. Be patient."

He grunted. "Because I'm great at that."

Colin laughed. "Bring her to a family dinner."

"I'm not sure she'll agree."

"You know she won't miss our engagement party."

Matt hadn't considered that. "I like the way you think."

$\sim$

"Aren't you at work?" Erin asked Matt. The man had called her every night he didn't actually see her. And he'd made plenty of excuses to be on the property since she fought the bottom of her sink with the back of her head.

"I'm not on a call."

"I would hope not." Erin sat on the patio by the pool as the sun dipped below the horizon. The late spring heat was bending a little and giving the air a cool edge.

"What are you doing?"

She looked at her laptop. "Attempting to work."

"Are you distracted?"

"Only by a man who keeps making excuses to talk to me every night. Most people just text."

"Texting is lame. I mean, I'll do it, but talking is much better. So much is lost in translation."

Erin closed her computer and set it aside. "Did you have a busy day?"

"You mean you haven't been watching your app?"

She feigned innocence with a gasp and then said, "I don't open it all the time."

Matt slowly chuckled. "See there. If you'd texted that to me, I wouldn't have heard that little noise you made, and I might even have believed you. But since we're talking, I know you're full of it."

"Are you calling me a liar?" She was smiling.

"Uhm, ah . . . ," he stuttered. "I'm calling you a skilled bender of the facts. A confession you made to me not too long ago, if I remember correctly."

Yeah, she had told him she'd become a chronic liar after leaving Desmond.

"Well, I hope people are on their best behavior and you can get some sleep tonight."

"Midweek is always a little less crazy than the weekend. Unless it's a full moon. And that's next week."

She laughed. "You know when our next full moon is?"

"Yeah. I rearrange my schedule if I can."

"That's nuts."

"You think that now. Just keep that app open and off silent mode on the next full moon and see how much sleep you get."

She was half tempted to do it.

"So, Colin and Parker's engagement party. You're coming, right?" he asked.

"I couldn't exactly say no. Parker asked me to bake a cake."

"Oh, no."

"What?"

"Cake. I haven't had your cake yet?" His voice carried a singsong tone as he spoke.

"Why did that sound sexual?"

He laughed. "I haven't had that yet either."

The word *yet* stuck out, but she wasn't about to bring attention to what he'd said. "You're impossible."

"I know. How's your head today?"

Every day, the same question. "It only hurts when I lie on it."

"I bet a hemorrhoid pillow would fix that."

The image said yes, the possibility of the smell said no. "I'll continue sleeping on my side, thank you."

He paused for a second. "How *are* you sleeping?"

With one eye open. "Not bad."

Matt hummed. "You don't have to pretend with me."

"It's a little hard when I roll over and catch the back of my head. I'm sure it will improve once the stitches are out."

"Erin?"

"Really, Matt. I'm getting enough." Yet as she was talking she found her mouth opening in a yawn. "I even nap during the day sometimes. Helps make up for what I don't get at night."

"I guess that's okay."

"Glad you approve. Now go back to work," she teased.

"I'll see you on Sunday."

"Ha. Does that mean you're not going to call the rest of the week?"

"Duh . . . no."

She didn't think so. "Thanks for checking on me," she said.

"Anytime."

She disconnected the call and imagined Matt walking back into the fire station. Was he wearing his blue uniform, or was he dressed down in a T-shirt and slacks? He kept his hair short and his jaw clean-shaven. At least that's what she'd noticed about his appearance when he was working. If he had a couple of days off, he'd leave his five o'clock shadow alone. She liked the contrast. Work Matt and play Matt.

He was being overattentive after their discussion about her past. It would be easy to feel guilty about taking so much of his time, but the reality was, she liked his attention and his concern. It felt as if she'd carried the burden of her abusive husband alone the entire time she had been with the man. When she'd told Renee, it was a hard delivery of facts without all the emotion that went with it. Yeah, she'd cried a couple of times, but when Erin was in the process of leaving Desmond she had been terrified he'd find out what she was doing and didn't give herself permission to fall apart.

And now she didn't want to give him the power to make her cry again.

She pushed Desmond out of her head and gave Matt the space. Before long, she was three chapters into the book she was editing, and the coolness in the air drove her inside.

CHAPTER SIXTEEN

Baking a cake was the easy part. Showing up at Matt's parents' home, on the other hand, made her want to vomit. Right when Erin was starting to put on the pounds she'd shed, here she'd lost her appetite simply by being around people she didn't know.

Mr. and Mrs. Hudson, Emmitt and Nora, she'd met a couple of times since they had accompanied Colin over to the property. Mallory's live-in boyfriend, Jase, was a cousin to Matt, so she'd met him. But then there was the rest of Matt's family, a grandmother that flew in just to meet Parker, an aunt on Nora's side with her husband, and a handful of family friends.

Yeah, Erin wanted to curl up in a corner and hide.

Instead Nora had taken the cake out of her hands when she hit the door, Grace placed a glass of wine in it, and Matt snuck to her side and greeted her with a kiss on her cheek. How had they become so familiar? She wasn't about to turn his affection away.

There was tons of chatter and music coming from speakers in the family room.

"I'm glad you're here," Matt whispered in her ear.

"You have a nice family, but . . ."

He placed a hand on her waist and moved her forward. "They won't bite. Grandma Rose will talk your ear off, but won't remember a thing you talked about tomorrow. Colin and Parker are the center of attention right now, not you. Relax and have fun."

No sooner did Matt's words reach her ear than his aunt walked up to them and reached out her hand. "I'm Aunt Bethany, you must be Matt's girlfriend."

Erin's jaw dropped.

"We're just dating, Aunt Beth."

Beth had the same eyes and mouth as her sister, Nora. But unlike Matt's mother's soft disposition, Beth carried herself a little more vocally. "Isn't that what I said?"

Instead of correcting her, Erin reached out her hand. "Pleased to meet you."

"Colin says you're Parker's roommate."

"I live in the guesthouse, yes," Erin told her.

Beth smiled. "Isn't that convenient. You can double date and never leave the house."

Yeah, Erin wanted out of this conversation . . . yesterday.

"How are Jasmine and Karl doing? I'm surprised they're not here," Matt said.

"Fine, fine. Busy." She leaned closer. "I think they're trying to get pregnant and she's ovulating . . . so . . ." Bethany lifted her eyebrows a couple of times before winking. "Can't wait to be a grandmother."

Matt turned to Erin. "Jasmine is my cousin, and she and Karl have been married for two years."

Bethany tapped a finger on the glass she was holding. "I'm not getting any younger."

"Hoookay, then. You know what, Aunt Beth, I promised Erin I'd show her that thing I did in the backyard."

"What thing?" Beth asked.

"You know . . . that thing, right, babe?" He looked at Erin and nudged her with his hand.

"Right. The, ah . . . artsy thing."

Matt's eyes lit up.

"You did an artsy thing?" Beth asked.

"It was when I was a kid." Matt waved her off. "Women like that stuff."

Apparently Aunt Bethany bought it. She dropped the subject and moved aside. "You must be Mallory . . ."

"On to her next victim," Matt whispered in Erin's ear as they walked away.

They chuckled as he navigated her out to the backyard.

Matt's younger cousin was outside with Austin.

"Escaping the chaos?" Austin asked him.

"Fresh air," Erin said.

He laughed. "Yeah, right."

"When is your graduation?" Matt asked.

"Thursday. The last day of school was Friday. I can't believe it's over."

"It goes by quick."

"I'm surprised you're not out with your friends." Erin sat her wineglass down after only one sip. She really didn't have it in her to drink around strangers.

"I have my whole summer to hang with them. Parker only gets engaged once."

Erin felt her heart swell. "You're a good brother."

He shrugged. "Don't tell her. She'll expect it."

Matt led her away from Austin and toward the back of the yard.

"Showing me your art project?" she teased.

"Actually . . ."

In the corner of a flower bed sat a stepping stone with three sets of handprints in it. "Just in case my Aunt Beth asks."

"I can't believe she told us her daughter was ovulating."

"My entire family overshares. It's a curse." Matt tilted his head and stared at her. "How's the head?"

"Fine. Stitches are out. I'm waiting a week and going to see my hairdresser." She shook her head, letting her hair fly. "I'm getting rid of the red."

"You mean you're not a natural redhead?" His tone was sarcastic.

"Oh, please."

He laughed, reached out, and touched the edge of her hair as it draped over her shoulder. "What are you going to do?"

"I don't know, but this doesn't feel right anymore." She was considering cutting it off. She disguised herself with the red, now maybe a new length. One she'd never worn before.

"What about purple?"

"Because *that* fits my personality." She rolled her eyes.

"I'm joking," he said. "What was it before?"

She leaned in with a whisper. "I'm a blonde."

Matt placed a hand to his chest. "Oh . . . my favorite. Probably a good idea if you don't go back to that."

"Why?"

"Because I'll never stop thinking about you if you do."

That made her smile.

"How are you?" She and Matt had talked and texted quite a bit, but he had yet to bring up their private conversation since they had it. "Everything quiet on that end?"

"Nothing's changed." Renee had touched base and informed her that they were still in a holding pattern because the judge had granted an extension.

"Are you still nervous?"

Erin reached for a nearby tree and pulled a leaf from it. Giving her hands something to do offered some stress relief. "You mean do I still look over my shoulder every time I feel someone watching me? Yeah. But I'm getting better."

He reached out and took the hand she was using to play with the leaf in his.

Erin found herself taking a step closer.

"What does your Thursday look like?"

"Are you asking me out?"

"Only if you say yes. Otherwise I just want to know what you're doing on Thursday. I could ask about Saturday, too, but there are a lot more people milling about on the weekends."

He'd given the day some thought. "Matt . . ."

"Before you say no, I have an idea that won't mean a ton of people."

"It's Austin's graduation, remember? Parker asked me to go with them."

Matt's eyes narrowed. "You ready for a stadium full of people?"

"I won't have to talk to any of them."

"Saturday it is," he said.

"I don't remember saying yes."

"In the absence of a no, the answer is yes."

She laughed. "I'm not sure that's how that works."

That grin. Matt had this boyish charm when he was trying to be endearing, but the sheer size of his shoulders and the way they tapered to his waist was a complete contradiction. The very thing that scared her before about the man was fast becoming the thing she liked the most. It was as if he was a chameleon, strong and protective when he needed to be, soft and gentle when he wanted to be.

"Someone's lost in her thoughts." He stepped closer.

"A little."

"Wanna share?"

His soft gaze created a fluttering of butterflies in her stomach.

"You used to scare me," she confessed.

His brow furrowed. "Was it something I did?"

She touched his arm. "No. Of course not. I've connected attraction with fear and pain. I'm trying to work through it, I'm just—"

He placed a hand on her hip, looked her directly in the eye. "I would rather cut off my own arm than hurt you."

Erin pointed to her head. "I know that here. But I'm not always in control of my impulses."

"I know that." His voice was so calm, so quiet.

"I'm a mess."

"I don't think you're as big of a mess as you think you are," he said.

"I wouldn't date me." Erin was delivering her disclaimer.

That made him smile. "Probably a good idea. Dating yourself might make people think you're crazy." When she looked at her feet, he gently brought his hand under her chin and forced her to look at him. "I understand what I'm getting into, Erin. And I'm still game. You've told me your secrets—"

She flinched.

Matt hesitated. "Some of them, anyway. I'm hopeful that you trust me enough to at least explore this thing we have working between us to see where it leads. What's the worst thing that can happen?" he asked.

The answer to his question appeared in her head like a news ticker during a newscast. She squeezed her eyes shut and tried to step back.

Matt loosened his grip but didn't let go. "Talk to me, Erin. What are you thinking?"

"We shouldn't—"

"I can't assure you of anything if you don't tell me your fears."

Her life was so unfair. She took a deep breath and released it. "What if we get involved and he finds me and I have to leave?"

Matt placed both hands on her shoulders and sighed as if he had the perfect answer to her problem. "As far as I'm concerned, we're already involved. I've tasted your brownies and I don't think I can face life without them again." He was grinning. "And if, *if*, he finds you, he's going to have to go through me to get to you."

"And if this attraction between us doesn't work out?"

"Is that what you're worried about?" He stepped closer until she had to tilt her head back to look him directly in the eye.

"Attraction fades. People change their minds."

He licked his lips, looked at hers.

She swallowed. Oh, damn . . . there was nothing boyish about the man looking at her as if he wanted a bite for lunch. Erin was pretty sure she leaned in. Her tongue slid out and licked her bottom lip.

Matt caught the movement. "Let's try it before we give it up."

His lips were warm, his breath hot. There was no hesitation this time. No question of was this really happening. It was. Matt was devouring her mouth with his, laying claim to her tongue.

Butterflies swarmed in her and built with every movement.

Her eyes closed, her thoughts fled. They'd been talking about something important but none of it mattered. He was touching her, his hands slid down her back and stopped at her waist. The way he pulled her into the frame of his body made her keenly aware of how long it had been to be handled with such care.

She felt his hand reach for hers and guide it around his waist. She took his guidance as permission to touch, and she did. Strong back and sculpted hips. Probably shouldn't move any lower, so she let her fingertips travel up. It was then she realized that his hands were following the same path on her as she was touching him.

Even now, while he kissed her breath away, he was letting her lead the way. No forcing or sudden movements. Just a slow, steady pressure of his tongue against hers, their chests molded to each other. And yeah, she could tell Matt was aroused. Jeans could hold only so much from the public eye. And right now that was pressed up against her but he wasn't satisfying himself with any movements that eased and excited. He didn't have to. His kiss was enough.

At least while they were in his parents' backyard.

It was then that Erin heard voices drifting to them from the party.

Matt's lips left hers, moved to her chin and the edge of her ear. "Through me to get to you, Erin."

His words were a promise.

One she wanted to trust.

~

"There you two are," Colin called out when Matt and Erin walked back into the house.

One look and Parker was shaking her head. "The bridesmaid isn't supposed to run off with the best man until the reception. You two are starting early."

Matt felt Erin stiffen beside him. He looked over at her, noticed the smear of her lipstick for the first time.

He wiped his mouth, and several people in the room started laughing.

Erin buried her head in his shoulder. Her cheeks were crimson.

"Art project, my foot," Aunt Beth boasted from her perch at the kitchen counter.

Matt noticed his mother watching the two of them with a wide smile. It was then that he placed an arm over Erin's shoulder as if to say, *Yeah . . . we're a thing.*

God, he hoped they were a thing.

Anything. Something. More than just a passing thing.

Yeah, she had baggage. Luggage big enough and full enough to make you pay double for it to be loaded onto a plane. But she kissed like an angel that needed someone else's wings to fold her in and keep her safe.

Matt had a distinct feeling he didn't really know Erin all that well, that maybe she didn't even know herself. Because while she was telling him they shouldn't start anything, her lips had an entirely different conversation. Her tongue was singing a different song until she started to let her fear take over. What would happen when the fear was gone and she was free of the ties to the past?

He didn't know, but he wanted to be there when it happened.

"So what do you guys think?" Colin asked.

Matt swiveled his mind back to the room and realized he wasn't following the conversation. He glanced down at Erin. She had the same confusion written all over her face.

"Come again?" Matt asked.

Colin pulled Parker into his side. "Best man?"

Parker looked at Erin. "Bridesmaid?"

Emotion swarmed inside Matt for the second time that day. Yeah, he assumed his brother would ask, but now that he had . . . Matt let loose of Erin and walked over to Colin. He skipped the one-arm man hug and embraced his best friend with emotions to fit the occasion. "I'd be honored."

"Love you, man."

"Love you, too, brother."

At his side, he saw Erin standing beside Parker. "We're such new friends, are you sure?"

"Erin, you're one of the most genuine people I've ever known. You've become one of the family. I want you to be a part of this."

Matt saw the internal struggle Erin was battling. He could damn near hear her crying. *What if we get involved and he finds me and I have to leave?*

"I'd love to."

They hugged, and Matt noticed the hesitation and worry written in every movement of Erin's body.

Matt's mom lifted her voice. "Let's eat before everything gets cold."

"It's mostly cold food, Mom," Grace teased.

Colin patted Matt's shoulder while the rest of the room started talking again. The noise drowned the conversation between Erin and Parker.

"I take it things are going well with you two," Colin said.

"She has more layers than an onion, but I'm in."

His brother patted his back. "Parker asked Mallory to be her maid of honor and Grace to be a bridesmaid."

"Sounds perfect."

"Yeah. I asked Austin."

Matt nodded. "That sounds right."

Colin pulled Matt a little farther away. "Parker and I were going to ask Dad to walk her down the aisle."

That had Matt twisting around to watch their father standing beside Grace.

"Damn. I didn't think about that."

The entire Sinclair family had been orphaned, and not having her own father to walk with her would probably be one hell of a bitter pill to swallow.

"She cried when we talked about it. We're going to take Mom and Dad out this weekend and ask him."

Matt swallowed hard and blew out a breath. "He's gonna love the spotlight."

"Yeah . . ."

Colin kept talking, but Matt's attention followed Erin as she slowly slid to the far end of the room and ducked out the back door.

"Colin . . ." Matt glanced toward the doorway. "I need to check on her."

"Everything okay?"

He slapped a hand to his brother's shoulder. "Nothing I can't handle."

Five steps and he was at the door. Six more and he was skidding in front of Erin.

She was breathing too hard, her face white. "Please." She stepped to the right. Matt countered.

"You're already involved and he isn't going to find you."

Erin's eyes snapped to his like a rattler striking its prey. "How do you know that's what I'm thinking?"

"Because I'm pretty sure the emotions you've connected to us are a bit like what they are to them." He motioned toward the house.

He saw the moisture in her eyes long before the first tear fell. "He's a dangerous man, Matt. If I smell him a state away, I have to leave or risk everyone. How can I commit to a future when I don't know what's going to happen?"

Matt reached out and pulled her into his arms. "You're not going anywhere." He held her as she softly cried and he whispered in her ear, "I've got you."

CHAPTER SEVENTEEN

Erin turned her head left, then right. Soft folds of her hair brushed against her shoulders and bounced with more body than she ever remembered having.

"Now *this* is your color." Manuela teased the ends of her hair with a tiny bit of wax and stood back on her heels, admiring her work. "I never liked the red."

Erin hadn't either. It was a means to an end. The soft brown with only a few highlights pulled through was different enough from her beach blonde natural color, but not shocking like the red had been. And the cut . . .

She shook her head and couldn't stop smiling. "I think the last time my hair was this short was when I was in third grade."

"It suits you. Everyone has the long straight hair. You have natural curls that only come out with shorter hair. This style is perfect for you."

They'd parted her hair on the side and added only a small amount of layers to allow hair to whisk in her face. "It's liberating," Erin said.

Manuela pulled the cape off Erin's shoulders and brushed any remnants of hair from her back.

Erin handed the hairdresser cash and thanked her.

"Now don't ruin my haircut."

Although she laughed, Erin knew the woman wasn't kidding. The one time Erin had bought dye from a grocery store would never be forgiven.

"I won't."

"And don't go home and hide. Grab a friend and go out. See how many heads you turn."

"Yes, ma'am," Erin agreed, knowing she had every intention of going home and avoiding any turning heads. "Thanks again." She headed out the door.

Santa Clarita was warming up. But as the hot breeze brushed up against the back of her neck, the feeling put an even bigger smile on her face.

Desmond had hated short hair.

She jumped in her car and rolled all the windows down. One glance in the rearview mirror and she sighed. She hardly recognized herself. Between the smile, the relaxed lines on her face, and yeah, the new hairstyle, Erin was feeling less like Maci and more like the woman she was attempting to become.

She turned over the engine and put the air conditioner on high.

Out of habit, she glanced at the app that told her if Matt was on a call. When it appeared that he would likely be at the station, she headed his way. Halfway there she started to feel uneasy. Showing up at his work just to reveal her new look was a little over the top. Now if she had some baked goods to give him and the crew . . . that excuse might be better.

Only she didn't have anything and it was getting too hot to heat up her small place.

Losing her nerve, she slowed her car as she passed the station.

The doors were down, and from what she could see through the high windows, it didn't look like the engine was inside.

Just as well.

Her mind made up, she headed for the grocery store. Because things cooled off at night and the smell of freshly baked brownies was a wonderful way to fall to sleep.

She pulled around the corner and into the parking lot.

The big red truck in the fire lane put a huge smile on her face.

Erin couldn't park fast enough and she was hopping out of her car, grabbing her purse, and buzzing into the store.

She walked by the row of cash registers and looked down each aisle. Erin found them in produce.

Jessie was fondling the fruit, and Matt was shaking his head.

She stopped when she saw him and waited for him to look up.

It didn't take long.

He glanced over, looked away, and then shot his eyes back to hers.

Matt dropped lettuce he was holding in the cart and was in front of her in five big strides. "Whoa." He reached out and touched the edge of her hair.

"It's different, huh?" she asked.

"I like it." He was smiling like he enjoyed what he was seeing. He paused. "Do you like it?"

"I love it." She shook her head from side to side.

"There's some blonde in there. Still not your natural color?"

"No. But it's closer."

He stopped looking at her hair and found her eyes. "You're beautiful either way, but I like the new do."

Yeah, that's what she was looking for. "Thanks."

He leaned closer. "I'd kiss you, and show you how much I like it, but I'm working."

She found his confession, and his restraint, endearing. "Being a professional is hard," she teased.

He laughed.

She glanced over his shoulder at the crew. "Getting stuff for dinner?"

Matt rolled his eyes. "Yeah, if we can move Jessie along. The man takes issue with his produce."

Tom looked over and waved.

She put a timid hand in the air. "I should say hi."

Matt took that as an invitation. Before she could say a thing, his hand was on the small of her back, and he was leading her to their grocery cart.

"Hi," she said.

A chorus of hellos followed. Tom continued with, "I hardly recognized you. I thought I might need to remind Matt he already had a girlfriend."

"Hey!" Matt snarled. "Ignore him," he told her.

She looked in the cart and only saw vegetables. "What's for dinner?"

"Nothing, at this rate." Anton gestured toward Jessie.

"You like my cooking, right?"

The three of them nodded.

"Then put up with my selection process."

Matt may not be able to kiss her in public, but that didn't stop him from touching her. He pulled her close and talked loud enough for Jessie to hear. "The rookie always cooks, and we lucked out with this guy. Except he hasn't caught on yet that we need to get in and out of the grocery store ASAP or risk a call."

She tilted her head. "What do you do when that happens?"

"Sometimes the food is in the rig and it does okay, if it's a short call," Tom said.

"Other times it heats up and can't be saved," Matt added.

"Most of the time we leave it at the store and pick it up after the call. But it would be nice to get it back to the station and in the refrigerator." Anton's last words were directed at Jessie, who seemed to get the hint and put the food in the cart.

Erin walked along with them as they scrambled around the store picking out food. "Why not shop before coming to work?"

"Believe it or not, this is easier. Once in a while we'll plan ahead and bring stuff in, but this way we pick out what we all want and split the cost." Matt moved to the other side of her, grabbed freshly baked bread from the shelf, and dropped it in the cart. The whole time he managed to keep one hand on her.

Halfway through the store she noticed the number of people watching them as they walked around. Mainly women. "You guys create quite a stir in here."

Tom laughed. "You get used to it after a while."

"We're the first responders that people like to see. After last year's fire, we were hard pressed to pay for a meal in this part of town. Restaurants took care of our meals, grocery stores had managers giving us big discounts and customers paying the difference."

"I know how thankful Parker was after the fire. I can only imagine that times hundreds of people," she said as they moved to the meat department.

Before long, the cart had all they needed, and they turned to the cashier and got in line.

Matt turned to her just as their radios went off.

Collectively, they sighed.

Around them, customers watched.

Anton listened intently to the call, and Jessie pushed the cart off to the side.

"We gotta go," Matt told her.

"The food?"

"The manager will hold it for us. We'll come back."

And risk another call? "Or I can take care of it and take it to the station."

Matt reached into his pocket and pulled out a set of keys. "That would be awesome." He pushed them into her hand. "Leave the key on the counter and lock the door on your way out."

"Thanks, Erin," Tom called as they all fled the grocery store.

Matt blew her a kiss and walked away.

Alone with their food she realized that several people were now watching her.

She squared her shoulders and pushed the cart forward. It felt good helping them while they ran off to help someone else.

It felt better to know Matt trusted her with keys and responsibility for his crew.

And even his air kiss didn't suck.

~

Desmond Brandt pushed down on the prescription pill bottle, removed one of the capsules, and swallowed it dry. He then leaned in his full-back leather chair and stared at the monitor on his desk. Beyond the door of his office, business ran as usual. With him in charge and people jumping to his every need.

But this bitch didn't seem to understand her place.

For an entire year he waited out his undeserved sentence. A restraining order. From his own wife. All the times he'd pulled her back from the dead and that was how she repaid him.

He ran a hand over his chin and grazed the perfectly trimmed beard he'd grown out with her departure. It added to his character. The jilted husband who was mourning his wife's absence.

For a solid year he employed three private investigators on two continents, one on the West Coast of the States and one on the East, and yet another in the UK. He was hours away from finding a fourth to search other portions of Europe when the image in front of him landed on his desk.

The small clip of video was an archived news feed from the winter.

Maci stood in the distance while a reporter was talking with a homeowner of a flooded property in California. This small taste of the original story was blipped on his PI's radar because the one-year anniversary of the fire that preceded the flooding was coming up.

Desmond was thanking a slow news day that prompted using old coverage to sensationalize an otherwise normal twenty-four hours.

There she was. Standing in a coat he'd bought her while they were on vacation. She'd actually bought it herself, but with his money. Therefore it was his. Everything about her was his.

She owed her very life to him.

Wasn't it he who pulled her out of their crumbled up car that could have caught fire? All while he himself had suffered a cut to the side of his face from the force of the crash?

He was by her bedside, bringing in specialists who worked with traumatic brain injury patients and the personality disorders that the accidents often caused. Or in her case, caused the accidents. They confirmed what Desmond had already learned. Maci wasn't right in her head.

"Wires get crossed." That's what he'd been told. That's what he made sure was written on her medical record.

So when she up and left him with nothing but divorce papers, a bitch of an attorney, and a goddamned restraining order, he took a long deep breath. A breath that resulted in the destruction of his stunningly beautiful living room. The pain he felt with her betrayal resulted in his demolishing everything. The whole house smelled of her. Reminded him of her.

The memory of that room once he'd finally felt like himself again flashed in his head like an old movie. Black and white with slashes on the film that made you squint at times to see what the videographer was trying to frame.

He blinked away the shattered image.

In its place was the reporter's interview that was nothing but a flash of the woman all those months ago and a pan through the property that Maci was standing on.

If it wasn't for the coat, he might not have recognized her. Long red hair. She looked like a whore.

Desmond pushed away from the desk before he was tempted to smash his monitor with his fist.

He crossed the room, opened a well-equipped office liquor cabinet, and poured two fingers of scotch.

Now that he had a lead, it was only a matter of time before he had a location.

He dropped half the contents down his throat in one swallow and absorbed the burn. Fighting the urge to wince fueled him.

Control fueled him. Much as he wanted to hire someone to take care of this for him, he questioned whether they would see his sick wife for who she was.

No, no . . . this was his to deal with.

Finishing his drink, he left the glass on the bar, crossed to the sleek, contemporary door of his office, and flung it open. "Keller," he barked.

His secretary stiffened his spine before shooting to his feet. "Sir?"

A slight thrill shot through Desmond at the man's response.

Desmond nodded inside his office and walked back to his desk.

At attention, Keller stood by with a pad of paper in his hand.

Desmond clicked the image of his wife off the computer monitor and sat. "I need you to clear my schedule."

Keller wrote that down. "For how long?" The man didn't look him in the eye.

"A month."

Keller looked up with wide, questioning eyes.

One glare from Desmond and the man pulled his attention back to his notepad.

"Is that a problem?" Desmond asked.

"Of course not, sir. There is a shareholder meeting next week."

He leaned his head back. "I am in control of fifty-one percent of this company. Tell the board to reschedule."

"Sir?"

The man was questioning him. "Did I suggest something you disagree with, Keller?"

The man looked away. "No, sir. I'll take care of it."

"Good."

"Would you like me to provide an explanation for your absence?"

He took a moment to think about what he wanted the public to hear. "Tell anyone who asks that I'm trying to find peace after losing my wife. And I have a sick family member in Greece I need to attend to."

Keller wrote frantically in his notepad. You'd think Desmond had asked for a regurgitation of the Declaration of Independence with how much Keller was scribbling. "When are you leaving?"

He had a strong urge to say now, but decided a little time would feel less . . . desperate. "Monday."

Keller sighed. "Got it."

Desmond watched his own fingers tap on his desk for several seconds. When he looked up, he was surprised to see Keller standing there. "That's all."

His secretary snapped his attention away and marched out of the room.

A month.

He would make everything right within a month.

CHAPTER EIGHTEEN

Wearing big sunglasses and twisting the curls her new hair afforded, Erin felt as if she were hiding in plain sight. Austin's graduation was at the local community college's outdoor stadium. She sat with Parker, Colin, and Mallory and cheered when they called Austin's name. Afterward they drove to the mall so they could sit in the lobby of a popular restaurant for forty minutes before being seated.

Halfway through the meal it dawned on Erin that she hadn't thought about hiding all day. She couldn't remember a day in the past year when she'd been out in public and hadn't ducked her head, sat in the back of a restaurant, or covered her face with sunglasses the entire time. Even a baseball cap did a fair job of changing her appearance. Sometimes her phone had a hard time recognizing her with the right eyewear and headwear covering her up.

It felt good.

Austin entertained them with how he would achieve world domination by the age of twenty-five. Which would start with a summer job, one Colin had helped him acquire with the county.

"The job is going to make you long for the days where Parker told you to clean the pool," Colin told him.

"But it pays better."

"So does this mean you're Austin's boss?" Erin asked.

"Only when he's on my team. Which strangely enough will happen next winter when we need to clean out the wash again." The winter had been nothing but a revolving door of dirt trucks and tractors scooping mud and moving it off the property.

Colin pulled his phone from his back pocket and looked at the screen.

The waitress arrived with their drinks and took their order.

"Matt is on his way. Says he has something for you, Austin," Colin said before tucking his phone back where he retrieved it.

Just hearing Matt's name put a smile on Erin's face.

"We wanted to invite him to the graduation but we only had four tickets," Parker told her.

Austin sat forward and rubbed his hands together. "That doesn't mean he can't stop by and drop some money on my graduating awesomeness."

That had them laughing. "You'll be thankful for whatever he gives you even if it's a card without cash."

Colin frowned. "What's the point of a card without cash?"

Parker nudged his shoulder in protest.

Mallory reached in her purse, pulled out an envelope, and handed it to her brother. "I didn't put cash in mine."

Austin frowned as he tore into it. As he opened the greeting card a piece of plastic fell out. "Sweet!" He waved the gift card in the air.

Parker shook her head. "Read the card. It's rude to just grab the money and not read the card."

It was interesting to watch Parker parent her brother. And it was even more entertaining to see Austin accept her guidance. He stopped rolling his eyes to read the card to himself. Soon his smirk fell and his eyes watered up. They all stopped the teasing and watched him.

Erin glanced at Mallory and saw her eyes glistening.

"What does it say, Austin?" Parker asked.

He wiped his cheeks with the back of his hand. "Mallory told me I'm her favorite brother."

Parker took the card Austin handed her to read. She glanced through it and went from grinning to swallowing hard. "Can I read this aloud?"

Austin nodded.

Parker cleared her throat. "'To my favorite brother. I'm really glad you kept your shit together and graduated. Because it would have been a sucky day if you hadn't. Losing Mom and Dad has been hard on all of us, but you most of all. You were robbed of time. I want to tell you today, a day where you have your entire future in front of you, that I will be with you during every special occasion, every milestone. And I will remind you of Mom's smile and how your laugh is just like Dad's. They loved you and would be so proud of you. I love you.'"

Emotion clogged the back of Erin's throat. "That was lovely, Mallory," Erin told her.

Parker reached out and placed a hand over Austin's.

For a few breaths they all let the moment sink in.

Matt walked up to the table and broke the somber mood. "Why the long faces? This is a day of celebration."

Erin scooted over in the booth to make room. "Mallory wrote an emotional message in her card to Austin."

Matt reached into his back pocket and tossed a card in Austin's direction. "Must be a girl thing. I just shoved money in mine." He winked at Austin, who brushed away the last of the tears and tore open the envelope.

As Matt scooted in next to Erin, he turned his face toward hers and smiled. Without hesitation, he kissed her. The kind of kiss that said they did that kind of thing all the time. The kind that made her look forward to seeing him again, and often. Under the table he placed a hand on her thigh and squeezed. "You look amazing."

"Aww, thanks, Matt. I didn't think you'd notice," Colin teased.

Matt laughed and started to lean across the table. "Do you want a kiss, too?" His kissy lips made plenty of noise and had all of them laughing.

Austin waved a hundred-dollar bill in the air. "Thanks!"

"Did you read the card?"

For some reason, Parker's question made them all laugh except Matt. "Why do I feel like I'm late to the party?"

When they finished their meal, Austin was already texting a few of his friends and making plans for the night. Mallory drove separately, and Colin and Parker were slated to take Erin back to the house. That was until Matt suggested he play chauffeur.

All that was well and good until he walked up to his motorcycle and handed her a helmet.

"You're kidding."

"Are you telling me you've never been on the back of a motorcycle?"

She looked around and realized that Parker and Colin had already left in Colin's car. "I have never gotten on the back of a motorcycle let alone dated anyone who owned one."

He walked straight up to her, placed a hand under her chin. "Well, you're dating someone who drives one now."

She snapped out of her motorcycle trance and into Matt's vortex. "Is that what we're doing?"

He grinned. "Do you trust me?"

She didn't have to think about it, but she hesitated nonetheless. "I do."

He lowered his lips to hers and took advantage a little bit more than he had while seated in the restaurant. When he drew back, his eyes traveled over her face, her hair. "I really like this new look." Matt took the helmet he'd just handed to her and placed it over her head.

It felt exactly how she thought it would. Snug, warm, and it filtered away the outside noise.

"We're really going to ride this?"

He adjusted the strap under her chin. "I'm going to drive, and you're going to wrap your arms around me and hold on."

Her stomach flipped. "Oh, God."

Once the helmet was in place, Matt took the leather coat he had swung over his arm and opened it for her to put on. "My mother wouldn't be happy if you weren't wearing this."

Erin positioned her cross-body purse before turning to let Matt tuck her into the coat.

It was a warm, late spring night, and the jacket was too hot.

"What are you going to wear?" she asked.

He winked and put his helmet on. "You."

He swung a leg over the bike and flipped back the kickstand. A turn of a key and the bike roared to life.

Am I really doing this? She was probably too naive about the bad things that could happen, and what replaced that was excitement over something completely new.

"You coming?"

Blinking away the anticipation, she tossed her leg over the bike and butted up right behind Matt.

"Put your feet here," he said, pointing to small foot holders on each side of the bike.

"Okay." Once her feet were up she felt unsteady. "Now what?"

He reached for her hand that was resting on her thigh and placed it on his waist. Then he turned to the other one and repeated the action. Once her hands were where he wanted them, he tapped down the visor of her helmet and then his. "Ready?"

Erin shook her head, smiled, then nodded. "Don't kill us."

He winked. "I won't."

The second he put the bike in gear and it started to move, Erin pushed flush against Matt, and her arms around him tightened. All the years of driving in cars with seatbelts and doors with windows, and now she was on something that could go just as fast . . . no, faster than a normal car, without so much as a single airbag.

"This is crazy," she said as they hummed through the parking lot.

"You're gonna have to talk louder if you want me to hear you when we're on the road." He turned the corner and waited at a red light to exit the parking lot.

"I said, this is crazy." It felt like she was shouting.

He placed his left hand over her arm. "I got ya." And the light turned green.

It was twilight and the roads were busy, but not stop-and-go traffic.

Erin felt her thighs tighten against Matt's legs to help stay on the bike. She liked to think she was adult enough to not get worked up over her position, but she'd be lying to herself to say she wasn't. It was exciting both sexually and emotionally. The closeness to the man and the realization that she did trust that he would get her home, in one piece, were as foreign as they were serendipitous. Instead of overthinking, she tried to relax and simply enjoy.

Once they got away from the traffic of the city, Matt pointed the bike down the canyon road that led to the house. As they cut around corners, and the walls of the canyon closed in, she was very thankful for the jacket. Parts of her body felt the pockets of cold but they didn't really bother her. She was too busy smiling and feeling the freedom of the ride. She compared it to cutting off her hair. Somehow the bike felt as refreshing as a cool dip in the pool on a warm day.

And she was curled around Matt like corn batter on a hotdog at the county fair.

She loved it.

From the buzz of the bike under her, to the warmth of the man in front of her, to the great outdoors all around her. She got it. Why people rode bikes. One trip and she got it.

Twilight was fading fast, and the half-moon night was closing in. When Matt turned up the long street to the house, she was actually disappointed the ride was over.

"What do you think?" he asked once he was driving at a slower pace up the residential street.

"I feel like a kid with a new toy."

He turned his head and looked at her with a huge grin. "Good."

Erin eased her grip and let one of her hands fall from Matt's waist to his thigh. The man was firm. He wore jeans, but she could feel the hardness of him through his clothes.

At the gate, he punched in the code and covered her hand on his thigh with his.

He drove the remainder of the way to the guesthouse and parked his bike next to her car.

Once he turned the bike off, Matt just sat there and looked down.

It was then she realized that she was spreading both her hands over his thighs and enjoying the sensation of him under her fingertips.

He was breathing hard. Aroused, she thought. Maybe as much as she was.

Is that what motorcycles did? Turned you on? She couldn't remember feeling this sexually charged in a great many years. Which was sad, since she wasn't even thirty yet. Here she was, wordlessly straddling a motorcycle with a good-looking, caring man in front of her, who was showing some serious restraint.

Erin moved her hands high on his thighs, almost to his hips and back down.

He blew out a breath and swiftly unblocked the strap under his chin and removed his helmet.

It dropped to the gravel drive.

She didn't stop touching him, and he didn't turn around. "What are you thinking?" she asked, surprised at the huskiness of her own voice.

"I'm thinking that if you reach those hands any higher you're going to realize exactly what I'm thinking."

She smiled, and her thumbs twitched in that direction.

He held his breath.

One touch won't hurt . . . will it?

Matt stopped her hand before she could touch him. His sudden movements made her flinch, but not in the way that said she was scared, more like excitement. "Erin?" Her name was a question.

"You don't want me to?"

That's when he shifted on the bike and looked at her. He unsnapped her helmet, removed it, and held it loosely in his hand.

His pupils were wide, feral with desire or adjusting to the night, she couldn't tell. Maybe a little of both.

He wanted her. She could see it, smell his need thick in the air.

"I want you to touch every part of my body," he whispered. "And I want to worship every inch of yours."

Yup . . . her heart couldn't beat faster without needing medical attention.

She wanted him, and he obviously wanted her. So what was stopping them? Erin licked her dry lips.

"Damn, Erin. I don't want to scare you."

She inched her fingers high on his thighs. "Do I look scared?"

A small shake of his head. His gaze dropped to her lips. "You look like you want to swallow me whole."

"Am I that obvious?"

"Yeah, babe, you are."

She inched closer, his mouth a breath away.

He hesitated. "If you get scared, need me to stop . . . I don't care how far we take it, I'll stop."

Was that even possible? The question must have been on her face.

"Watermelon," he said out of the blue.

"What?"

"It's your safe word. You say *watermelon* and I'll stop."

"I don't know if we need that," she told him.

"We don't know if you do." He was serious. And the fact that he'd actually thought about this moment enough to give her a safety net made her want him even more.

"You're right. We don't know. But I'd like to find out." Erin stretched the final distance and pressed her lips to his. She tasted surprise, and it was scrumptious.

Matt fiddled with the helmet in his hands before she heard him cuss under her kiss and it dropped to the ground.

The twisted position he was in on the bike trying to kiss her became a source of irritation. He broke their kiss long enough to crawl off the bike and returned with an even bigger fever.

Erin reached for the back of his neck and closed her eyes. Every time they'd kissed before, touched before, there had been people around. Not this time. This was all them, permission slips signed. She smiled under his kiss with the thought.

She was still on his bike, one leg over each side, and wishing he was between them. Erin wasn't sure how to crawl off without tipping the thing over while he was finding all the sections of her mouth with his tongue.

Matt was very talented with his tongue.

"We need to . . ."

"Yes," he said over her lips. "We do."

Without effort, he placed a hand under one of her thighs and the other under her butt and lifted her off the bike. "Hold on," he instructed before he went right back to kissing her.

Erin wrapped her legs around his waist and did just that. Suddenly, the sheer strength of the man was nothing to fear, and everything to enjoy. He carried her, kissed her, and managed to get them both to the front door of her house. He wiggled the knob to the locked door.

Instead of letting her down, he pressed her back against the outside of the door while she fiddled with her purse and searched for a key by feel. The very hardness of him pressed against the softness of her and shot distant stars in her head.

The keys . . . she felt the . . .

He pressed into her again.

"We'll never get inside at this rate," Erin said.

"No one is home," he said as he kissed the length of her neck.

"Got 'em," she said, removing the keys from her purse. For a second, it felt like he was going to drop her, she drew in a sharp breath and squeezed her thighs harder. All he was doing was shifting positions and taking the keys from her hand.

While he attempted to open the door, she ran her fingers through his hair and kissed the side of his mouth and grazed her teeth on his jaw.

Three times he attempted to put the key in the slot while not letting her go.

"You can put me down," she said with a laugh.

"I'm not a quitter."

Now she was really laughing, and he was trying hard to kiss her and work the key. Finally the door opened, and they both nearly fell into the room.

Matt kept them upright and kicked the door shut as the burglar alarm blared.

He walked her to the kitchen counter where the keypad was and only then did he set her down. Butt on the counter, she kept her ankles locked around his hips.

Free of her weight, Matt roamed his hands up her thighs, much like she had done while they were on the bike.

She pressed in the four-digit code to stop the alarm and set the monitor aside.

The feel of his thumbs pressing along her hipbones and tracing the curve of her ass shot her awareness to full throttle. He was firm but gentle as he explored her through her cotton pants, his fingers pulling the fabric away from her skin.

He was making good on his promise of worship. His pursuit was slow even though his kisses were urgent with need and desire.

The heat of his jacket became too much, and she leaned away and tried to shrug it from her shoulders.

Matt's hands stripped it from her body, and his lips pressed into her collarbone and the open V of her shirt.

So this is what real passion feels like, she told herself. And for one dark moment she felt her brain comparing when there was absolutely nothing comparable about what Matt was making her feel and what the monster she'd been married to had convinced her she felt.

"You okay?" Matt asked.

Her dark thoughts fled. "Better than okay."

Those soft eyes bore into hers. "No discussion of your produce needs?"

Erin reached for his chest and slowly dropped her hands past the waistline of his jeans. "Is this a banana in your pocket . . . or are you just excited to see me?"

He pushed into her hands and she gripped him through his clothing. "I'm in trouble."

With slow, measured movements, Matt played with the neckline of her shirt and worked on the first button. Once it was unhooked, he kissed the spot his hands had caressed and moved to the next.

She wondered briefly if Matt took his time opening gifts and enjoyed the discovery of them, or if he tore into them with frantic abandon.

His mouth detoured from the button to the tops of her breasts.

It was hard to breathe. Her chest reached for him and the tingling in her nipples told her they wanted contact. Only Matt didn't seem in a hurry.

Maybe it was time to show him what she wanted.

Erin tugged at his shirt and slid her hands under it. This was perfect; the feel of his taut body under the splay of her fingers, his lips on her skin. The touch of a loving man whose goal was to bring her pleasure and not pain.

He popped the last button free and slid her shirt to meet his jacket on the counter. In turn, she pulled his shirt over his head and dropped it on the floor.

The laughter over the fumbling of keys and opening of doors was gone; replacing it was a concentration of energy that buzzed like an open circuit in the room.

Matt reached for her, scooting her closer to the edge of the counter, and wrapped her in his arms. Chest to chest, skin touching, he accepted her tilted head and kissed her hard. Without warning, the clasp on her bra released and Matt shoved the unneeded clothing aside.

Hard lips softened when he moved his attention to the needy tips of her breasts. His tongue rolled one nipple and moved to the next.

Erin's head fell back between her shoulders, and her legs tightened around him. "This feels so wonderful," she told him.

"Yes, it does." He cupped the breast he was inspecting with his mouth, held the weight of it. She'd not been blessed with large breasts, but the size of them seemed to suit her frame, and from the way Matt was latching on, he appreciated what she had.

Her bottom was losing feeling the longer she sat on the kitchen counter, and the desire to feel Matt stretched out alongside her was becoming a physical need.

"I have a bedroom," she reminded him.

He nibbled on her nipple.

"Oh . . . the couch is closer," she sighed.

Matt seemed to have other ideas. He tugged at the button on her pants and stopped kissing her long enough to gauge her expression.

Damn . . . she was really starting to love that smile. Confident, cocky. Matt.

"It's going to be a little difficult to take those off with me sitting on them."

He looked down. "You have a point."

She giggled.

Matt swooped her off the counter. This time he held her ass with both hands and squeezed as he took the few steps to the couch and sat her on the arm.

"Lift," he instructed.

She did and he wiggled off her pants and panties at one time.

Erin reached for the button of his jeans.

He pushed his hips away. "Not yet."

"Shy?"

Strong hands encouraged her to sit on the edge of the couch. "There is nothing shy about me. And when I'm done with you, you'll wonder where I've been all your life."

She shook her head. "That sounds like a line."

His eyes lost focus as he dropped to his knees. Their gazes locked. "No. I simply want you to think the same way I am."

It took a moment for her brain to wake up to the meaning of his words. As it did, Matt pushed her knees farther apart and lowered his kiss to her sex.

Erin lost it. All thoughts of bad lines and the fact that Matt wasn't completely undressed fled. His touch and the way he worked to find the spots she responded to the most, and the constant pressure that teased just enough and delivered even more, was too much.

She braced herself with one hand behind her, her back arched until she couldn't hold herself up any longer. Her back met the sofa and her hips were up on the arm like an offering plate full of sexual sacrifices. And Matt took and took. And the moment when she felt the heat building she reached for his head and held on as he pushed her over the edge of sanity. He kept touching her until she had to push him away or risk screaming.

So completely lax, she didn't have it in her to be embarrassed. Even when he smiled at her.

"Is it working?" he asked from the intimate space between her legs.

"What?" Were they talking about something before he took her away from the universe?

"Not sure?" he asked, teasing. He lifted her hips off the arm of the couch and scooted her whole body up. "I have more."

She honestly couldn't remember what they'd been saying.

It didn't matter. Matt was kicking away his jeans, his erection fully prepared to do more.

He was a beautiful man. In every way.

"How do you want to do this?" he asked as he looked down at her.

At first, his question caught her off guard. Then she realized he was considering how she might feel if he was on top of her. Holding her down. And yeah. That might not be the best way this first time.

Erin sat up and pushed to one end of the sofa. "Lie down."

He handed her a condom and took his time stretching out.

The packet in her hand laughed at her. "It's been a long time since I've seen one of these."

Matt ran a hand up her arm. "Do you remember where it goes?"

The man made her laugh. She couldn't remember ever laughing during sex. But then, she . . . No! She wouldn't go there. This was about the two of them, and all thoughts and emotions that would follow had to come later. They couldn't be allowed room to fester now.

Erin tore the packet open and removed the wet latex.

Matt guided her hand to him. The color of her fingernail polish caught her attention as she wrapped her fingers around him slowly. When she looked at him, his eyes were closed and that seemed to give her permission to touch him more. And she did. Part of her wanted to touch him the way he had her, but that might be pushing her into the past a little too quickly. And the last thing she wanted to do now was find a need to talk about summer fruit.

So she gave him pleasure with her hand, her fingers finding the soft places, the hard places, and the ones that were adding lubrication without the condom.

Without realizing what she was doing, her fingertip caught a drop and she brought it to her lips. He tasted different. Smelled like heaven.

"Ah, damn."

Matt had opened his eyes and was watching her.

She bit her lip and smiled. The condom went on, and she crawled up the length of him. Their lips met and Matt's arms circled her back and ran over every place on her body he couldn't touch before.

He seemed content just like this. Kissing her, touching her. Not once did he attempt to take control. Then, as if he caught her thoughts, he stopped kissing her long enough to direct those soft eyes on hers. "Your pace, your time."

So many emotions swelled and threatened to bring tears to her eyes. Erin blinked several times to stop them while she bent her knee and draped it over him. Like the motorcycle, the man under her hummed. "Slow. Okay?" she asked.

Matt ran his hands to her hips and helped lift her at the right angle.

He was right there. "You sure?"

She braced her hands on his shoulders and nodded.

Together they met in the middle and paused. The length of him, the feel of him, was filled with pleasure and pressure. Because she knew he was waiting for her cue, Erin leaned down, kissed him, and started to move.

Matt whispered in her ear saying all the things she wanted to hear. How she was making him feel, how beautiful she was, how he wanted her to crave this time together. Only when the intensity became too much, and her hips moved faster, frantic, did Matt stop talking. Her orgasm was fast approaching and instead of keeping it from him, she told him and he kept the pace steady until she called his name. Her body pulsed around him, his breath so labored with the force of his resistance she could tell was torturing him.

"What do you need?" she asked him.

His knees came up and he found an even deeper part of her body that sparked an unexpected groan. "More from you," he told her. "One more for you."

"I'm—" She was going to say *done*, but he thrust his hips again and picked up speed and a second more intense orgasm washed over her as his strangled moan told her he'd found his release with her.

She collapsed on top of him as they slowly made their way back to earth.

Erin tucked her head in the space between his shoulder and his chin. "Where have you been all my life?"

He waved a victorious hand in the air. "Yes. Mission accomplished."

CHAPTER NINETEEN

They'd moved to her bed. His T-shirt covered her a little too much, and Matt had pulled his boxers on so he could be present in their conversation and not keenly aware that he was completely naked while she was all kinds of hot in his shirt.

The moment they'd caught their breath, Erin announced how hungry she was.

He didn't point out that they'd just had dinner. He followed her into her kitchen and helped make sandwiches, and when those were done, she heated up brownies.

Matt waved the bit of chocolate goodness in the air. "You've been holding out on me."

She sat cross-legged on her bed while he lounged against the headboard. "How so?" she asked between bites.

"You warmed them up. This takes the madness to a new level."

He loved her smile. "I don't know why I'm so hungry."

He dropped a hand on her naked thigh. "I have a guess."

"These are pretty good, huh?"

Apparently Erin liked to eat . . . *after*. Matt found himself fascinated with how much she was enjoying her food. "I think you might want to patent the recipe and make money off of them."

"You mean like Betty Crocker?"

He looked her up . . . and down. His shirt covered her, but he knew damn well she wasn't wearing panties. "A hot version of Mrs. Crocker."

"How do you know Mrs. C. wasn't hot? She could have been the blonde you crave."

His jaw slacked. "I'm all about the sassy short-haired brunette."

"I wasn't fishing for a compliment, Matt."

"You're going to get one anyway."

Her gaze grew distant, and he nudged her knee with the back of his foot. "Where did you go?"

She blinked a few times, put the food she was eating aside. "Was this . . . was I . . . ?" A question hung at the end of her incomplete sentence, and Matt knew exactly what she was thinking about.

"It was, and you were."

She smiled and looked away.

"Tell me what you're thinking," he said.

She shook her head. "I don't want to ruin this moment."

Matt sat up and moved so that she had to look him in the eye. "First of all, nothing can ruin what just happened. But the only way to preserve it is for us to be open and honest. When I leave I don't want you asking yourself a bunch of questions that I can answer and getting them wrong." He paused. "Talk to me, Erin. Is this the first time since . . ." He didn't mention her ex-husband. He didn't have to.

"Yes."

Much as he didn't want to know the truth behind his next question, he felt the need to assure her that her thoughts and feelings were normal so they could push past them. "Did you think of him . . . at any time?"

She squeezed her eyes shut, and his gut twisted the brownie inside into a knot.

"My mind tried to go there. But I forced it out, Matt. I hate that there was even a ghost of my past clouding what just happened."

He blew out a sigh and leaned forward. With a hand on her naked thigh he said, "Please don't hate anything we've done. You were with him, he hurt you . . . I can't imagine putting myself in a position that I once felt pain. Considering everything, I think we did pretty well."

Her hands were doing the wringing thing. A sign he recognized as stress. "I never thought I'd enjoy sex again."

"Well, unless I'm a complete clueless asshole, I think you enjoyed yourself tonight."

She smiled for the longest time, and then he saw moisture in her eyes. "You were so thoughtful," she said as her voice broke.

Oh, God . . . she was going to cry.

Matt hated seeing a woman cry.

He pulled her into his arms.

There wasn't a possibility in the world that he could imagine what she was thinking right at that moment. So instead of suggesting he had a clue, he simply held her until she gained control. While she did, her arms tightened and she sucked in short breaths through her nose. "I'm sorry."

"Don't be."

She cried almost silently. "I wish we didn't have to have a safe word."

He stroked her short hair and rubbed the back of her neck as he did. "Did it make you feel safe to have it?"

Erin nodded.

"Then we keep it."

"We didn't need it tonight."

Much as he liked to think every time would be this easy . . . well, it took some serious work to hold himself back at several moments during their lovemaking. He'd seen enough in his short career to know that old trauma could flash inside someone at any time. "We keep it," he repeated. "You need me to stop, take notice . . . anything to know you're not okay, *watermelon* is the word."

"I'm sorry."

"Please stop saying that. I'm a zillion percent into what we're doing here. I'm in with my eyes open and your past in front of us."

She nodded into his shoulder.

"Now . . . the next question is where am I sleeping tonight?" He didn't want to go home. Didn't think Erin being alone was a great idea after . . . well, after.

She pushed off his shoulder and wiped her eyes with his shirt. "I want you to stay, but I don't know if I can do it."

"Do what?"

Her lip quivered. "Fall asleep with you in my bed."

Matt reached over her, took the plate of half-eaten food, and put it on her nightstand. "We won't know until we try," he told her.

"Matt . . ."

"If you need me to leave, I will. I'll sleep on the couch if I have to. But let's try."

Her tears had dried up, and she hid a yawn with her hand. "I feel like I ran a marathon."

"Have you ever run twenty-six miles before?"

"No," she said, laughing.

He pulled the covers back, patted the bed, and hesitated. "Which side do you sleep on?"

"In this bed . . . everywhere. But the left."

He hated to ask, but he needed to know. "And with him?"

"The right. He made me sleep on the right."

He moved to the side of the bed that would make her the most comfortable and fluffed his pillow. "I have to leave early for work."

She stared at him for the longest time. "Why are you so kind to me?"

Leaning past her, he twisted off the light on the nightstand. Plunged into darkness, he reached up and touched her face. "I like to think I'm kind to everyone. But with you, it's because you've rocked my world since the night we met, and now that I'm half-naked in your bed, I wouldn't do anything to mess that up. Kindness is the minimum, Erin. You deserve so much more."

She sunk down into the bed beside him. Her leg grazed his as she settled. Her body rolled toward him, and he wrapped her slender frame in his arms. For several seconds they were both silent. Slowly, he felt her starting to relax.

"If you need me to—"

Her soft inhale and deep exhale told him she wasn't listening.

Erin was already asleep.

Matt kissed the top of her head and rested his hand on her hip.

This . . . the whole thing, was profoundly good.

~

When she woke up, he was gone, and the sun had been up for hours. Light filled the room, and the small air conditioner hummed. She hadn't remembered turning it on.

Erin rolled over, pulled the pillow that had held Matt's sleeping head, and hugged it to her face. It smelled like him. Her senses warmed her body, and her memory of the evening lit her soul. She lay like that for several seconds and imagined that he was still there stroking her hair and talking to her as she fell asleep.

Damn, she felt good. Better than she had in, well . . . forever. Matt had taken such care in assuring her that she was safe. And yet he didn't handle her as if she were made of glass. He drank his fill and nibbled every part of her, and holy cow, she couldn't wait to do it again.

Erin forced her eyes open to look at the clock.

It was after ten.

A low chuckle rose in the back of her throat until she lay there laughing. Not since she was a teenager had she slept in until ten.

She stretched like a cat, wiggling her fingers and toes in opposite directions. It was then that she realized she was wearing Matt's shirt.

The thought of him riding his motorcycle home half-naked had her laughing all over again.

The bathroom called her name so she swung her legs off the bed. Her naked butt met the air-conditioned chill in the room that made her shiver.

"What happened to your panties, girl?" Her question to herself kept her mood light.

In her small bathroom there was a sticky note by her toothbrush. *I used your toothbrush. I see there is room for one more in here so I'll bring one over. Matt.*

When she was done, she took his note with her in search of coffee.

She found another sticky note on her discarded panties on the floor. *I actually considered taking these. But I'm a grown-up and I didn't. Matt.*

She giggled, picked up her underwear, and went back to her room and tossed them in the hamper. Back through her home, Erin found another note on top of the kitchen counter. *This is my official favorite spot in your house. Matt.*

"Mine, too."

Another note on her plastic container that housed the leftover brownies. *I totally ate one of these for breakfast. Matt.*

The last note she found was in the cupboard next to her coffee cups. It was longer and took up several sticky notes.

You're beautiful when you sleep, stunning when you explode under my touch, and brave to let me see you in these vulnerable moments. I wanted to wake you with a kiss but couldn't disturb my sleeping beauty. Please text me when you're up so I can remind you how much I enjoyed last night. How much I enjoy every moment I'm with you. Have a spectacular day. Matt.

She crushed his love notes to her chest with a smile.

After pulling her cell phone from her purse, she noticed the low battery light blinking and plugged it in. Leaning against the kitchen counter, she shot Matt a text. I just woke up.

Within seconds, three tiny dots flashed, and she eagerly waited for his response.

Give me two minutes.

She set the phone aside and turned on her one-cup-at-a-time coffee maker before retrieving creamer from her fridge.

True to his timeline, her phone rang within the hundred and twenty seconds Matt had told her.

"Good morning." His voice was a purr.

"Almost afternoon," she countered.

"I'm jealous of your bed."

Her fingertips grazed his notes. "Someone had a lot to say before he left."

"Yeah, well . . . I would have said it all to you in person, but you were out like a light. I even made noise, and you didn't so much as sigh in your sleep."

"That's unusual. I haven't slept that good in a long time."

He paused. "I like to hear that. What are you doing now?"

"Making coffee wearing your shirt. What did you drive home in?"

He laughed. "Costume. I looked like one of the Village People riding my bike with only my leather jacket on."

She giggled.

"You think it's funny, huh?"

"Gives new meaning to the walk of shame."

"Oh, darlin', there is nothing shameful about last night." He sighed. "How are you feeling about it? No regrets?"

"That hasn't entered my mind. I feel good, Matt. Really good. Like maybe I'll go jogging this morning."

"I didn't know you were a runner."

"I haven't been. Not in a long time. But I think that's what I'll do. It's such a beautiful day." Like someone had tossed the blinds up for the first time since she changed her name. Matt had done that.

"God, I wish I was there to see the smile on your face."

And that's exactly what she felt on her lips. "What are we doing on Saturday?"

"Are you asking me out?" he asked.

She reached for her coffee that had finished percolating and killed it with creamer. "Actually, you asked earlier in the week."

"Oh . . . that's right."

She sipped her coffee. "I have an idea."

"Let's hear it."

"How about a ride on your motorcycle and a picnic lunch up in the mountains?"

"God, woman . . . where have you been all my life?"

Erin smiled into her cup. She didn't know, but now that she was there, she wasn't going to waste any time.

CHAPTER TWENTY

Matt felt like he was picking up his date for prom, only without the suit. He drove up to the gate and pressed the button to call the house.

"Hey, Matt. Come in," Parker's voice called out from the box.

He waved at the camera mounted on the fence post and waited for the gate to open. His bike announced his arrival, and he noticed Erin pop her head out her front door as he cut the engine.

"You kids be careful," Parker yelled from the porch of the main house.

"Yes, Mom," Matt teased.

He took the package he had strapped to the back of his bike and left his helmet in its place. He'd gotten off work, went home to change, and then headed straight over to pick up Erin. He'd thought about her constantly whenever the day calmed down. Now that she was only a few feet away, his body hummed with anticipation.

"Knock, knock." He walked in her open door to find her sticking food in a backpack.

"Come in."

Her jeans were snug, wrapping around her ass in a way that made his mouth water. "Don't you look appetizing."

"Ha. You mean the food."

"I mean you!" He set the package on the counter—his favorite part of her home—and walked up behind her and wrapped his arms around her waist. He pressed his lips to the side of her neck, and she stopped what she was doing and leaned back.

"You're distracting me."

"Yes, ma'am, I am."

She twisted around and placed her hands on his hips. "Hi."

He leaned down until he felt her breath. "Hello."

Damn, she tasted good. Summer and apple pie good.

When she started to melt, he pulled away. "We won't be going anywhere if we start that."

Erin licked her lips and twisted back around.

He rested his chin on her shoulder and kept her in his arms. "What are we having?"

"You said you weren't picky."

"I'm not."

"Good. It's a surprise." She zipped up the backpack and scooted it aside.

"Speaking of surprises." He put a little space between them and handed her the package he'd brought. "For you."

She looked at the box. "What's this?"

"It's for you."

"It's not my birthday." Erin tugged a finger through the tape holding the wrapping paper in place.

"I think you'll like it."

She pulled apart the paper, sat the box on the counter, and opened it. Her jaw slacked. The red leather jacket came out of the box and went straight to her cheek. "This is beautiful."

"If you're riding with me on mountain roads, you need the right clothes."

She handed it to him and turned around so he could help her put it on. "When did you have time to get it?"

One arm at a time and she twisted back in his direction.

The fit was perfect.

"I had a little help. I did some recon online and called Parker when I found a place in town who had this in stock."

Erin pushed past him and over to a mirror she had by her front door. "You had Parker go shopping for you?"

"I needed a woman to help with sizing. I'd screw that part up." He walked to her and zipped together the sides of the jacket. He stopped just shy of her breasts and took the liberty of making sure the girls were properly displayed.

"Having fun?" she asked.

"This is fantasy stuff right here."

She turned back around, twisted to look at the back in the mirror, and then smoothed her hands over the front. "I love it. Thank you."

Yeah . . . he did, too. "My pleasure. I have one more surprise."

"Matt!"

"It's necessary. Trust me." He looked around her place, grabbed the backpack. "You ready?"

"Let me set the alarm and I'll meet you outside."

He stepped out and shut the door. Seconds later she joined him by his bike, and he handed her his second gift. "These helmets have a built-in communication system," he told her. "Check it out."

Erin pulled the helmet over her head. It, too, was red to match her jacket. There was a whole lotta sexy wrapped up in one woman. "This fits better than the other one."

"It's meant for a woman." He reached for his helmet.

"You mean you bought this for me?"

He winked. "You said you liked the bike, and, honey . . . I'm going to do everything I can to keep that going."

He adjusted his and helped her with hers and then activated the Bluetooth headsets. He turned away and whispered, "Hey, sexy." He was rewarded with a pat on his ass.

Facing her again, he asked, "Can you hear me?"

"Oh, yeah."

"This way we can talk while we're on the road."

He helped her with the backpack, started the bike, and counted his lucky stars when she straddled the bike and him in turn. "Let's do this."

She held on, and he took off.

He took her up Angeles Crest and into the forest. Unlike other parts of the world, Southern California forests weren't densely wooded and filled with lakes. Most of the time the temperature didn't even drop as they climbed the altitude needed to call a hill a mountain. Still, it was a break from the city and great roads to show Erin the fun one could have on a street bike. He wondered if he could interest her in camping in the desert once the weather cooled in the fall. From the way she was holding on and the ohhs and ahhs he heard in his earphones, he figured he had a chance that she would.

Once they reached the ridgeline, he kept going past the burn areas of the past season's forest fires, and he found a day camp area that he knew was up there. He was also aware that the place was almost always deserted. In fact, there weren't any cars in the small lot, and the only thing he could hear once he cut the engine was the wind in the tall trees above his head.

They walked hand in hand down an overgrown path to a creek that was still flowing after the heavy rains they'd had all winter. It was by no means something they would want to go into, but it did make for a nice sound and a sense of serenity.

"This is really beautiful, Matt."

"I haven't been up here in a while. Glad to see it's still being maintained despite the lack of visitors."

They found a shade tree, and he stretched out a small blanket he'd rolled up and put on the bike before he left his place.

She unzipped her new jacket and put it to the side.

"Have you always ridden a motorcycle?"

"Yeah. We grew up on them. Dad was a motorcycle cop, and he made sure we all knew how to ride early on."

"Even Grace?"

"Yup. I'm the one who kept it going after we grew up and moved out." He explained that his father had a bad spill that resulted in a long hospital stay, and his mom nixed family vacations that involved motorcycles, but he'd never lost the passion for riding.

"You like the adrenaline rush," she told him.

He nodded. "Guilty. And it's in everything I do. My job, the bike, my vacations."

They talked for some time about the high-octane adventures he'd been on and how his buddies he'd met through firefighting were all similar in their hobbies. "It's rare to find a woman who likes it, so imagine my excitement that you're asking to go out."

"I'm probably being naive about the dangers."

"There is risk in everything. You minimize that by being smart, wearing the right gear, and paying attention on the road."

She handed him a sandwich. "You pay attention to the road, and I'll be mindful of where I rest my hands." She peeked over her sunglasses, suggestion written all over her face.

"I multitask better than most men, feel free to rest your hands wherever they land."

They ate lunch in the shade and talked. Erin asked a lot of questions about him. What was his childhood like? The best and worst parts of being a firefighter? The list went on. It dawned on him that she asked another question every time he presented one of his own.

"Enough about me."

"I like talking about you," she said, smiling.

He was leaning back on his elbows, the food forgotten. "Did you always want to be an editor?"

She shook her head, then nodded, and shook it again. "Not of novels. I thought I wanted to be a reporter. I like research and writing. I fell into editing fiction."

"Do you like it?"

She shrugged.

Matt took that as a no. "So why not get a job as a reporter?"

"Editing novels is a lot more isolating. Less exposure. Reporting news or writing commentary would mean getting myself out there. And that can't happen."

Because of her ex. "So you just give up on your dreams forever?" He hated that idea.

Erin looked away and up into the sky. "I'm out here with you on this beautiful day, and for the first time ever I don't have to wonder if I'm going to do or say something wrong. I feel free. I'm not going to mess that up by exposing myself any more than I have to and risk all that going away. Editing pays my bills. And if it dries up, I'll figure out something else."

"Some reporters make good money."

"Name one outside of who you see on TV?"

He couldn't name any.

"Money isn't everything."

"Only people with money say that," he said.

Erin nodded. "It's true. I'll never drive fancy cars again or shop in Paris. That life came with a huge price tag. I'm much happier baking brownies for my boyfriend and playing with my friend's dog."

He squeezed her hand. "I've never been to Paris."

She sighed. "It's fabulous."

"Why do I get the feeling you're not talking about a precollege backpacking experience through Europe?"

He could see her struggling with her words long before they came out of her mouth. "He, who shall not be named, had money, Matt. Money and influence. And before you ask or assume . . . no, I didn't marry him for any of that. I was born with a silver spoon and a dad who was just as big of an asshole. He didn't beat us, but he did ignore us."

Lots of questions formed in his head. "Us?"

She looked at him, looked away.

"You can trust me."

"Sister. I have a sister. She's older. Married, has a family." Erin smiled into a memory only she could see. "Barely out of high school she eloped with her first love. My dad pretended to be furious, but he barked about it for all of ten minutes, then moved on to me. Only I was younger so he had to wait. Then at some point he realized that I could become a bargaining chip with his colleagues."

Matt narrowed his eyes. "I'm not following you."

Erin ran a hand through her hair. "My father introduced me to my ex. In the beginning, the two of them spent almost as much time together as we did. My ex joined me in a dislike for my dad, which made me think we had more in common than we did."

Matt sat up. "If your ex hated your dad, why spend time with him?"

"Pawns in a game of chess. De—my *ex* suggested we keep my father happy so that he would give me a significant wedding gift."

"A wedding gift? Like what, Grandma's china?"

She laughed. Matt wasn't trying to be funny, but Erin was laughing hard.

"No, Matt. I don't think my grandmother ever had china. We're talking shares in a company they were both a part of. It was something my dad had stock in, but really didn't care about. But Desmond did . . . he wanted—" Erin slapped a hand to her mouth.

Desmond . . . her ex's name was Desmond.

Matt crawled across the blanket and placed both his hands on her knees. "Babe. C'mon. I don't care. His name means nothing to me." Yeah, it did. He could now place a name on his punching bag and have at it.

"I shouldn't have . . ."

"What did he want, Erin? What did your ex want that he married you for?"

"His shares in the company combined with what my father gifted him when we married gave him controlling interest. We got married, and my dad washed his hands of me."

"It's like you were chattel."

186

Erin looked at him. "I could have said no. I cared for my ex in the beginning. He grew up with a single mom who brought men around that treated him poorly. He convinced me that we had a lot in common. And I said yes."

Matt could see her kicking herself for that decision. "Did your dad ever find out what a douche you married?"

"My sister did, and she went to our father. They never talked, and it was rare they ever saw each other, but she realized that in order for me to get away, I was going to need some financial help."

"So your dad did step up."

Erin started rubbing her hands together. "No. My dad told my sister that life wasn't fair and for me to grow up and figure out my own problems without running to Daddy."

What the fuck? Who did that? "Damn, Erin . . . what did you do?"

"Promise not to judge me?"

"I'm judging all kinds of people right now, but you're not in the pool."

She patted her feet. "I sold my shoes."

He wasn't sure he heard that right. "Shoes?"

She smiled. "I saw this movie where a princess wanted to help out her lover, so she went on a spending spree buying all kinds of things. The prince didn't care that his wife spent money on stuff, but he wasn't about to hand her cash. So she sold the stuff and gave the cash to her lover. So . . . I sold my shoes. Desmond would have noticed my jewelry missing, so I sold what he wouldn't miss. I kept the boxes in the back of my closet and emptied them one at a time until I had enough money to start over."

He blinked several times, looked at the sneakers on her feet, and grinned. "Shoes?"

"Designer shoes. They're pretty spendy, Matt. Women will pay seventy-five percent of retail on a lightly worn pair of Ralph Laurens."

"I'm going to have to look up Ralph when we get home."

187

She started to relax. "Would have been easier and faster to just sell his ring. But my attorney said he might use that against me in the divorce and say it was theft on my part. So I left it in a box on my dresser."

"What did your dad get out of it? You said he used you as a pawn."

"He lost credibility when my mom ran off and when my sister eloped. He had a new girlfriend who was only a little older than my sister, and she wanted me gone. So when he married me off and made a grand gesture of making sure I was provided for by means of giving Desmond controlling shares in the company, he was praised as the best dad in the world."

"What an asshole."

"The ugly underbelly of money. I don't want it. Any of it. Desmond can have the money. They can all rot with it."

He clasped her hand with his. "You're the strongest woman I've ever met."

"A strong woman wouldn't have allowed herself to be used the way I did."

"No, babe. Strong people find themselves in hard situations all the time. How you deal with and get out of them is what really shows your power."

He could tell by her expression she wasn't buying what he was selling.

"Maybe someday I'll believe that," she said.

Matt pulled her over to him and lay back on the blanket. "Maybe someday I'll prove it to you."

She relaxed against his chest as a summer breeze brushed along their skin.

"I don't have a ton," he told her. "But I could probably take you to Paris if I saved up. Not sure if we can invite Ralph, though."

Erin's slow laughter put a huge smile on his face. And when she looked up, he took advantage of the lips she was offering.

CHAPTER TWENTY-ONE

Now that the seeds had been planted, Erin found herself finding reasons not to work. What if she could work behind the scenes as a reporter? Did that kind of thing exist out there? Could she write a column for an online publication? Never meet the people she interviewed in person? Like a fake profile on a dating site, maybe she could reinvent herself again in a world where she could follow that dream.

Matt had brought her home after their ride and had made love to her in the shower before going home. He'd picked up a shift the next day and needed to sleep. They both knew that wasn't going to happen if he stayed another night with her.

She found herself chasing the "What if" rabbit down the Wonderland hole until she fell asleep.

And she started to dream.

Erin was walking down a hall wearing shorts and four-inch pumps she'd sold. In her head she kept wondering how it was possible that she had the shoes on her feet. They weren't even her favorite pair of heels, yet there they were making clicking noises as she walked the endless hall.

She followed the light and walked through double doors, and Matt was there on his bike telling her to get on. She looked around for her helmet but didn't find it. Still, Matt beckoned.

Erin smiled, and her tongue ran over her teeth.

One was missing and the others didn't feel right. Like they were moments from falling out of her mouth. She covered her lips, hoping Matt didn't see her broken smile.

I'm dreaming.

Only it felt so real.

Wind was flying through her hair, which felt wonderful, but she wasn't wearing a helmet and what happened if they crashed? All her teeth would fall out.

Wake up.

She looked over Matt's shoulder and saw a stop sign. On the right was a car.

Desmond sat in the driver's seat.

"Stop!"

Erin shot up in bed, her hand reached for her mouth. She pressed on her teeth, sighed, and flopped back against her pillows.

The clock said three in the morning.

She rolled back over with her eyes wide open.

Outside she heard the cry of a coyote, and before long another joined the chorus. The emergency lights outside the house clicked on.

She covered her ears in hopes of blocking out the sound and falling back to sleep. Twice she dozed, and twice the animals woke her. Giving up, she crawled out of bed and flipped on her porch light to scare the coyotes off.

It didn't work.

Eventually the animals moved on, but by then, Erin was wide awake. Her dream buzzed in her head.

Back when she was with Desmond, she'd often have dreams of missing teeth, or walking naked in a crowd. The counselor she'd once talked to said it was a sign of insecurity. That the subconscious made you vulnerable in your dreams so you would wake up to what was wrong in your life.

So why now?

Things were steady and secure.

The only thing she could come up with was that she was revealing her truths to Matt. The man was slowly extracting her past from her and making her think about it all over again.

He was also giving her hope that she had a future that didn't involve running and hiding. She'd been warned that would happen. The counselors in the program she'd found to help battered wives told her that once she finally felt comfortable, her mind would settle and she'd go through a growing period where she would battle the demons of her past in order to move on. If that didn't happen, they would always lurk in the shadows threatening the new life she was attempting to live.

It would seem her toothless dream was the start of her moving on.

Instead of fearing her dream, she removed a notepad and wrote down her feelings about it. Words of a song drifted in her head. *Write it down and it won't live inside of you.*

So she did. And when she was done, she opened her laptop and researched the phases of letting go of the past.

The sun crested the horizon in shades of pink, and by the time she finished her first cup of coffee, Erin had five pages of notes and it was almost eight.

She'd gotten lost in the work of battling her demons.

Surprisingly, it made her feel good. "I won't let you control me any longer," she said to the man in her past.

~

"What are you doing now?"

Matt glanced up from his tablet, met Tom's eyes, and looked back down. "Wasting time."

"Really? You've been on that all afternoon."

Yeah, they'd had a slow day. He wasn't complaining.

Here he thought Desmond was a unique name, one a Google search would pull up very few of and give him some direction.

He thought wrong.

He'd looked up Desmond Fleming. Looked up Erin Fleming. Used searches in celebrity weddings, elite magazines. CEOs, Fortune 500 . . . He realized early on that Erin wouldn't have kept her married last name. In fact, she probably changed it. No telling if Fleming was her maiden name. Again, if he was hiding from someone who had that information, he wouldn't use it. Erin was smarter than that.

All he had was her ex-husband's first name, the fact that he held controlling interest in a company, and that he abused women.

He needed more information. A birthday . . . a location to start. Something to narrow his search.

"Earth to Matt?"

He closed his tablet in frustration. "Sorry."

"You're up to barbeque," Tom told him.

Matt unfolded from his seat and tossed his tablet to the side. "On it."

Tom shook his head as he walked by. "Woman. Has to be a woman."

~

Matt was at work. Colin was at his house, and Austin was out with friends.

Parker pulled a cork out of a bottle of chilled wine while Erin tossed a salad. "Girls' night. We absolutely have to keep doing this once I'm married."

"Yes. You do. Friends are important in the mix. Trust me."

Parker poured wine into two glasses and handed one to her. "You speak from experience."

"Much as I wish that wasn't the case."

Parker lifted her glass. "Cheers."

They sat on the porch as the heat of the day faded.

"Soooo, Matt?" Parker wasted no time.

Erin instantly smiled.

Parker rubbed her hands together and squealed. "Tell me everything. Don't leave out one detail!"

She felt like a schoolgirl talking about her first kiss. "I'm blaming the motorcycle. That darn thing is like an oyster on the half shell."

For the next hour, Erin told all. From butterflies to orgasm . . . Parker knew every detail. "But what really threw me was how I knew that if I had to throw in the towel and yell *watermelon*, he would stop. I never doubted that for a second."

"It's the Hudson charm. It's a real thing."

"He's so darn perfect. Here I come with all kinds of baggage and he's like, 'Let me get those for you.'"

"It's a Hudson thing. I can't find a whole lot wrong with Colin either."

"Does he snore?"

"No. Does Matt?"

"No." She stared into her wine. "You'd tell me if I was missing something, right?"

"In a heartbeat. And I'm not just saying that because Matt's going to be my brother-in-law."

"Good," Erin said. "And I'd do the same. No sugarcoating."

They clinked their glasses together as if it were a sacred girl-promise.

"Damn, I'm happy for you," Parker said into her glass.

Erin giggled and put aside her thoughts that she was missing an important undesirable personality trait. "I'm pretty happy for me, too. Is that bad?"

"I don't know a woman more deserving. And the fact that you told Matt about your ex-husband tells me you're really invested."

Erin sipped her wine. "Not quite."

"Not quite what? Invested?"

"No. I'm in when it comes to Matt. My ex . . . he's not quite an ex."

Parker lost her smile.

"The divorce isn't final," Erin admitted.

"Excuse me?"

"He refuses to sign the papers. My ex is an ass, Parker. He thinks he can prolong the inevitable forever. But he can't. Eventually he has to let go."

"My God, how long has it been?"

"I filed about three months before I moved in here."

"That's almost a year."

"I know. My attorney assures me it won't be long now."

The phone inside the house rang twice. A signal from the gate that someone was there.

"You expecting anyone?" Erin asked.

Parker shook her head and went inside to answer the call. When she returned, she tossed the phone on the table. "It's Grace."

"Oh, good."

"Maybe she can give us some dirt on her brothers."

Erin laughed. "No comments about the ex, okay? The less people that know . . ."

"I get it. Don't worry."

They watched Grace's car make it up the drive and park. She got out and waved a bottle of wine in the air. "I brought provisions."

They greeted her at the top of the stairs. Scout slapped his tail on the deck and licked Grace as she walked by.

"I'm here . . . the party can start. But please, I really don't want a picture painted of how my brothers have sex. I really can't go there."

God, she loved Grace. The woman was spitfire and energy.

"Who says I'm having sex with your brother?" Erin asked, half joking.

The three of them walked into the house, and Parker removed a wineglass from the cupboard.

Grace leaned on the edge of the kitchen island while she rolled her eyes. "He missed the game with my dad. The man lives for baseball. There is only one thing that would keep him away from a game and that's sex. And since your lipstick was smeared all over his face at the engagement party, I put two and two together."

"You sure you don't want to hear about it?" Parker asked.

Grace frantically waved her hands in the air before taking the glass of wine Parker offered. "No! Please. It's going to make the Game of Life difficult at Christmas."

"How so?" Erin asked.

"Because I'll know just how he managed to have a car full of pink and blue pegs."

"Well, if you don't want to hear about our sex lives, tell us about yours," Parker said.

They moved back out on the porch and got comfortable. "I don't have a sex life. I swear my vagina is going to shrivel up and fall out if I don't meet someone soon."

Erin laughed. "Where are you looking?"

Grace kicked off her shoes and tucked her feet under her bottom. "I'm back to online dating."

Parker groaned. "That's the worst."

"Well, I'm not going to date anyone I work with, and I really don't do the bar scene. So unless you know someone you wanna set me up with . . ."

Erin certainly didn't. She glanced at Parker.

They both shrugged.

"What about Matt or Colin? They both work with men, certainly someone on their list is single and worthy."

"I dated one of Colin's work buddies early on and realized that when it doesn't work out, it makes things uncomfortable for everyone. So I forced that train to leave the station a long time ago."

"I've met some of Matt's friends, and they're a pretty good-looking group," Erin said.

"And married, or recently divorced and looking for a replacement. Or already have kids . . . Yeah, I've met his friends, too. But no thanks. It's okay. I actually have a couple guys I've been chatting with online. I'm meeting one for coffee next week."

Parker set her wine down and scooted out of the chair she was sitting on. "Well, if it gets past the coffee stage, let us know."

"I will."

Parker stood and started for the door.

"Where are you going?"

"To grab my bridal magazines. Since you're here and we're done talking about sex, it's time to look at flowers and stuff."

Grace jumped up, too. "I have some in my car."

"Wait." Erin stopped them midstep.

Grace and Parker both turned around.

"What?" Grace asked.

"Are Colin and Matt perfect?"

Grace's expression twisted several different ways as she contemplated her answer. "You mean outside of childhood pranks and blaming me for their parties and porn?"

That had Erin smiling. "Yeah."

Grace rolled her eyes. "Yeah. And it's annoying as hell."

CHAPTER TWENTY-TWO

"We need to talk."

"That doesn't sound good." Erin had picked up the phone knowing it was Renee. They went through their normal code and then she was hit with . . . *We need to talk.* "Let me guess. Desmond figured out another way to delay the divorce."

"In a manner . . . yes."

Erin pushed her laptop aside and put her phone on speaker. "What's he doing now?"

"First of all, he left the country."

"He does that all the time. He's never gone long."

"This time he told his attorney he had a family emergency in Greece or someplace like that."

"He doesn't have family in Greece."

Renee sighed. "I never thought he did. I told his counsel this tactic wasn't going to work. That if I could represent you and you never show up in court, his counsel needed to do the same."

"What happened?"

"The judge delayed based on personal hardship. The next day Desmond's attorney called to tell me that your discovery was missing several components."

"I thought we finalized this months ago," Erin said. "There's nothing to discover. I left with my clothes. I didn't touch the bank account."

"According to Desmond, he took your jewelry in for appraisal and found several pieces had been replaced with fakes."

Erin's jaw dropped. "I did not . . ."

"Maci, I need you to be honest with me. If you did this, I can work around it—"

"I wish I had thought of it, Renee. Then maybe I could buy a decent car. But I didn't."

Renee sighed, almost like she wasn't convinced. "You did sell your shoes."

"And I told you about those."

"And Desmond finally clued in to that and is now looking for anything else you may have 'taken' from your marriage."

Erin stared down into her phone. "Taken? I sold *my* shoes. Not his!"

"And he realized, or was advised, that he wouldn't get anywhere with the shoe debate. But jewelry obtained during your marriage is another subject."

"They were blood gifts, Renee. Every earring, every necklace. I didn't want them then, and I don't want them now. I left everything in his home . . . our home." The entire thing was ludicrous.

"They filed a motion and we have to respond. They're prepared to bring in experts on this."

"To serve what purpose? I'm asking for nothing. I want nothing from him. I just want him to go away. This isn't about any money he thinks I've taken. You know that." So she could get on with her life.

"No, Maci. This is about money he wants from you."

Her head was starting to pound. "I don't have any money."

"No. You have something more powerful."

Now Erin was completely confused. "Really? Because I'm feeling rather powerless right now."

"Shares in the company, Maci."

"What are you talking about? That was a gift from my father to Desmond on our wedding day. Like selling your daughter with a flock of sheep." The whole thing was disgusting.

"I told you I had a colleague of mine look into Desmond to see if we could find another trail of abuse or coercion with your doctors. She stumbled upon some financials that you and Desmond jointly share, and the company came up."

"The stock belongs to him."

"It doesn't. It belongs to both of you . . . I think. It's actually murky. I'm leaning toward it belonging to you."

"That's not what Desmond told me."

"This is the man who beat you, Maci. Do you think he wanted you to know that you owned a part of his company? He wanted you isolated and broke so you needed him. It's classic. I've seen this a hundred times."

Erin closed her eyes. "I don't want the company. I want nothing from that man."

"I understand. I do. But as your attorney, I'm going to advise you to learn exactly what you're giving away. And here's the deal. Desmond hasn't asked for this from you as of yet. He hasn't even hinted that you own any part of the company. Which leads me to believe that this jewelry bullshit is his way of setting you up to be forced to sign over your interest in the shares before the divorce is over."

"I didn't fence my own jewelry. I wouldn't even know how."

"I believe you. I have my investigator digging so he can testify in your defense when the time comes. For now, just do nothing."

"Do I have a choice?"

Renee didn't answer her.

"You might have your friend look up my father and ask how he *gifted* the shares. I remember handshakes and pats on the back and being told that I was going to be fine now that my husband owned controlling interest of the company. Daddy came out looking like a saint in the financial news world."

"I'll do that. And if you remember anything, call me."

"I will."

"How are you otherwise?"

Erin's mind shifted to the good things in her life. "I met someone."

"A *man* someone?"

She found her smile. "Yes. He's nothing like Desmond."

"I can't imagine you'd make the same mistake twice."

Erin had to laugh. "Most battered women fall into a pattern of abusive relationships. But that's not something I have to consider when it comes to Matt. He's kind and caring and a firefighter."

Renee sighed. "I'm having a hot flash just hearing about him."

If you only knew. "He reminds me that there are good men out there."

"You deserve one. I have a call on the other line so I've gotta let you go. But call me with anything."

"I will. And let me know when the asshole is back in town."

"That's what I like to hear. Be angry with the man, it's more productive than giving him the power to make you cower and hide. I'll be in touch."

Renee hung up, and Erin sat there staring at the phone.

Cower and hide. Exactly what she was doing and had to do. But she didn't have to hide from life or cower from the people in it now.

~

"It's time to say yes to a dress!" Parker was pumped up on adrenaline and caffeine. Erin could see it in her eyes.

Grace leaned forward between the seats. "Take a right at the next block."

Erin was driving. For the first time in years, her car was full. Parker took shotgun, and Grace and Mallory were in the back seat.

"You think we're here for you, but really . . . we wanna make sure you don't pick out bridesmaid dresses that look like Tinkerbell threw up," Mallory said.

"Ha ha!" Parker's fake laugh was aimed at her sister.

"She's half right," Grace added.

In the rearview mirror, Erin noticed Grace and Mallory fist-bump. The two of them were a lot alike. They said what they were thinking even if it wasn't completely politically correct.

"You're with me, right, Erin?" Parker asked.

Erin stopped for the pedestrians jaywalking in the middle of downtown Los Angeles. "You bet I am. Our dresses should complement yours. And if you want to float down the aisle with fairy wings and taffeta, we will, too."

"Suck-up," Mallory chided.

They all laughed.

"Take the next left and start looking for a parking garage." Grace was their navigator. At first she suggested she drive since she knew the fashion district in LA and Erin didn't. But then there was talk of toasting with champagne and a designated driver, so Erin volunteered to stay sober and drive.

Erin didn't know the streets and found herself hyperaware of everything going on around them. The homeless sat at corners of buildings, while everyone else scurried around them doing their best to avoid their path.

Mallory tossed her hand between the seats. "Parking on the right."

Erin hit the brakes a little hard to avoid missing the turn. "Sorry."

"Better than going around the block again," Grace said.

It was midweek and the lot was packed. They found a spot in the lowest level in a corner.

They jumped out of the car and started toward the elevators. Grace patted her oversized purse. Inside was the champagne. "Let's get this party started."

Parker was all smiles. "I can't believe I'm doing this."

"Me either," Mallory agreed and dropped an arm over her sister's shoulders.

~

It wasn't even ten in the morning, and Grace popped open the bottle as soon as Parker headed into a dressing room with a dozen dresses.

They were on a budget, and it was tight, which was one of the reasons they were in the fashion district instead of some boutique shop being waited on hand and foot.

Erin recalled her experience and couldn't help but compare the two.

She'd been excited to get married. The act of tying the knot was full of days like this. Girlfriends, champagne, and giggling. Silk, lace, and satin. And since Erin's mother wasn't involved and her father didn't care, it was up to her and her sister to plan everything. She'd had the help of a consultant and a rather unlimited budget.

What she wouldn't do to have the money they spent on flowers alone. That would probably pay for Parker and Colin's wedding in its entirety . . . or come close. Her one-time dress had cost fifteen thousand dollars and then another five hundred to have it cleaned and preserved in a box.

Damn shame.

It all felt so superficial now.

Parker was trying on three-, five-, and eight-hundred-dollar dresses, and looking like a million bucks simply because of the beaming smile on her face.

The first three dresses Parker tried on warmed them up and had each of them running to the racks to follow a direction. "I really think you can pull off something long and sleek," Erin told her.

Parker was wearing a sleeved princess dress with entirely too much lace. Not quite Tinkerbell, but close.

"I never imagined something formfitting."

"Well, you'll never get a chance to try them on again so you might as well while we're here," Mallory encouraged her sister.

Back to the racks they went.

When they returned, Parker had come out in something less lacy but covered in beading.

Mallory shook her head with a frown.

"Yeah, I don't think so either," Parker said.

Grace unzipped her, and they both disappeared into the dressing room.

"Ohhh," Grace said a few minutes later.

"What?" Mallory asked between sips of champagne.

Around them other bridal parties were doing exactly the same thing. The people-watching was fascinating. It was fun to pick out the spoiled brides, the reluctant brides, and the mothers that wished they were the brides. Of everyone in the room, the four of them were having the best time with the whole ordeal.

Parker emerged in silk . . . or at least something that resembled silk. It was sleek and hugged Parker's figure without being an hourglass. It was the first dress that made them all sit back and wistfully sigh.

And Parker was smiling. Full-on ear-to-ear happiness. "This is definitely a contender," she announced.

"It's beautiful," Mallory said.

"It flatters everything. Turn around," Erin instructed.

The back was low cut and a little daring.

"I'm not sure about the back," Parker said the minute she looked at herself from the side.

"Tape keeps it from gaping," Erin told her.

"Oh."

And so it went.

Three hours later, the shiny moment of truth came when Parker found a beautiful combination of sleek silk that didn't drop so low in the back but that capped right at her shoulders and flattered her bust. There was beading and lace but only a small amount along the sleeves and the back where it buttoned up.

It wasn't overdone or understated. It was perfect.

Erin, Grace, and Mallory spent quite a bit of time searching for similar themed dresses for them while Parker stood through the painstaking task of having her measurements taken for the alterations.

Mallory took several pictures of Parker in the chosen dress and did the same with the handful of gowns the three of them had put on. Sadly, there wasn't a hit when it came to the bridesmaids' dresses, but they all agreed to continue their search in a couple of weeks.

They had a late lunch and worked their way back to the parking garage. The place had cleared out quite a bit, making it easier to drive around.

Grace was chattering from the back seat, occasionally shouting directions to get them out of the city and onto the freeway.

Parker sat turned in her seat to give her attention to those in the back. "I think we should look in the mall. There are so many formal gowns that could work just as well as anything we saw for you guys today."

"Probably cheaper, too," Grace said. "If not, there are several other places in the fashion district we didn't get to."

Erin followed the line of traffic getting on the freeway. She'd hoped they would have gotten out of the city before it backed up too bad, but that never seemed to work in LA.

"We need to pick a day."

"Wednesday is my only day with no classes during the week," Mallory said and went on to keep talking about her schedule.

Erin moved slowly onto the freeway where the traffic picked up slightly. Confident she could get them home now without any directions from Grace, Erin felt her shoulders relax in the drive.

"I can get to the local mall and check a few places, and if that doesn't work, get to a bigger one in the valley."

No sooner did Erin press the gas than she was hitting the brakes. The car didn't respond as quickly so she pressed them harder.

They all jolted forward. "Sorry."

Parker shrugged. "Stop-and-go traffic. What are you gonna do?"

Erin's neck started to strain again. Ten miles an hour turned into twenty-five. To avoid jostling her passengers, she kept distance from the car in front of them and took her foot off the gas.

Again she hit the brakes. This time the pedal sunk farther down to the floor, then it caught. It was then that she glanced at her dashboard. The check brakes light was on. She tapped the dash. "That's weird." She tapped it again, the light flickered and went back on.

"Something wrong?" Grace asked.

"My brake light is flashing."

"You probably just need service," Parker said.

She pumped the brakes a couple of times. "They don't feel right."

Grace leaned forward. "Did you notice anything on the way down?"

"No, nothing."

She sat back. "Well, brakes don't go out that fast. Just get it in for service. Or ask Matt. He knows his way around a car."

"I can't ask Matt to work on my car."

"Why not? He wants to work under your hood," Parker said, laughing.

The rest of them picked up on the joke and started laughing.

Cars started to move.

"So how is he, Erin?" Mallory asked.

"Oh my God . . . no. Just don't go there," Grace whined.

Mallory laughed the hardest. "Everyone in this car is having sex with someone in your family."

Erin saw Grace in the rearview mirror. The woman was squeezing her eyes shut.

"I'm the only one not having—"

Erin saw the red lights of the car in front of them, hit her brakes. Nothing happened.

"Shit." She hit them again and the pedal went to the floor.

"What?"

Frantically, she pumped them. The brakes weren't working. "Hold on." In a split second, Erin looked around them. Cars on both sides with nowhere to go and avoid a crash.

Metal hit metal, and someone in the car screamed. The airbags exploded and horns blared. The second punch came from behind and jolted them a second time.

Erin's heart sped. She first looked to her right. Parker was coughing around the substance that had deployed with the airbag. Mallory was grasping her left shoulder but awake, and Grace was holding the top of her head.

Erin saw blood.

"Oh my God. Are you okay?"

"Yeah." Grace moved her hand away, saw the blood. "I think so."

"You're bleeding," Parker cried.

"Just my head."

Someone outside the car knocked on the window. "You guys okay?"

Erin looked around. The cars around them moved but the one in front and the one that hit them from the back were at a standstill.

Erin started to shake as adrenaline dumped and memories surfaced. "It wouldn't stop." Her breath came in short pants.

"It's okay. We're okay."

"It wouldn't stop."

CHAPTER TWENTY-THREE

Matt received the call from Colin. He heard the words *the girls* and *accident on the freeway,* and his blood pressure jumped. The next thing Colin said eased him slightly. *They all walked away.* Traffic was bad so they weren't going at freeway speeds. But fast enough to hammer the front and back of the car when the car behind them couldn't stop in time.

Much as Matt wanted to take his bike and swerve in and out of traffic to get to the hospital, he didn't trust himself not to become part of the problem, so he took the truck.

Grace needed a couple of stitches. That's all he knew.

Colin said he'd call the second he got there, and he was only a few minutes closer than Matt.

He white-knuckled all the way in. His phone rang as he was parking the truck.

"Are they okay?" He jumped out of the truck and double-timed his steps to the emergency room doors.

"They're fine. How far out are you?"

"I'm walking in now."

His eyes searched the lobby as he entered. Without a familiar face in sight, he approached the receptionist.

The hospital was in Glendale and not one he was familiar with. "My family was just brought in from a car accident." He gave them Erin's name and then Grace's.

He was directed to a room in the far back of the department. A good sign no one was seriously injured. Matt saw Grace first. She was sitting on the edge of a gurney with a bandage on the left side of her forehead and laughing. On another gurney Colin sat next to Parker, his arm over her shoulders. She, too, was giggling. Mallory was in a chair to the side.

Erin sat in a corner, eyes wide, her lips in a straight line.

"You didn't have to rush," Grace said when she saw him enter the room.

"And miss the party? What are you laughing about? I thought this was a serious moment." Matt moved to his sister and wrapped her in his arms.

"Grace was hitting on the doctor," Mallory told him.

That sounded like his sister.

"You okay?" he whispered.

"I'm fine. Erin's pretty shook up," she whispered back.

He moved from Grace, around the gurney, and to Erin's side.

She looked at him with a blank expression.

Matt knelt down and took her all in. Both her forearms were wrapped in bandages. He touched one and she finally spoke. Her voice wavered. "The airbag burned my . . ." Her voice floated off and she started to shake.

He carefully took both her hands in his. He could only imagine what she was feeling. What thoughts were racing through her mind.

"So what exactly happened?" Colin asked.

Matt listened while his eyes stayed on Erin.

"We were on the five. Traffic was crazy. Erin said something about the brake light," Grace explained.

"They didn't work. I slammed on the brakes. The car didn't stop," Erin said a little louder this time. Her eyes finally met Matt's.

He squeezed her hands, realized that might hurt her arms, and eased up.

"Next thing we knew, the airbags were exploding and another car was slamming us in the rear," Grace finished.

"Erin's car is jacked," Mallory said.

"But we're all okay, and that's all that matters," Parker said. "It's not your fault, Erin."

"One of the other drivers tried to limp the car off the freeway and even he said the brake pedal wasn't catching. They had to tow it."

"Did you come in on an ambulance?" Matt asked.

Grace rolled her eyes. "They insisted, but I refused the backboard. I have no time to be tied down by your people," she teased.

Matt wanted to laugh, but Erin was still staring out in space.

"I'm so sorry, guys."

Another round of "It's not your fault" ensued.

Twenty minutes later, a doctor came in the room. Matt had taken up residence behind Erin and kept his hands on her shoulders to make sure she knew he was right there.

Grace offered a smile to the fortyish-year-old doctor who didn't seem to notice her attention. He introduced himself and shook both Colin's and Matt's hands.

The doctor pointed to Mallory first. "Your shoulder is going to hurt, but nothing is broken." He turned his attention to Erin. "You're not broken either. Looks like you have old fractures."

Erin nodded. "I do."

"I'm glad you agreed to the X-rays. Swelling in these airbag burns can be pretty intense and might make you think you refractured something. Now you know."

Matt kissed the top of Erin's head when the doctor looked away.

"Stitches out for you in five to seven days."

Grace smiled. "Should I come back here?" Her voice was breathy and hardly sounded like her.

Mallory started to giggle.

"Ah, no. Your regular doctor can do it without an ER visit."

"That's too bad."

Matt noticed the doctor's blush. He turned to Parker. "And it looks like the only one to escape without a scratch is the bride."

"They gave me the most champagne. I didn't tense up when we hit."

"You guys were drinking?" Colin asked.

Parker patted his hand. "Only the three of us, and we finished the bottle before noon. Erin didn't have a drop."

All eyes went on Erin.

"One of the nurses will be in with your discharge orders in a minute." He left the room with Grace watching his backside as he walked away.

"Good Lord, could you be more obvious?" Parker teased.

"I could slip him my phone number when I walk by as we leave."

Erin offered a practiced smile but didn't find the humor the way everyone else in the room did.

Colin pulled Matt aside before they walked out to the parking lot. "I'll take the others back to the house. Are you going to take Erin back to your place?"

"If she'll let me. If not, I'll be right behind you. Try and get her to let me stay. She's pretty shook up."

"Thankfully she wasn't drinking. That would have made everything worse."

Matt couldn't imagine.

They met back up with the women, who did a group trip to the bathroom, and walked outside. Matt kept close to Erin. He led her to his car and opened the door. "See you guys later," he said as they walked past his truck.

Matt started the engine and waited for it to warm. "Erin?"

"I'm okay."

No, you're not.

"It's not your fault."

"I was driving. It was my car. If my brakes failed because I was supposed to do something with them, it's totally my fault."

He turned and leaned over the center console so she had to look at him or ignore him.

"How old is your car?"

"Four years. It was a lease return. I bought it used."

That didn't sound right to him. "So it was from a dealership?"

"Yes."

"Were there any warning lights before today?"

"None."

Matt shook his head and reached to take hold of her hand. "Then, hon . . . this isn't your fault. You couldn't have known something was going to fail. Be thankful that you weren't going seventy. This could have ended much differently."

She turned to him and her eyes began to swell.

He leaned over and hugged her the best he could across the console.

~

Erin woke the next morning feeling like an 18-wheeler had run over her . . . twice.

Matt had insisted she stay at his place, and she was too emotionally and physically exhausted to utter an argument. And even though she felt guilty for being high maintenance with him, she knew being alone would result in nothing but self-degradation and blame of herself. And that wasn't healthy.

She rolled over and found the other half of the bed empty. Matt had held her the night before and let her cry. Now her eyes were swollen and her head pounded. She needed aspirin and caffeine.

Wearing one of Matt's T-shirts, she padded barefoot through his house, following the scent of coffee.

In a pair of shorts and without a shirt, Matt stood in front of his sink with his back to her.

Erin must have made a noise because he turned and smiled. "Good morning, beautiful."

She ran a hand through her hair, winced at the discomfort in her arm. "I look like something the cat dragged in."

He crossed the room and placed both hands on her hips. "Are you saying I have bad taste?"

She curled into him, set her cheek on his chest.

"I'm saying you may be a little blind to reality right now."

He chuckled.

"How about some coffee?"

"Oh, God, yes."

"You sit. I'll get it."

Erin did as he asked and watched him move around his kitchen. The simple domestic chore of pouring her a cup of coffee and mixing it up the way she liked was an oddity.

He handed the cup to her and sat across the table. "Did you get any sleep?"

The java swished in the back of her throat, making her sigh. "Yes. More than I expected."

"You tossed and turned quite a bit," he said.

"I'm sorry."

"Don't apologize."

"You don't manage decent sleep when you work, so you should get it when you're at home."

He reached out and toyed with her fingertips. "I slept ten times better with you here."

"I doubt that." The second sip of coffee was better than the first.

Matt rolled his eyes at her comment. "We have a lot to do today."

"We do?"

He stood and moved to his refrigerator. "Phone calls to your insurance company. Getting the information on where your car is. We need the police report. Is it totaled, or can it be fixed? Then there's the trip to the rental car place." He stopped looking for whatever it was he was searching for to look at her. "Do you have rental coverage on your insurance?"

"I have no idea."

"Regardless. You'll need a car." He removed eggs and milk. "You can use my truck . . ." He stopped again, looked at her. "Have you driven a big truck before?"

"No."

"Probably better off with a car, then. Trucks take some getting used to, and having another fender bender now will probably scar you for life."

He had put a lot of thought into this. "It sounds like a long and frustrating day. You sure you want to be a part of all that?"

He set everything on the counter, turned, and leaned against it. "Does all that stuff need to get done?"

"Yes."

"Am I taking something away from you if I'm helping you do it?"

"No."

He tilted his head. "Do you want my help?"

She paused.

Matt waited. "Listen. From what you've told me, you probably weren't given a lot of choices as to when, where, and what your ex-asshole was involved in. I never . . . ever . . . want you to think I'm pushing my ideas of how your life should be. I woke up this morning with a to-do list that needs to be tackled, and I'd like to help. Since I'm not working today, I'm available. But if you don't want me to, I get it." He stopped his monologue long enough to take a breath. "Well, I don't get it, but I'll respect it and step aside and wait for you to ask for help."

Erin sat there holding her coffee and staring at him. By now he'd crossed his arms over his bare chest, and he was staring right back at her with a perplexed look on his face.

"Thank you," she said.

"For what?"

"Taking the time to not only figure out everything I haven't even considered after yesterday's freeway debacle."

He uncrossed his arms and rested them on the counter behind him. "You're welcome."

"And for going the extra mile to consider what I might be feeling on a personal level."

He flashed his charming smile. "There's no point in you opening up and telling me everything you did if I'm going to carry on as if you didn't have the past you've lived through."

"Really, Matt. You're five steps ahead of me here. All I was thinking was a cup of coffee and a good morning kiss."

He took one step away from the counter, placed both hands on the table in front of her, and pressed his lips to hers. "I forgot about the kiss," he said, staring down at her.

"I may need two."

He took his sweet time delivering her second request. "What's the verdict?"

"*We* have a lot to do."

CHAPTER TWENTY-FOUR

There was more color in Erin's face as they moved through the day. They'd gone to her place so she could get a change of clothes and call her insurance company. The car was in Glendale, but the station for California Highway Patrol was closer to them. They started with CHP, got stuck in a ton of their red tape, and left without a report.

By the time Matt laid eyes on Erin's car, it was two in the afternoon.

It sat in the back of a collision repair center where it appeared to have been dropped the day before.

"Whoa." Breath left Matt's lungs like he'd been punched. He put an arm around Erin, thankful she'd walked away. The car had turned into an accordion.

"Is it possible it looks worse today?" Erin asked.

"You were preoccupied when it happened." He ducked his head inside the open window and looked at the passenger space. The car had taken the impact in the front and the rear, but where the women had been sitting didn't have collapsed metal inside. The safety mechanisms of the car had done their job.

"Hello?"

Matt and Erin both turned to see a man emerge from inside the repair shop.

"Hi," Matt said.

"This belong to you?" the man asked.

"It's mine," Erin told him.

He glanced her way and extended a hand. "I'm Ed."

They introduced themselves, and Ed continued talking. "I was going to call you in the morning if you didn't. I've learned to give these a couple days to settle. Takes the insurance company at least that to get their act together."

"Do you think it can be repaired?"

Ed nodded, then shrugged. "I haven't looked into the weeds yet. Depends on how much of a hit the engine took. But even if it can be fixed, the question is how much and if the insurance company has to pay less to fix it or pay you off for it."

"When will we know that?"

"I need to get it up on a rack. Now that you're here I need some information from you and I can put a couple of my guys on it. I write a report and we wait for the insurance company to approve the repairs." Ed scratched his head.

"At first glance, what do you think is going to happen?" Matt asked.

Ed didn't miss a beat. "They'll total it."

Erin winced.

Ed walked around the car pointing out what he saw and the numbers involved with fixing them. "Back bumper, trunk, and side panels. Same with the front of the car. And here . . ." He walked to the driver's side. "Driver's door is trashed. Were you driving?" he asked Erin.

She nodded.

"Did someone pry the door open for you to get out?"

"Yeah, it was stuck."

Ed bobbed his head like one of those dolls. "Right. So not only is the door going to have problems, but chances are the frame of the car is compromised, too. And fixing that is expensive. The radiator was leaking when it was brought in but we need to dig and see what else is damaged. On the interior, the airbags, dashboard, steering wheel." He stopped and sighed. "It's a lot. And since it's not that new of a car, and not that expensive of a car, the repair will likely exceed its value, and that's when the insurance company says no thanks, they give you a check, and you start over."

"Will I be able to replace it with the check they give me?"

Ed laughed. "Not in my experience unless you have great insurance. And this is where the blame game starts."

"What do you mean?"

"This was on the freeway, right?"

"Yeah."

"The guy behind you will say you stopped too fast and he couldn't avoid hitting you. Or maybe he was on your butt and he is at fault. Same for the car you hit. Were you too close, or did he slam on the brakes? It all becomes a bunch of finger-pointing. And if all the cars have insured drivers, the insurance companies look for fault so that the other company pays."

Erin walked to the front of the car. "My brakes gave out. I tried to stop. I couldn't."

"Did you recently have them worked on?" Ed asked.

"No. And they were working fine when we drove into the city."

Matt knelt down to look at the wheels. "You said you noticed a problem after you got on the freeway, right?" Matt asked.

"I guess the first time was as I was merging on."

Ed rocked back on his heels. "I'll look at 'em. Check to see if there is a recall of some sort. Insurance companies love going after the manufacturers, and if that's the case, and you can prove it, you'll probably get more money and afford to replace this one."

Matt stood and shook the man's hand. "Thank you. It helps knowing what's coming."

"I've been doing this twenty years. I can usually call 'em."

Before they left, Ed had both their phone numbers and all of Erin's insurance information. Erin had collected everything personal from the car, and they were hitting traffic on the same road she'd crashed on the day before.

"Rental car next?" Matt asked.

"How long do you think I'm going to need it?"

"You heard Ed. He didn't think the insurance company will move fast. I'm thinking minimum two weeks."

"I need to look at my finances. Besides, I'm not in a hurry to drive right now."

Matt glanced at her. "You're going to need a car."

"I know. But I can put it off for a few days. And if the insurance company says they're going to fix it instead of writing an insufficient check, then I can afford to rent something for a while. If not, then I'd rather spend that money on something else." She looked out the window and muttered, "I don't have any more shoes to sell."

"But you're going to be okay, right?"

She nodded. "I have some money saved. I want to be smart. The old me would have been all, 'Let's go rent something.' The new me is trying to be responsible. And since I work from home and don't have to leave the house every day . . ."

"I get it. That's smart. And besides, you have me."

She smiled for the first time in the past hour. "When did that happen exactly?"

Matt laughed. "At the risk of sounding like a drunk in a bar, I'll say it was when you said, 'Hello, my name is Erin.'"

"That was at Christmas." She sounded surprised.

"What can I say? I'm a sucker for sad eyes with a beautiful smile."

She stared in her lap. "I really want the sad eyes to go away."

He placed his hand between them, palm up.

Erin laced her fingers with his.

The sadness was starting to dim. She just needed more time.

~

It took three days before a lack of car became a complete pain.

Ed was right. The insurance company wasn't in a hurry to make any final decisions.

Her income was paying her bills, barely, but she knew bigger ones were coming. Renee was a bleeding heart for the abused wife, and Erin knew she was being given a big discount taking into account she was going to try and make Desmond pay for her attorney fees. But Erin knew the bill was coming.

She'd sold her shoes and even a few pricy dresses, and the money had given her a plane ticket, a new identity, and enough money to buy a used car and pay her rent at Parker's for almost a solid year. But when she really took a good look, there wasn't enough in her account to keep her going for long. She needed to either work a heck of a lot more, or cut her expenses. Buying her next used car would be completely dependent on the check from the insurance company. Erin wasn't proud to admit that the idea of being broke was foreign to her. Even when she'd left Desmond, she had enough money to get by.

Instead of letting it get to her, Erin worked extra hours over the weekend and accepted another two manuscripts to put in her already busy schedule. The answer was to make more money and not bitch about what she didn't have.

Matt convinced her to join him with his parents for a Sunday dinner, and she welcomed the break. Because he was off the following day, she stayed the night at his house.

The routine they were falling into was chipping away at the deep sadness that had lived inside her for years. She even found herself watching baseball with him and his dad, taking the time to learn the game. Erin didn't see herself wearing a Dodgers jersey or dying her hair blue, but she enjoyed it enough to make a comment or two about the players. Mainly which ones were easy on the eyes.

Matt took her ribbing and offered his own, but never went too far.

When Monday morning rolled around, Erin promised herself she'd get up early and have Matt drive her home so she could get to work.

He threatened to rent a car for her if she didn't do so by midweek.

So when the phone rang while they were drinking coffee, and Ed identified himself, Erin was feeling pretty confident that maybe they had some answers.

That wasn't the case.

"Good morning," Erin said. She placed her phone on speaker and put it on the table between her and Matt.

"Good morning. I have my report ready for the insurance company. But I wanted to call you before I sent it in."

"How bad is it?" she asked.

"Actually, the engine is in pretty good shape. But the bodywork inside and out is gonna be expensive. I've seen insurance companies go both ways on jobs like this. I'm still leaning toward them sending it to the scrap yard."

"Hey, Ed, it's Matt. We have you on speaker. Any chance you found a recall?"

"Well, that's why I'm calling."

Erin's hope surged.

"There wasn't any brake fluid in your car."

"That explains why the brakes didn't work," Matt said.

"So the question is why. We found a hole in the right rear brake lines."

Erin watched Matt for direction.

He shrugged. "So there's the issue."

"Yeah, but since it was late on Friday and we wanted to get this off the blocks, I had two guys looking at it at the same time. And we found the other line with a bigger hole in almost the exact same place."

"That doesn't sound right," Matt said. Concern danced on his face.

"I don't understand," Erin said, mainly to Matt.

"Me either. I came in this morning and took a second look. The hoses were in great shape. Shouldn't have worn out for another couple years. Again, I figured it must be a manufacturer issue. One hose I can chalk up to a bad line, but two that are in the exact same place and clean cuts . . . If this had been a fatality accident, someone would be taking these hoses to a forensic lab to find out what happened so someone could be sued."

"A recall?"

"Has to be. Only other time I saw something like this on a newer car was when a woman got mad at her boyfriend and cut the line on purpose." Ed laughed.

Erin laughed with him for the space of two seconds, then she froze. *Desmond.*

Matt was staring at her. "You know what, Ed . . . can you take those lines off and maybe give us a contact on who to send them to, to look at further?"

"No problem."

Matt finished the call and hung up.

Each breath became difficult.

"Erin?"

"What if this wasn't an accident?"

"We don't know that."

Erin saw just enough doubt in Matt's eyes to scare her more. "He said he would find me if I ever left."

"Let's not jump to conclusions."

She stood, felt the need to move. "Are you suggesting this didn't cross your mind when Ed laughed at the scorned woman?"

"What crossed my mind is that you would jump to that end point. Does cutting a brake line match your ex's MO?"

"I wouldn't put it past him."

"Think, hon. Has anything else even remotely felt off? Anyone following you? Strange phone calls? Anything?"

She couldn't think. "No . . . I don't know. But I know he doesn't have any family in Greece."

Matt narrowed his eyes. "I'm not following you."

"Renee, my attorney. She called last week to tell me he was delaying again because of some family emergency in Greece."

Matt started to smile. "See. He's not in the country. He couldn't do this."

"He could have paid someone to do it." Even as she said it, she knew Desmond wouldn't give someone else the task of harming her. He liked to do that personally.

"Does that sound like him?"

Erin sat back down. "No."

"Deep breath. Okay. There is a rational explanation. We'll find it."

~

Desmond sat across the bar twisting his wedding band and watching people as they occupied the seats in the busy establishment. His patience was growing thin. If things didn't start going right for him, someone, somewhere was going to have to pay.

Slowly each seat at the bar started to fill until there was only the one next to him. Twice someone attempted to sit beside him. Twice he politely suggested he was waiting for someone.

The bartender was somewhere around twenty-five and had tattoos on both arms and a purple streak in her hair. She'd actually introduced herself when he sat down and reached across the counter to shake his hand. He felt strangely violated and didn't offer his name. When she wasn't looking, he wiped his hands on the cloth napkin at his side. At least this shithole could carry off a proper napkin.

He looked at his watch. Almost showtime.

That's when he saw her.

Desmond skirted his eyes to the side and pushed over on his barstool and stared into his drink.

She walked up to the bar and sat a bag on the stool. "Hey, Maddie."

So she knew the bartender.

Maddie turned around and lifted a hand. "Hey."

The woman beside him caught Desmond's eyes and she paused. "Is this seat taken?"

He shook his head. "No, no. Please."

She smiled and slid beside him.

Maddie walked over and pointed at a wineglass. "Chardonnay, or are you thinking red?"

"Better stick with white. Red goes to my head faster."

"Isn't that the point?" Maddie asked.

"I'm meeting someone for the first time, I don't want to look like a professional."

The two of them laughed.

"Who's the lucky guy?"

"A right swipe."

Maddie groaned. "The worst. If you need an exit, let me know. I'll help you out."

The two of them fist-bumped before his companion sipped her wine and looked at her phone.

Desmond waited a minute before he directed his words to his left. "I'm sorry," he said. "What's a right swipe?"

She looked up at him like he'd just landed on the planet. "You're kidding, right?"

"I'm sorry. I shouldn't have asked." He reached for his drink and made sure his wedding ring hit the glass.

She took notice and laughed. "Oh, you're married. I guess that makes sense. It's a dating app. You right swipe when you like the person on the other end." She made a sweeping motion with her hand.

"Oh . . . is that how it's done now?"

"Sometimes."

"And it works?"

"Not very often or I wouldn't be sitting here. Well, I might be sitting here, but I wouldn't be waiting on someone who's late." She glanced at her phone and took another look around the bar.

Desmond forced a sigh. "I suppose I need to figure that out."

She did a double take. "Excuse me?"

He waved his left hand in the air. "I lost my wife in a car accident a couple years ago."

"Oh, damn. I'm so sorry."

"No, no . . . I didn't tell you that to gain sympathy. I just don't want you to think I'm a complete jerk. The idea of dating makes me a little sick. I haven't done it in years."

She looked at his ring. "Well, the first thing you might wanna do is take the ring off."

He faked a laugh. "I probably don't want to date anyone where a ring isn't a deterrent."

She laughed. "That's a special kind of ugly when a ring is a turn-on."

"You're right. So a dating app, huh?"

By now she was turned around in her seat and no longer watching the door.

"It's a way to break the ice. But you might ask a friend to help with a profile. A good-looking widower who dresses nice is the first profile a woman will think is fake."

He made sure his smile was slow, and he met her eyes. She was too short, too curvy, and completely too independent. "People do that?"

"Men trying to scam women out of money. Shitty people are everywhere. Like the one who stood me up."

Desmond lifted his drink. "His loss."

She smiled back. Touched her glass to his. "I'm Grace, by the way."

"Dylan. It's nice to meet you."

CHAPTER TWENTY-FIVE

There were many perks of being a firefighter. The public loved you, kids adored you, women hit on you . . . and the police respected you. And in Matt's case, his station was often a lunch and pit stop for the local sheriffs when they were out on patrol. Add to that his father was retired law enforcement, and Matt never worried about getting a ticket in town.

Right now he was looking up at a uniformed friend, who tossed him a ziplock bag filled with Erin's brake lines.

"That was fast."

"It took Pete less than five minutes."

Draped in a utility belt filled with cuffs, a Taser, a radio, a gun, and everything else a cop needed to stay alive while at work, Ty made a lot of noise as he took a seat opposite him. It was the end of both their shifts. Matt had given Ty the hoses the previous night before going to bed. He must have had whoever Pete was looking at it late.

"The verdict? There's a logical explanation, right?"

"Yeah. Sure . . . Who'd your ol' lady piss off?"

Matt's stomach fell. "What?"

Ty stuck his hand inside the bag and removed one of the lines. "Pete took one look and said foul play. See here?" He pointed at the cut. "If this were worn, it wouldn't have dissected the threads of the tube like this. This is a vertical cut across the threads. Just to make sure, he looked under the scope. The image was clean. Nothing frayed. Nothing the road could re-create with hitting it in just the right spot."

"Jesus."

"Sharp knife and a grudge can do a shitload of harm. Whoever did this was dedicated. The placement isn't the easiest to get to."

Matt stood and ran a hand through his hair. "She was right."

"Any idea who did this?"

"Yes . . . no. She knows." All Matt had was a first name.

"In the right court, this could go down as attempted murder."

Matt started to pace. "Son of a bitch." He looked at his friend. "What the hell am I going to do?"

"Do you think he'll do this again?"

The visceral fear Erin was just starting to shake moved into his veins and took up residence. "She's still breathing."

Ty sat back, crossed his arms over his chest. "If I were you, I'd get a tail on this guy and catch him in the act. And I'd keep my lady close."

Matt raised his arms at the station surrounding them. "When I'm at work?"

"Family, friends . . . I'm happy to take a shift."

Where was Erin now? Home . . . she hadn't rented a car. He was grateful now that she hadn't.

Ty shook his hand and left with the promise of taking an extra swing through Erin's neighborhood.

Matt was an hour away from his shift change. They were drinking coffee and praying they didn't get a run. Matt was doubling the call to fate to let him off on time.

Erin was going to run. He had an hour to find a way to make her stay.

~

227

The sun woke her early. Or maybe it was because Matt hadn't slept over. She slept better with him by her side, and she wasn't sure if it was because he exhausted her before they fell asleep, or if she simply felt safer with him there.

Both, she decided.

She padded around her small home and made a cup of coffee. Because the night had cooled off, the windows were open to let the air in. Jasmine bloomed in a hedge outside her kitchen and added a fragrant scent to the air.

After turning on her radio, and overfilling her coffee with cream, she walked outside in her nightgown and sat under the pergola by the pool. She loved the open space and quiet mornings before the world woke up. Funny, she'd lived on large properties before. Estates with manicured lawns and help, but none were this peaceful.

Her father's home was lacking emotion, and her marital home was a giant nerve she tiptoed around.

This home, the one she was making for herself, she was finding herself. She really hoped nothing was going to mess that up.

From down the street, she heard the roar of Matt's motorcycle and stayed in the chaise she was perched on as he drove up.

She crossed her legs at her ankles and hiked her nightgown up above her knees.

He took his helmet off, placed it on his handlebars, and turned her way.

The smile she was expecting wasn't quite as wide as she'd hoped. "Did we have a morning date?" she asked.

Now his grin grew and his eyes traveled her body from head to toe. "If this is your morning look when I'm not around, then count on me every day."

He sauntered her way, dropped his hands on both sides of her hips, and leaned in for a kiss.

"Mmmm, good morning to you, too," she hummed.

He pulled back, placed a hand on her cheek, and kissed her again. This time with an open mouth and a sigh of his own.

When he'd drunk his fill, he straddled her chair and placed her feet over one of his thighs.

"Did you want some coffee?" she asked.

"No. I had some at the station."

He stroked her leg and slowly lost his smile.

Much as she tried to keep the one he'd placed on her lips just by being there, she felt the air shifting. "What is it? Did you have a bad night at work?"

He shook his head.

She sat forward, put her coffee aside. "What is it, Matt?"

Twice he opened his mouth to talk, twice he shook his head.

"I need to tell you something, but I need something from you first."

Erin was having a hard time getting a read on him. "If you were the girl, I'd swear you were going to tell me you're pregnant."

That had him grinning.

"Do you trust me?"

"You know I do."

He waved a hand between them. "Do you think we have a good thing going here? Like maybe we have a future?"

Now she was really confused. "Everything about us has been fabulous. As for a future . . . I mean, when things are good they keep going and when they aren't they end. You know I'm not in a place to offer more commitment than we have right now."

Matt shook his head. "I'm not going about this right. For the first time in forever I feel a real connection with someone, you, and I'm scared to death you're going to run away."

She covered his hand with hers. "Matt, why would I run . . ." And then it hit her. The only reason she would run. "Desmond." When he didn't immediately deny the sheer mention of her ex, she panicked. "What do you know?"

"The brake lines weren't an accident or a recall. I had a friend at the sheriff's station take a look. They were cut, Erin. The first thing Ty asked was who had a grudge."

The back of her throat constricted, and suddenly she felt entirely exposed, half naked and lounging by the pool. All the while in the back of her mind, she knew this was going to happen. Suspected it at the first mention of her brake problem being an anomaly.

Matt watched as she absorbed the information.

She needed to leave. That's why Matt was talking the way he was. He knew.

"Running isn't the answer," Matt said. Both hands were on her knees and squeezing.

"So I sit back and wait for him to slice something better next time?"

"First"—he held up a finger—"we need to talk to this lawyer of yours. The one who said he was in Greece. She helped you get away from him before, right?"

"Yes." *I need to pack.*

"She knows everything, right?"

I don't have a car.

"Erin?"

"What?"

"She knows everything, right?"

"Yes . . . no. She doesn't know where I am."

"Really?"

"No. We used a complicated paper trail so Desmond couldn't track it." She swung her feet off Matt's lap. "I went through a lot of effort so he could never find me. How the hell did he find me?"

Matt followed her into the house. "What are you doing?"

She didn't know where to start. *Just the essentials.*

"Erin?"

She twisted around and yelled. "What?"

"What are you doing?"

"I'm panicking, Matt. I need to go." Just saying that made her want to weep. "I don't want to. But he won't stop until I'm dead." Her gaze fell to the bandages on her arms. "He did this. He could have killed all of us." She twisted again. "Oh, God."

"Erin, please. Let's talk about this logically. You're reacting and not thinking clearly. What if he wants you to run so he can get you alone?"

"Then at least he won't hurt anyone else."

It was Matt's turn to panic. "No. I won't let that happen." He walked up and grabbed her arms. It was the first time he'd ever touched her with anything less than gentle hands. All she had to do was look at his hands and he flexed his fingers and softened his hold. "You have people here who can help you. We need facts. Is he here in the valley or did he send someone to do this for him? If it was someone else, you won't even know who to watch out for if you leave."

His words started to clear the fog.

Matt kept talking. "If he is here, and we have proof that your brakes were vandalized, then we get your lawyer to slap another restraining order on him. We have police confirmation of foul play and an accident report. We might even have probable cause to bring him in for questioning."

"He has a lot of money, Matt. He won't be in jail for long, if at all."

Matt pushed into her personal space. "Please don't run. I can't protect you out there. But here, with all the people I know, those my dad knows . . . Colin's team. Doesn't that sound like a better chance than you out there alone?"

"I don't know, Matt."

"If your logic is to leave so he can't hurt those you care about, he already knows they exist and will hold that against you. Isn't that why your sister doesn't know where you are?"

Matt was right. Could she forgive herself any less if Parker was hurt, or Mallory, Austin? Any of them? Erin leaned against the arm of her sofa.

Matt knelt in front of her. "Let's call your lawyer."

Erin found herself nodding, and Matt reached around her and dropped his head in her lap.

CHAPTER TWENTY-SIX

Matt waited while Erin showered and then handed her a second cup of coffee while they sat in her living room.

With her cell phone in front of them, she made the call.

He held her hand in his and watched every emotion wash over her face.

"Hello, Renee."

"How are you? It's great to hear your voice. Did you try that beet juice I told you about?" The attorney's voice was like a cheerleader. Upbeat and timed as if she were chanting. And what was up with the beets?

"I'm . . . it's not good. And yes, I did."

In an instant, Renee's voice dropped an octave. "What's going on? Talk to me."

Erin glanced at Matt.

"You know the man I was telling you about?"

"Oh, please don't tell me he ended up being a douche."

Erin smiled for the first time in the last hour and looked at him.

Matt pointed a finger to his chest and mouthed, *Me?*

"No . . . he's a pretty amazing man. You would definitely approve."

"Oh, so what, then?"

"He's sitting right here, actually. I have the phone on speaker."

Renee was silent.

Matt looked at the phone. "Did she hang up?"

"What about the coconut water . . . did you like that?" Renee asked.

"Yes, Renee. I did. I'm okay. Well, right now. I told Matt everything."

"You what?"

"He knows about Desmond."

"Hoookay, and you called to tell me that?"

Erin swallowed hard and had a difficult time finding the right words so Matt jumped in.

"Hello, Renee. Listen. We need to know if Desmond is in Greece. Actually we need to know if anyone knows exactly where he is right now."

"Why?"

Erin found her voice. "Because he found me."

"God no, Maci. Are you sure?"

Matt turned his head, narrowed his eyes. "Maci?"

Erin waved him off. "Someone sliced holes in my brake lines . . ." For the next five minutes, she explained to her attorney what had happened.

"Are you absolutely sure this was foul play?" Renee asked when Erin finished her story.

"Yes," Matt answered. "If we can prove Desmond is in town, can we get a restraining order again?"

"We can ask for one, but if he isn't home or at work to receive it . . ."

Erin closed her eyes. "What do I do, Renee? Do I disappear again?"

"If he knows your new name and your location, then we need to start at zero. There's no point in leaving until we have those things in place."

Matt found himself panicked all over again.

"And until we're absolutely sure this is Desmond, don't tell me where you are or your name. Just in case you're wrong."

"What about a police report?" Erin asked.

"The first thing the authorities are going to ask is if you have a name. You give them Desmond's name and if he doesn't know where you are, you'll be handing yourself over. If we can prove he's close, then yes. Give me twenty-four hours, Maci. Don't go anywhere. If I have news sooner, I'll call."

"Do you think I'm wrong?"

Renee paused. "I don't believe in coincidences. Desmond's unreachable and you start having problems. Remember one thing. He's a coward. He preys upon you when no one is looking. If he's reduced himself to slicing up cars, then he's getting desperate."

"I don't like the sound of that."

"Is your firefighter still there?" Renee asked.

"I'm here," Matt told her.

"Don't leave her alone. Desmond is smart, charismatic, and has a way of making people believe whatever lies he spins. He's a true narcissist that believes his own shit. He won't confront you. He'll be the one who gets you to make the first move and then play victim. And, Maci?"

Erin . . . who apparently had changed her name from Maci . . . glanced at him before answering. "Yes?"

"Have you shared a picture of Desmond to your new friends?"

Erin looked away. "No."

"Now might be a good time. I'll call tomorrow. Nine in the morning my time."

"Thank you, Renee."

"Be careful."

~

"Where the hell are you?"

Desmond pulled his cell phone away from his ear, looked at it as if it were a foreign object, and put it back. "Excuse me?"

"Listen, Brandt, you pay me to be your divorce attorney, and I agreed to deal with the restraining order as it applied to the basis in which your wife asked for the divorce. However . . . and this is a big however . . . I'm not a criminal defense attorney. So let me ask you this question one more time. Where the hell are you?"

"I told you I'm in Greece." Desmond looked out his hotel window onto a golf course in Valencia.

"What time is it there?"

He flexed his fingers. "Is this the goddamn Spanish Inquisition?"

"Simple question."

"Fuck you."

"Attorney-client privilege works really well for shit you did, but it won't cover my ass if you're about to commit a crime."

"What's this about, Schwarz?"

"Maci's attorney is filing an emergency restraining order."

Just knowing he'd gotten under her skin made him smile. "On what basis?"

"Attempted murder."

Desmond couldn't help it, he laughed. "That's a stretch." He reached for his medicine and popped a pill in his mouth.

"Give me proof you're in Greece and I can make this go away."

"Fine." He took a swig of water . . . shook his head.

His attorney paused. "You have proof?"

"I'll get it to you."

"I need it now, Desmond."

"Is that all, Schwarz? I have a date."

Schwarz cussed under his breath. "At one in the morning? Because that's what time it is in Greece right now."

"You're beginning to annoy me. I'm going to hang up, and you're going to do your job. You tell that bitch that's representing my wife that I have assured you I'm out of the country. And if slanderous accusations of my character surface, I'll be forced to sue my wife in order to sustain my good standing in the community." Desmond didn't wait for Schwarz to comment. He hung up.

~

"His name is Desmond Brandt. And he's my husband."

Matt peered at the image Erin had brought up on her computer. So many things caught him at the same time.

First, this wasn't a picture that she had in her files but rather an image she pulled off the internet. A picture from the society pages of the *Chicago Tribune*.

Second, Erin looked like a completely different person than the one in the images she clicked through.

Third, she was more beautiful now.

"My name has been legally changed from Maci Brandt to Erin Fleming. My social security, driver's license, passport—everything—is legal."

Matt glanced over to his brother. They'd called for a family meeting . . . well, one for the immediate people involved, which in this case was Colin, Parker, Austin, and Mallory. And since Mallory was living with Jase . . . Jase was there. Matt had called Grace, but she hadn't picked up. He left a voice mail asking her when was a good time to meet at their parents'. This disclosure of the truth was a trial run. Erin asked that they get through this round and then move to his parents the next day. Considering it was his mom's bunco night and Dad was elbow deep in poker with a bunch of retired law enforcement, he deemed them safe.

"Desmond was—is—a dangerous man. I'm ashamed to say that I stayed with him even though he was responsible for . . ." Her words trailed off, and tears began to swell behind her eyes.

Matt reached over and took her hand in his.

". . . for many broken bones and shattered dreams. I was too frightened to leave and too scared to stay. He threatened to hurt anyone I loved if I left. So when I did, I cut all ties. My sister has no idea where I am or who I've become. My father . . . no one. I moved here because this city is large enough to get lost in and small enough to feel comfortable."

Erin looked around the room. "I'm sorry I lied to you. I hate that I've lied about anything. But I truly had no choice. The people that helped me escape this man gave me a blueprint of how I was supposed to behave. What I was supposed to say. I've stuck to that as much as I could to protect you and me."

Colin met Matt's gaze.

"So why tell us now?" Colin asked.

"Because I think—"

"*We* think," Matt interrupted.

Erin tried to smile.

"*We* think Desmond is in town. Or at least knows where I'm at. I need you to know what he looks like so that if you've seen him or anyone like him, you know to stay away."

"How dangerous is he?" Colin asked.

Erin looked around the room and physically recoiled.

Matt spoke for her. "The leaky brake lines on her car weren't an accident."

Colin swore, and Parker placed a hand on Erin's arm.

Matt explained what Ty had told him to offer weight to Erin's concern.

"I'm sorry. I'm so sorry. I left Chicago, spent time in Washington State, and then came here in the hopes of avoiding this."

"Soooo, what exactly does this have to do with us?" Austin asked.

"He told me he would hurt the people I loved to get to me. And I care very deeply for everyone in this room. It would gut me if he hurt any of you."

Matt noticed Colin shifting in his chair. "Erin's attorney told us to show his picture to everyone. Have any of you seen him?"

The room filled with affirmative nos.

Parker, God love her, sat back and huffed. "What exactly does he think he's going to gain by hurting any of us? This guy"—she pointed to the forgotten computer screen—"looks like he has a lot to lose if he's caught slicing up someone's brake lines. Does he really think you'll come running back if he threatens us?"

Erin paused.

Nausea rose in Matt's throat.

"I'll do whatever I have to. And make him stop," Erin said.

Parker moved forward in her chair and looked Erin straight in the eye. "That's Maci talking. Whoever the hell she was. Erin . . . the woman I've known for almost a year, she's spent a lot of time empowering herself and taking control in her life. This . . . this douchebag thinks he can come in and screw with this family? I don't think so."

Parker squeezed Erin's hand, and Colin looked Matt in the eye. "We need to talk to Dad."

"I know," Matt said.

"Love, greed, notoriety, revenge, or a severe case of mental illness . . . or a combination of all. Those are the motivations of the kind of man you're describing. That's what Dad always says." Colin repeated what they'd been told their entire life. Anytime they'd watched TV and witnessed the truly evil, their father would calmly, and pragmatically, explain the motivation of why people turned bad.

"Right. So we're looking at love," Matt said.

Erin shook her head. "No. Maybe. The first time he hit me was on our honeymoon. A man in love wouldn't do that, right?"

Matt's heart broke all over again. "No."

Mallory leaned forward, grabbed the laptop, and pulled it toward her. "This ex-asshole. He has money, right?"

"Yes."

"What are we talking? Is he rubbin' noses with Buffett or some hotshot that made it big on YouTube this week?"

Erin shook her head. "Not Buffett . . . somewhere in between."

Mallory clicked on the computer while the rest of them talked.

"Revenge?" Parker asked.

"I don't see it. I met him through my father. They both had stock in the same company, went to the same functions. To my dad, we were meant to be."

"The father who wasn't there to help you when you went to him for help," Matt pointed out.

"My dad isn't like yours. He's self-serving. Much as I hate to admit it."

"Vertex!" Mallory called out.

Everyone turned to look at her.

"Yeah, that's the company," Erin told her.

Mallory set her chin on her fist and read. "It says here the company pulls in over 11.3 billion . . . with a *B* . . . in annual revenue."

Matt narrowed his eyes. "That's the company Desmond works for?"

Erin shook her head. "Owns. Well . . . he has majority stock. Which means he has veto power in the company."

"So it's public?" Jase asked.

"Right."

"And your father has stock?" Mallory asked.

"No. He signed it over to us as a wedding present. Gave Desmond the inch he needed to control the company. My father told me I was set and would never have to worry about something as dirty as money."

Matt felt his brain starting to itch.

"He really said that?" Austin asked.

"My father has stock in a lot of very lucrative businesses. His only real job is investing and making money."

Jase blew out a breath. "I'd like in on that action."

Mallory nudged him. "Not at the expense of your soul."

"Your ex has stock? Or you *both* have stock?" Parker asked.

Matt felt his head bopping from one person to another like a tennis match. Only he didn't watch that kind of sport.

"Him . . . only my attorney thinks the stock was in both our names. One of the hiccups in the divorce. I walked away. I didn't want any of it. But Renee thinks the stock belongs to both of us. We're still investigating that."

"You don't know?" Austin asked.

Matt had the same question.

"I didn't care," Erin said. "I went from my father taking care of me to Desmond. I went to college but never truly understood what I was going to do with my life. I got married and became a punching bag." Erin looked at Matt for the first time in the conversation. "Then I had one life goal. Get away from the narcissistic monster before he killed me."

Considering all the parts she'd left out of her tale for those at the table, Matt considered what she said an understatement. Erin escaped with her life and was happy for it.

"Narcissist?" Mallory asked.

Erin moved her gaze to Mallory. "Yes."

"You mean he believes his own lies?" Mallory's major in college was psychology.

Erin shook her head and closed her eyes. "He could run through a red light and by the time he stopped at the next, convince himself, and anyone else in the car, that the light was yellow . . . maybe orange, but he didn't commit a moving violation." She paused. "He's that good."

"You fell for that?" Austin asked.

Matt wanted to hit him . . . but the kid was barely shaving.

"I'm not proud, Austin," Erin said.

Mallory sat back. "A narcissist looking to keep power. I don't think we've gotten to that chapter yet, but it doesn't sound good."

"I'm pretty sure my father gave the stock to him. That's what I was told."

"By the narcissist who didn't run the red light?" Mallory asked.

Erin blinked several times as if the computer in her brain finally started to reboot after an update.

CHAPTER TWENTY-SEVEN

"I found her." Desmond pulled out every emotion he could as he spoke.

"Is she okay?"

"It's gotten worse, Lawrence. She's changed her name, her identity. And now she's hurting other people. I don't know what to do. I've lied to my lawyer in an effort to find her, and now that I have I'm afraid it's going to backfire."

"Where is she?"

Desmond wasn't about to disclose that. "I have an in with the people she's deemed her new family."

"New family? What are you talking about?"

"A family. A new sister . . . two, actually, and a brother. She has a lover." Desmond sobbed. "I don't care. I don't care. For better or for worse. I'll take care of her. Make sure she gets the help she needs."

"Let me help. Maybe she'll listen to me. I am her father."

"I have this . . . Dad. Now that I've located her I'll bring her home."

"Desmond . . . I really think we should do this together."

His father-in-law saw it his way. "Give me a couple of days. If I can't convince her, I'll call you."

"Desmond—"

"Thank you for your help."

"Desmond!"

He clicked off the line, tossed his phone on the vanity, and straightened his tie.

~

The weight of the world lifted from her shoulders.

It was barely nine thirty and Erin was crawling into bed feeling like she could sleep for the next month and be just fine.

Matt emerged from the shower with one towel tied over his hips and another in his hand.

He took one look at her and stopped drying his hair. "You okay?"

"I'm exhausted."

"That makes two of us." He ducked back into the bathroom, lost the towel, and emerged in his boxer shorts.

Erin scooted over, leaving room for Matt to crawl in beside her. Once settled, she burrowed into the crook of his arm and latched on.

She could lie with her ear resting on his chest, listening to the beat of his heart . . . the air moving in and out of his lungs . . . for hours and never tire. Matt ran his fingertips along her arm in slow strokes. When he kissed the top of her head, Erin sighed.

"Thank you," he said quietly.

"For what?"

"For trusting me . . . us. We're going to get you through this."

"I . . ." *don't deserve you.* She shook the negative thought away before she said it out loud. "I come with more baggage than a reality star on *Paradise Hotel.*"

He chuckled. "You're worth it."

She lifted her head to see his eyes. "Really, Matt. I should be apologizing. I brought all this on you and your family just by being here."

"You can apologize, but I'm not going to accept it. You aren't the problem, *he* is. Taking him out of the shadows and giving us a face and a name to the person who has haunted you gives you the power. If he's in this town, we'll find him." He kissed her forehead and encouraged her to lie back down.

Erin sighed in the comfort of his arms. "And then what? It's not a crime to be here."

"We file a police report, give them Desmond's name, location, and history. The only business he has here is to screw with you. He took it to a new level when he targeted three other women in this family. He might have gotten away with what he did to you all those years, but he won't get away with this now."

"Right after I left, when I was absolutely certain that everyone I came in contact with could see through my fake name and bad hair color, I would dream about him finding me. Each time he dragged me away from the life I was trying to create and lock me in the house. Only recently did those dreams change."

Matt held her tighter. "How so?"

"I pull away . . . yell and scream. I fight back. In my dreams I fight back. I never did when I was with him." *Not once.* Every day she told herself she would, and every day she cowered and protected herself by lifting her arms to keep her face from taking the brunt of his attacks. When he was done she would clean herself up, put on broad-rimmed sunglasses, and avoid anyone she knew. She adopted lies about her injuries and knew when people saw through her.

"Your dreams should be a testament to who you are now. Maci was a victim. Erin is a fighter."

Something about Matt's statement punched right into her solar plexus. Gooseflesh rose up her spine and down her arms. Once again she lifted her head from his chest and looked at him. "You really think so?"

Matt smiled. "Don't you? Maci took the path of least resistance. Even if it involved pain. Erin forged her own path and isn't afraid of saying no." He pressed a finger to her chest. "She's pretty badass, if you ask me."

Not once in her entire life had anyone ever referred to her as *badass*. "You make me feel things I never have before."

He reached for her face and tilted his head. "I don't hold the monopoly on that."

Erin reached for his lips with hers and fell a little deeper into the vortex she called Matt.

~

"You have nothing on this phone. How is that possible?" Grace sipped on her second glass of wine while they waited for their food. Already her cheeks were flushed and her laugh came easy. The phone he'd purchased two weeks before was free of everything but what the manufacturer loaded in at the factory. Grace attacked it with both thumbs as she downloaded a dating app to help Dylan discover the love of his life.

"I find people who spend all day on these things annoying."

Grace shrugged. "A sign of the times, I guess. Human contact is taken in small doses."

Desmond frowned. "That's unfortunate. I'm rather fond of human contact."

Grace looked over the top of the phone and grinned. "If you're going to flirt with me, is there a reason to download this?"

Women are so easy.

"You're much too put together for someone like me."

Her brow furrowed. "Pretty sure that's a line." She went back to clicking away on the phone.

"I might have a few I can dust off and use," he teased.

She rolled her eyes, and Desmond's jaw started to hurt as he ground his teeth together. Nothing was more disrespectful than an eye roll.

"We need a picture." Grace lifted the phone and pointed it at him. "Smile."

"We're in a restaurant." *A five-star one at that.*

"People take pictures of their food all the time. Smile."

He put a hand in front of his face. "We can do that later. Outside."

She relented. "Okay, fine. What are your hobbies?"

The waiter showed up with their salads, which forced Grace to set his phone down. When she turned to ask the waiter for more water, Desmond slipped the phone off the table.

She filled her fork with lettuce and lifted it to her mouth. "I saw that."

While she chewed, Desmond talked. "What are *your* hobbies?"

For three courses he asked questions and she answered them . . . elaborately. She spent time at Dodgers games and occasionally camped with her family. Once she mentioned her brothers, Desmond pried. He already knew about the man screwing his wife. The other one, he'd seen going in and out of the property where Maci lived. The home with gates and cameras and signs that said "No Trespassing" and "Beware of Owner." Why couldn't Maci have rented a normal home on a simple street? One where he could walk in the back door and drag her back where she belonged.

"I feel like I lost you right then," Grace said, bringing him back to the room.

Desmond put his fork down, found the smile he'd placed on his face since walking in the restaurant, and did all he could to direct it at Grace. He knew how to make her believe she was the only woman in the room. "I'm fascinated. A successful woman who's comfortable in her own skin who watches baseball. You're quite a catch, Grace."

She laughed a little too loud, and Desmond had to stop himself from looking around the room to see if anyone was watching them. He hated loud women. Despised them.

"Tell the single men in this town that."

He leaned forward and placed his hand next to hers on the table. "Their loss. My gain."

"That's another line, isn't it?"

"Is it working?"

She rolled her eyes but then brought them back to his.

Yeah, it was working.

They stepped out of the restaurant, which sat right outside the city's mall. Across the street was the only decent hotel in town.

"How about a nightcap?" he asked as he guided her steps. She had consumed three glasses of wine with dinner, assuring him the rest of his plans would fall into place.

"I have to work tomorrow."

"Coffee, then."

She started to look around and he felt the moment slipping.

He guided them away from the people walking on the sidewalk and stopped her by stepping in front of her. "Tell you what," he said. "Let me do this. And if you hate it, we'll call it a night. And if you don't, I'll fill you with coffee and maybe share an overpriced dessert."

Grace tilted her head back and licked her lips.

Desmond placed his hands on her elbows and leaned over her. Kissing was one of the many tools in his arsenal. And it appeared that Grace had plenty of practice. He brought both hands to her neck and stroked his thumbs along her windpipe. So easy.

He let the kiss linger before she pulled away.

"Well? Coffee?" he quietly asked.

She smiled, and he knew he had her.

"Grace?"

Desmond stiffened, and she turned toward the male voice. He glanced over his shoulder.

Two uniformed police officers approached them.

"Hi, Miah."

Grace stepped around Desmond and accepted a hug from the cop. She greeted the second one by name as well.

The desire to shrink away, to go unnoticed, became a physical need. Only one of the cops was looking at him with eyes that only law enforcement seemed to have. Questioning, accusing, and judging.

Desmond lifted his chin and let Grace introduce him. Anything else would have been met with a whole lot of trouble.

Somewhere in the handshakes and names that he quickly forgot, Desmond heard Grace say, "They worked with my dad before he retired."

"Is that right?"

"A lot of us knew Grace when she was in a training bra."

Grace slapped a hand to the cop's chest. "Don't listen to him, Dylan. I never wore a training bra. I went straight to a D cup."

The older of the officers closed his eyes. "Too much information, Gracie."

These men were entirely too familiar with her.

"Fine, fine . . . go away. You're crashing my date."

More kisses to cheeks.

"Nice meeting you, Dylan. Be careful with this one. She's loved in this town."

Grace laughed and made shooing motions with her hands. "Police harassment. Get lost."

As they walked away, she was all smiles. "How about that coffee?"

Desmond lost his fake grin and took a step back. "I can't."

It took time before his words reached her ears. "What?"

"I lied to you." It was time to turn this around. "I can't do this."

She crossed her arms over her chest. "Lied about what?"

"My wife . . . she didn't die. She's divorcing me."

Grace rolled her eyes and dropped her arms to her sides. "You've got to be kidding me."

He took a step forward. "I know. I'm sorry. In my defense, everything else I said was the truth. I haven't dated in years and have no idea—"

"Stop." She held up a hand. "Just stop. What a douche."

"Please don't hate me. My wife is mentally ill and as much as I'm trying to let go, I still feel responsible for her."

"Is that supposed to make me feel better? Do you feel justified?" She shook a hand in his direction. Made giant sweeping motions. "My dad always told me not to date a guy in a suit. The shoe fits." She turned a one-eighty and walked in the opposite direction.

"Grace?"

Her middle finger waved in the air as she strode away.

CHAPTER TWENTY-EIGHT

Twice Erin had woken up in the night with fractured dreams, and twice Matt wrapped her in his arms and reminded her she was safe. Although she hadn't slept the whole night through, she managed to step to the kitchen before Matt rolled out of bed. When he joined her he slipped behind her, wrapped his arms around her waist, and rested his chin on her shoulder. His familiar greeting was something she felt herself craving when he was in the room.

"What are you making?"

"Pancakes."

He kissed the side of her neck. "To help replenish my reserves after last night?"

"Yes and please."

He laughed and moved away to fill a cup of coffee.

"You look like you're feeling better," he said.

"I am. I like that we have a plan that doesn't require me to change my name and deplete my entire bank account on another move."

He leaned against the counter wearing nothing more than a pair of jeans and a smile. "I like a plan that keeps you close."

She walked over, kissed him softly, and turned back to their breakfast. "We have about an hour before Renee calls. I say we enjoy the morning before the next round of chaos."

They sat outside and watched the world wake up while they ate, slowly marking time until they were both watching the clock.

"Don't you work tomorrow?" Erin asked.

"I switched shifts. Until we have a handle on this ex of yours—"

"You need to work."

"Don't worry about me. I'll figure it out."

She glanced at her phone for the time, 8:50. "Ugh."

"We have dinner at my parents' at five thirty. Grace answered last night's text this morning, said she'd be there."

He was making small talk.

"What should I bring?"

Matt's eyes lit up. "Brownies."

"You're going to turn into one of those at this rate."

He placed a hand to his chest. "I'm already too sweet, I should probably share."

As she started to laugh, her phone rang. They both looked at the phone while she answered. "Hello, Renee."

"Hi. How are you?"

"Good."

"Did you like that watermelon cooler I told you about?"

"Yes, I did. It was wonderful."

Matt glanced at her. "What is up with that?"

"I take it your firefighter is still there," Renee said.

"I am."

"Good. I have a lot of news."

Matt reached out and grasped her hand in his. "We're listening," she said.

"I spoke with Desmond's attorney last night and again this morning. Last night he assured me Desmond was in Greece and went on to say that he is threatening legal action if you go forward with another unfounded restraining order."

"Someone tampered with my car."

"I might have suggested that Desmond might need to seek a criminal defense attorney that handles domestic violence and attempted murder." Renee chuckled. "That shut him up."

"Only we don't have proof it was Desmond."

"Right, but his counsel doesn't know that. And I only tell him what he needs to know. Then this morning I received word that Schwarz filed a motion to withdraw from the case."

"What does that mean?" Erin asked.

"It means Desmond's attorney no longer wants to represent your husband in this divorce."

"Can he do that?" Matt asked.

"He can try, but a judge has to sign off on it," Renee explained. "Our clients can fire us without any fuss, but it's a lot harder for us to fire our clients. Schwarz has to have grounds."

"Did he tell you what they were?"

"What he quoted boils down to he and his client don't agree on how to proceed with the divorce."

"Irreconcilable differences?" Matt asked.

"Basically. I call bullshit. I think Schwarz suspects Desmond is up to something and he's cutting his ties so he can't be held accountable."

Erin's head started to spin. "How can Schwarz be held accountable?"

"Okay . . . let's say you were accused of murder and you hired me to defend you. Then you told me, under attorney-client privilege, that you did in fact murder the son of a bitch and stuffed his own balls down his throat . . ."

"Wow, Renee."

"Sorry. A girl can have her fantasies. Anyway. As your attorney I'm legally obligated to defend your innocence so long as that is your wish. I need to do everything in my power to represent you and have you acquitted of your crimes. But . . . if during a conversation you tell me you were *going* to cut off Desmond's balls and feed them to him—"

"You become an accessory to the crime," Matt finished for her.

"Exactly. So Schwarz motions to be removed from the case at the same time we're threatening another protection order. You see where I'm headed here?"

"Schwarz knows Desmond isn't in Greece." Erin looked at Matt. They had already concluded that. "We still don't have proof he's here. We showed his picture to the family last night. No one recognized him."

"I have more people to share his picture with today," Matt told Renee. "My father's a retired sheriff. We know a lot of people in the community."

"Perfect. I'll start the process."

"Thank you."

Erin thought they were through, but Renee kept going. "And another new development."

"What?"

"Your father called my office this morning."

"What?" Shock came in the form of a shout.

"Yup. My assistant spoke with him. He said he knew I was your attorney and that he was flying to Seattle to meet with me."

Erin glanced at Matt and shook her head. "Why? When?"

"Not sure why. When is in the morning. I don't have to speak with him if you don't want me to."

A swarm of emotions she couldn't name washed over her. "He must want something. Desmond probably convinced him I'm sick or something. What was his latest . . . munch-something?"

"Munchausen. And maybe. Or your father may have come to his senses. I've had many clients' family members contact me once they adopt a new identity. Remorse, regret . . . lots of reasons. A dying family member. He's flying in from Chicago instead of sending an e-mail. Which tells me he doesn't want a paper trail for whatever he has to say. I suggest I take the meeting and report back to you. It can't hurt."

"Okay. You're the expert here."

"In the meantime, keep your head up. It sounds like you have a pretty good support system there. You didn't have that the last time. Use it. I might have news by the end of the business day. If not, same time tomorrow."

"Thank you, Renee."

When Erin hung up, she realized her focus was on one of the giant oak trees in the middle of the lawn. There was a steady hum in her veins without her heart beating a rapid tune in her chest.

"You okay?" Matt asked.

"My father always sided with Desmond. I'm sure he's meeting Renee in person to try and threaten her with some kind of legal action or something."

"Don't spend your time worrying about Renee. She seems like a smart woman. I particularly liked how she wants to feed your ex his balls."

Matt always made her laugh.

"I'm pretty fond of that myself," Erin added.

"But I'm fairly certain they house male and female inmates in separate prisons . . . so let's hand him his balls figuratively."

She dropped her head on his shoulder.

~

"You can't fucking quit. I will sue you. Have you disbarred."

"It's a divorce case, Brandt. One where your soon-to-be ex-wife isn't asking for half a house, alimony, or even pain and suffering. Which we both know she rightly deserves. My resigning as your counsel will hardly cause you any financial pain."

Desmond did not see this coming. "Are you accusing me of something?"

"Of course not. I don't foresee any reason for the court to not grant me leave of this case. So between now and trial I suggest you seek a new attorney. You're going to need one."

He ran a hand over his beard. "What the hell does that mean?"

"Your wife's attorney is moving forward with the protective order. I'm obligated to tell you that. Now that I have, I'm done. My final bill will be sent at the end of the week."

"Fuck you. Sue me for it."

"Okay."

Schwarz hung up and Desmond lost it. His phone went flying across the hotel room. It died a quick death and left him wanting something bigger to punch. The dive he'd checked into after Grace walked away was in the San Fernando Valley. The entire place was a pit. But he didn't risk staying in Santa Clarita where the sheriff's department had a close relationship with the Hudson family. That would have been a nice tidbit to know before he approached Grace in the first place.

He realized now that had been a mistake.

But he had this. A couple more days was all he needed.

And new clothes.

Wearing a suit in this town was attracting attention.

He had all the doctors in place back home and an institution ready for his sick wife when they got there.

Only now there was a need for some desperate measures.

Yes . . . sometimes you needed to take matters into your own hands to help the ones you love.

~

Matt didn't bother knocking on his parents' front door. It was never expected and, frankly, frowned upon when he did.

Erin had taken a few extra steps to look her best when they left her house. He knew that only because she put on three different outfits before settling on the very first one she had picked out. They stopped by his place, where he packed a bag with a few changes of clothes and some essentials for an extended stay. And since the Santa Ana winds were forecast over the next few days, he brought a uniform with him as well. He may have managed to switch one of his shifts, but if a wildfire got going, he'd be forced to report. Besides, after speaking with his parents, and especially his father, they'd have to come up with a better game plan than Matt sticking by Erin's side one hundred percent of the time.

Erin straightened the edges of the summer dress she picked out and ran a hand over her hair as they walked in the door.

"You look like a breath of sunshine," he told her.

With the batch of brownies she'd cooked up in one hand, and her hand in the other, Matt walked them down the short hall to the open family room and kitchen in the back. "Hello?" he called out.

"We're out here," his mother yelled from beyond the sliding glass doors leading to the back yard.

Outside, his dad stood in front of the barbeque, and his mother and Grace were sitting under the shade of an umbrella covering the patio furniture.

Grace bounced up and hugged Erin before moving to him. "Sorry I couldn't make it last night," she said with a grunt.

"How was your date?" Erin asked.

"A complete disaster."

"Oh, no."

"It started out fine. We had a great dinner, decent conversation. As it was ending he informed me that he's married."

"Isn't that a question you ask before the date?" their dad asked from his perch.

"We covered the subject and, news flash . . . he lied to me. Story of my life."

Erin draped an arm around her. "I'm sorry."

"Me too."

Matt moved to the barbeque beside his father and looked down at the grill. "Don't get too excited. It's only chicken. Doctor says my cholesterol is high and your mother put me on a diet."

"It isn't like you miss many meals, Dad."

"Wait until you're my age and not running around chasing fires. You'll have a dad belly, too." Emmitt patted his stomach. "This is your future, hotshot."

Matt looked over his shoulder and saw Erin laughing at something his sister was saying. "If my future involves a woman who loves me enough to make me diet so she can keep me around for a few more years, surrounded by my family . . . I'll take the spare tire that goes with it."

His dad lowered his voice. "I like this one, Matt. She's good for you."

"I'm falling pretty fast."

"The feeling mutual?"

Matt nodded. "But it's a little complicated."

"How so?"

"That's why we're here. There's something we need to talk to you guys about. Get some advice."

"Sounds serious."

Matt nodded. "It is."

Twenty minutes later the chicken was off the grill and a summer salad with corn on the cob was dished up.

Halfway through the meal, Matt noticed Erin stop eating. He knew the pending conversation was weighing on her and she wanted it behind them. So instead of waiting for Erin to broach the subject, Matt took a shot at covering the details.

"You're probably wondering why we asked for an unplanned family gathering," Matt said.

"I never need an excuse to spend time with my children," Nora said.

"I know, Mom. But we could use some advice, and more importantly, we want you to be aware of a situation that has come up."

For the next ten minutes Matt regurgitated the conversation he'd had a few times in the last couple of days. First when learning of Erin's past. Then when speaking with her attorney as things unfolded, and then again the night before when they'd talked to Colin, Parker, and her family.

One by one, each of his family members stopped eating and sat back in their chairs to take it all in.

On his father's jaw, a nerve started to shoot against the right corner of his lip. Matt always thought of it as a warning light to his father's anger level. It would twitch, like a tic that someone can't control, until it finally blew.

"So this man is responsible for the accident," Emmitt concluded once Matt finished the whole soap opera story.

"That's what we believe."

"When would he have cut the lines? While we were dress shopping?" Grace asked.

"The garage was compact and dark, so . . . ," Erin said.

"Have you filed a police report yet?" Dad asked.

"We have the accident report. The second Erin identifies Desmond as a possible suspect, he will be privy to her new name and location. So we're waiting on her attorney or evidence that he has been anywhere in town. There are a couple of things boiling."

"Like?" Grace asked.

Erin spoke up. "Desmond's attorney quit. My attorney has filed a second emergency restraining order."

"Sounds like this man is losing his team," Emmitt said.

"He has money. He'll hire a new one."

Matt watched as his father stood and started to pace. "What's his motivation? He can always find another woman to hit. Men like him seem to attract the weak." He looked up. "Sorry."

"No, it's okay," Erin said with a brave face. But Matt knew his father's observation clashed hard.

"He's delayed the divorce . . . why? Are you asking for a hefty check every month?" His dad kept firing off questions.

"No. I walked away. I don't want his money."

"What about him . . . is he asking something from you?"

Erin sat forward shaking her head. "He hasn't asked for anything. But according to my attorney, she recently found that in the discovery, the stock in Desmond's business that my father gifted us is in both our names. She thinks Desmond is setting me up to have to give him my shares."

"What are we talking?" Grace asked.

Matt looked at his sister. "It's a billion dollar company."

"There you go!" Emmitt sat back down. "Money is a powerful motivator. Follow the money and you'll find the criminal."

"So that's a good thing?"

Emmitt shook his head. "Not in my experience. Crimes of passion are something only you two would have to worry about. He'd come after you since you're with Erin. And he'd come after Erin to keep her to himself. When money is the driving force, he's going to do whatever he needs to make it good for him. Which is why the brakes on the car. He doesn't care who he hurts to get to you," Emmitt said, pointing at Erin. "If you own stock in his company and he's afraid of losing it in the divorce, the only way to keep it is for him to inherit it upon your death . . . or somehow deem you psychologically unfit."

Matt exchanged glances with Erin. "Munchausen," he muttered.

"Excuse me?" Nora asked.

Erin shook her head. "Why didn't I see this before? He's been building this up for years."

"Erin's attorney explained that Desmond has argued Erin has Munchausen syndrome. Which is a disorder . . . or mental illness, that makes people pretend to have an illness or even hurt themselves for the attention someone gets when ill." Matt grasped Erin's hand and squeezed. "He will try and prove that you cut the brake lines."

"I don't even know where they are," Erin said.

"This man sounds crazy," Nora said.

Emmitt patted his wife's hand. "Crazy, but not stupid. All he has to do is convince one psychiatric doctor that Erin is a threat to herself, she says one thing in a way that can be spun to support the man, and she's put on a seventy-two-hour hold. Then it's all about proving you're not. And the more you yell you're not, the more they think you are."

"Or pay a doctor off," Erin said.

"Damn . . . and I thought I was having a hard week. I'm so sorry, Erin," Grace offered.

All that settled in, and everyone sat quietly. Finally Matt asked, "What do we do, Dad?"

"The man cut the brakes . . . or hired someone to do it for him. He's already crossed the line. We circulate his picture to my friends and yours. We let the family know to be on the lookout. I don't care what your attorney says; you get down to the station and file a report. Offense and defense. Who has the power?"

"The one punching first," Matt said.

His dad pointed at him. "Right."

Matt felt better knowing they had a direction and a plan. Much as he wanted to trust Renee, he trusted his father more.

"So what does this asswipe look like?" Grace asked.

Erin removed her phone from her purse and started scrolling.

"Try not to worry, son. It clouds your head. We'll get you both through this." His dad reached over and patted him on the back.

"Here he is." Erin handed the phone to Grace.

Grace expanded the image and made a choking sound in the back of her throat. Color drained from her face, and she jumped to her feet and ran inside.

"Gracie?"

Matt hurried behind her with the rest of the family on his heels.

Grace ran straight to the nearest bathroom and lost her dinner.

"I hope that wasn't my chicken," Emmitt said, turning away.

Erin moved behind Grace and held her hair back while Nora turned on the faucet and dampened a washcloth.

"Oh, God."

Matt was about to walk away.

"Desmond was my date last night."

CHAPTER TWENTY-NINE

Growing up in a home where your mother disappeared before you reached a double-digit birthday, and your father tolerated your existence by hiring nannies and sending you to camp in the summer, Erin's sense of family was grossly distorted. Now she sat in a conference room at the police station across from one detective and one uniformed officer that was a friend of Matt's. Mr. and Mrs. Hudson sat by her side along with Matt and Grace. The sheer support and understanding from this family rendered her speechless. If this had been her family all these years, she wouldn't have stuck around after the first hit. And chances were, Desmond eating his balls would have been a harsh reality.

Emmitt had told everyone to get in the car the second Grace had rinsed out her mouth. He marched into the station as if he was still in uniform.

For two hours they gave statements and documented everything they knew to be true. And since they couldn't prove otherwise, and it was in their best interest, they moved forward on the assumption that the vandalism to her car had taken place in Santa Clarita prior to the trip into LA.

Grace was painfully silent during the whole ordeal, and when they exited the station, she walked beside Erin and laced her arm with hers. "I feel like such a fool."

It was Erin's turn to comfort Grace. "He's a master manipulator with charm and charisma. He should spend his time writing a book on the art of bullshitting and getting away with it."

Grace laughed at her side as they walked through the parking lot. "You sound a lot calmer about this now than you did earlier."

Erin drew in a deep breath with fresh air. "Walking in there and finally working toward legal action that would actually make Desmond pay for what he's done to me . . . to all of us . . . felt like I'd just run a marathon and won. Yeah, I'll be sore and tired when it's all through, but right now it feels great. He fed on my fear, and you know something? I'm not on the menu anymore."

"Why do you think he approached me?" Grace asked.

"To prove he could. To scare me into submission."

Grace stopped beside her parents' car. "Clearly he didn't expect that you'd grown proper chesticles since your separation."

Erin glanced down at her breasts and started to laugh right along with Grace. She hugged the other woman hard. "It would have killed me if he hurt you," Erin said in her ear.

Grace pulled back, looked her in the eye. "Well, he didn't. And it wouldn't have been your fault if he had. He won't get a second chance."

Kind words, even if Erin didn't completely believe them. "Did he at least buy dinner?"

Grace laughed again. "Yes. And I ordered the expensive wine, too."

Matt joined them along with Nora and Emmitt and clapped his hands together once. "Okay, then. Mom and Dad are taking you to your place to pack a bag. You can either stay with them or us," he told Grace.

"Oh, please—"

"Gracie?" Emmitt's voice stopped the argument.

"Fine. At least the bed in the guest room was my old one. It will be better than listening to you guys go at it and remind me that I'm going to be single forever!"

Matt patted his sister on the back. "I was actually thinking you'd stay up in the main house with Parker and Colin."

"Like that's any better." Grace rolled her eyes.

Nora moved in for a hug. "Anytime you need anything . . ."

"Thank you," Erin said.

"Daily updates," Emmitt announced.

"I really am sorry I brought all this on you guys." And she was.

"Young lady?" Emmitt found his dad voice. The one Erin knew existed in the wild but had never heard before.

"Yes, sir?"

He looked her dead in the eye. All amusement vanished from his face. "Let that be the last time you apologize for actions that are not your own. Do you understand me?"

And then he opened his arms and pulled her into a hug.

~

"I have your father in my office. I think you might want to hear what he has to say."

They'd called Renee the night before to inform her they had proof Desmond was in the area and that they'd gone to the police. Now it was nine in the morning, and Renee had called on schedule.

"He hasn't said anything worth hearing for years. What's changed?"

"Regret is a strong emotion. I'm happy to tell him to take a hike if you want me to, but I'm going to act in your best interest, and right now I think that's you hearing what he has to say."

She and Matt were lying in bed drinking coffee when Renee called, and right at that moment he was staring her way. "Up to you. Listening to him doesn't mean you need to act on anything."

It was time to face her demons. And talking to her father was one of them. "Fine."

"Give me two minutes. I'll be back in my office and put you on speaker."

She held the phone in her hand and closed her eyes.

"Anytime you wanna hang up, the button's right there, babe. It's as simple as that."

"You always say the right things," Erin told him.

Matt winked. "I took a class."

The phone made a clicking noise. "You still there?" Renee asked.

"We are," Erin replied.

"Okay, Mr. Ashland. You're on my time and I bill five hundred an hour."

The deep tenor of her father's voice filled the line. "Maci?"

"I'm here."

"Damn . . . I was starting to think I'd never hear your voice again."

Not the words she expected. "I'm pretty sure that's what you wanted when you told me to grow up and solve my own problems." She threw his words at him so fast she hoped his head spun until he was spitting up split pea soup.

"I deserve that."

"Is there a point to this conversation?" Because she had no desire to fan the flames of the past.

"I called your attorney to make her aware that Desmond had located you. And since your desire to disappear under a new name went as far as to cut your sister off, I knew I was wrong about the man you married. Cutting me off, I understood. I was a shitty father."

"You can say that again."

"Anyway—"

"No. You can say that again. I'm not sure I heard it the first time."

To hear her father take a deep breath and admit it again was worth all the tea in China. "I was a horrible father. I didn't deserve you or your sister and didn't realize how empty my life was until I was following

Home to Me

Desmond down the crazy hole and believing that he was right about you."

"Which was?"

"He said you were sick and that he'd been hiding your illness since you married. When Helen showed up on my doorstep a month after you left, she ripped into me. Blamed me for every bruise. She showed me letters that you'd sent to her the week you left."

Erin remembered the letters well. It was her goodbye to her sister in writing and a warning not to try and find her or risk Desmond using her as bait, or locating her, which would have devastating results. Each letter outlined, in order, what a nightmare her marriage was. It wasn't evidence so much as a testimony should something happen to her. Erin knew Helen would fight in her memory if it came down to that.

"I'm sorry I didn't listen to you, Maci. I truly am."

Erin closed her eyes. "I'm not ready to accept your apology."

"That's fair. The fact that you're listening to me is enough. Now, other than hearing your voice and assuring your sister that you're safe, I came to your attorney's office to lend emotional support, if you'll have it, and financial—"

"I don't want your money."

Renee cleared her throat. "Five hundred an hour, Maci. Take the money."

Now wasn't the time.

"I also have some insight on a few things," her father said.

"This is where it gets good. Listen up," Renee said.

"I brought Renee a copy of the gift I gave you and Desmond in regards to Vertex. Collectively you and Desmond own fifty-one percent of the shares of the company."

"I know that."

"*Collectively.* Independently you own twenty percent and Desmond owns thirty-one. I gifted the shares to you as an inheritance. This isn't

267

something Desmond can take from you when you divorce. I did see that as a problem for the daughter of a wealthy man."

"Desmond told me it was a dowry and you gave it to him."

"I gave him the right to be able to control Vertex, which you showed no interest in doing, but the shares belong to you."

"That's not how it was explained to me."

"I really should have insisted that you take business classes in college," he said. "Anyway, since you filed for divorce and your sister gave me a come-to-Jesus moment, I have slowly started buying out or trading shares of my other holdings and now have thirty-three percent of the total sprinkled about under various names. You're not the only Ashland who can make up names."

"To serve what purpose?"

Her father sighed. "I live in a financial world. I'm not known for going into a bar and starting a fight to flex my weight. I am, however, gifted in the art of corporate takeovers. You and your sister now own fifty-three percent of Vertex and have the ability to kick out the CEO and replace him with someone mentally competent."

Erin's jaw dropped. "You're kidding."

"I suck at being a dad," he told her. "But I'm pretty good at being an asshole."

Matt squeezed her hand.

"I'm looking at the paperwork from the wedding gift, Maci. This is ironclad. I'm sure Desmond knows this and that's why he's losing it."

Matt spoke for the first time. "Once Desmond finds out he's been removed from the corner office, it will make him even more dangerous."

"Who's this?" her father asked.

"My name is Matthew Hudson, Mr. Ashland. And I have no qualms about flexing my weight with fists if it means protecting your daughter."

Erin smiled at the sentiment and lifted his hand to the side of her face.

"You have a valid point, Matt. Which is why Mr. Ashland and Helen haven't announced anything yet," Renee told them.

"I've spoken with the authorities both in Chicago and California. We think it's wise to lure Desmond back to the office where we can keep track of him while this becomes public knowledge. Which might be the best way to keep you safe."

Erin's brow furrowed. "How did you know I was in California?"

"You were spotted in LAX back in May. I might have hired a few dozen people to find you."

"Dad!"

"I'm sorry. I know it's not what you wanted, but I had to know that Desmond hadn't found you first."

"He did find me."

"Yes, I know. It's against my nature to ask permission but in this, I am. I'd like to come to you and escort you back to Chicago—"

"My life is here now." Erin looked at Matt as she spoke. "There are people here who love me."

"It's not forever. It's to lure Desmond away from those you care about."

"I need to think about this."

Matt nodded his approval.

"I'm on standby."

A gust of wind rattled the bedroom window.

Erin sat in an awkward space of not knowing how to say goodbye.

"I'm not in a position for asking favors," her father said. "But I'm going to anyway."

"Okay . . ."

"Call your sister."

Erin placed a hand to her chest. Could she? "Renee?"

"Cat's out of the bag. No reason not to now."

Just the thought of her sister's voice had tears in her eyes. "Thank you."

"I'll check back with you at the end of the day," Renee said. "This is all good news. But watch your step. If Desmond gets wind of any of this . . ."

"I know. Trust me. I know what the man can do when he's angry."

Matt picked up the phone. "Thank you, Renee. Mr. Ashland. We'll be in touch."

After the call ended they both stared at the phone.

"I can call Helen!" Erin leaned forward, kissed Matt, and grabbed the phone.

She dialed the phone and put it to her ear.

"Hello?" The second her sister's voice came over the line, Erin started to cry and Matt walked out of the room.

"Helen, it's me."

"Maci? Maci!" Helen all but screamed her name. "Are you okay? Please tell me you're—"

"I'm fine."

"Did he get to—"

"No, Helen. Well . . . not . . ." She didn't want to get into all that. Not yet. "It's so good to hear your voice."

Helen started to sob. "I never thought I'd hear from you again."

"That makes two of us."

"What changed?" Helen sucked in a breath. "Oh, no. No, no, no . . . he found you. Christ, he found you, didn't he?"

Much as she wanted to deny it, for ten minutes, Erin explained what had happened.

"I'm protected. I have such a strong support system now."

"Where are you? I want to come see you."

"I need you to hold off on that. We know Desmond is close by. You coming would give him a new target. Once the police get ahold of him, it will be safe for you to come."

"I want to see you, safe or not." Her sister always was more direct than she was.

Instead of encouraging that, she said, "I spoke with Dad."

"Did he tell you about the stocks?" The change of subject worked.

"He told me everything. It's like I wasn't talking to the same man."

"After you disappeared, I went off on him. Apparently something I said stuck. At first I think he passed me off as being dramatic. Then Desmond got in touch with him and started in on your mental illness. That's when he realized how serious the issue was. He assured me he was working with private investigators to find you, and then he told me about the stocks."

"How do you feel about all that?"

"Sis, I'm willing to do some jail time to put a dent in that man. Hitting him in the pocketbook is the least I want to do. But it's legal and it will hurt, and my babies need me."

Erin curled into herself on the bed and talked about her niece and nephew for the next hour. By the time she hung up, she was sitting on the floor by an outlet with her cell phone plugged in and talking about Matt and Parker and Colin and everyone. Their conversation jumped back and forth from Desmond, to Erin's new life, to Helen and her family. In the end Erin promised to check in daily, even with a text, to let her know she was all right.

When she hung up, she realized it was long past time to hit back. And if returning to Chicago was a step in that direction . . . that's what she needed to do.

But her home wasn't there any longer. So her return would have a purpose and a round-trip ticket.

CHAPTER THIRTY

Desmond may have been on vacation, but he always checked in. As any good CEO would. He looked in the mirror as he called in to the office. The man staring back looked nothing like him. The normally trimmed beard dangled after only a few days without a trim. He wore a godawful baseball cap, short-sleeved T-shirt, and pants that belonged on someone in the armed forces instead of a boardroom.

He'd found a hiking trail that backed up to the property Maci lived on, and with a pair of binoculars, watched from a charred hillside.

She was never alone.

He nearly caved and hired help to put this problem to rest. Easy to do when you found the seedy side of the block. Only he didn't trust that the job would get done without implicating him. Then, as evidence that he was right in his desires, the weather forecast devastating winds.

What went better with winds in California than a tossed cigarette on the freeway? Means justifying the end and all that.

For today, he looked past the mess that reflected back at him and promised himself a trip to his tailor when he returned home.

"Good morning, Keller." See . . . he was a great boss. Even greeted his secretary with pleasant salutations.

"Mr. Brandt. Yes, good morning."

"How are things stacking up in my absence?"

Desmond listened for ten minutes while Keller rattled on about corporate accounts and a strike in the shipping that came in from China. He had people in every department to deal with all the issues, which he pointed out once Keller stopped rambling.

"Sounds like I've got everything under control," he told Keller.

"Yes, of course you do, Mr. Brandt. I was told to inform you, when you called in, that there is a shareholder meeting scheduled for Friday."

Desmond rubbed the bridge of his nose. "Right. Well, my business in Greece isn't over yet. Tell them to reschedule."

Keller paused. "Uhm, about that. Yes, they told me to inform you that the meeting will go on with or without you, sir."

Desmond dropped his hand and stared at his reflection. "Who are *they*?"

"Sir?"

"They . . . who are the *they* who told you to inform me of anything?"

"Mr. Forrest's assistant said it came from him."

Forrest . . . his chief financial officer. "Put me through to him."

"Yes, sir."

His call was picked up immediately.

"So you're not dead." Forrest didn't sound happy.

"What the hell is going on there? I leave for a simple vacation and suddenly people are telling me what to do?"

"You've been gone for weeks. We're not Europe. We don't close down for the season."

Desmond wasn't about to be chastised by a man beneath him. "Reschedule the shareholder meeting."

"I can't do that. I'm not a shareholder . . . just the CFO."

"Tell Al to do it." His VP of operations did most of the legwork and held a small percentage of the company.

"I don't think that's going to happen. Al's been out all week. Some kind of stomach thing."

"Damn it, Forrest—"

"Before you start cussing at me, I think you might want to know that there aren't as many names on the list of shareholders as there were six months ago."

"What are you talking about?"

"Less. You know. People buy and sell every day."

Desmond's palms started to itch. "What are you suggesting?"

"I've seen this before. Shareholders demand meetings when big changes are coming. I have to know . . . Did you sell out?"

"Sell what? My company? Are you mad?"

"Hey, I had to ask. Someone is forcing this meeting, and if you're not here to represent, there's no telling what can happen."

"This is pissing me off."

"It's scaring the senior staff. Some are whispering takeover, and others are looking for new jobs."

"There's no damn takeover. I own fifty-one percent of Vertex. It's business as usual. Tell Al to get back in the office and puke in his private bathroom. I'll be back by Friday to remind everyone that I own Vertex and if they want to keep their jobs they'd do well to remember that." He hung up the line. "Fucking hell."

~

Austin walked up to the massive dining room table that sat in the front of the house with windows that overlooked the entire property. In his hands was one of the shotguns the Sinclairs owned. He set the gun down and looked up. "I really don't see the problem. I may only be eighteen, but I do have balls. Parker could outshoot anyone and Erin's not going quietly. And if that's not enough, Colin will be home before dark, right?"

Colin nodded. "He's right, brother. We've got you covered."

"It's been quiet," Erin told him. "Go to work. I really want you there on Friday, and if you take off now, someone is going to start bitching."

They'd made the decision together. Something Erin was adamant about. He tried to explain that this was all her. And that he'd support whatever she wanted to do. But it wasn't until they'd debated for hours that they concluded the best thing to do was take her father's offer and get Desmond out of her life once and for all.

He didn't like the thought of leaving her until Desmond was accounted for.

"I hate this."

"Wait until you're standing with me in front of the media when we make our announcement. Then you'll really know what hate is."

He'd been warned.

"Fine. I'll call in. Let them know I'm available." Otherwise he had to report first thing in the morning. With the winds blowing with gusts upwards of fifty miles per hour, he really hoped they could ward off any sparks until it all died down.

As they walked out of the main house and down to the guesthouse, Matt took a shotgun with them. Austin stopped him and handed him a box of shotgun shells. "Change it out. It has snake shot in there."

Matt thanked them and said good night.

Outside, ash from the previous year's fire blew everywhere. The familiar smell actually put a smile on his face. He would always be a firefighter. It was truly in his blood.

Inside Erin's house, he closed the door behind them and set the alarm. He dropped the gun on her kitchen counter along with the box of ammo as Erin walked behind him and wrapped her arms around his waist.

He paused in that moment and smiled. "You feel so good."

"I'm going to be all right."

"You're going to be better than all right. It's me who's a mess."

"Well, don't let me distract you from your job. You need to be focused out there to come home to me."

He twisted around and settled his arms on her shoulders. "I can say the same to you."

"What do you mean? I'm not going anywhere."

"You're going to be a rich woman again really soon. It's me who wants you to come home to me."

"Oh, Matt. Are you actually worried about that?"

"It's crossed my mind. I clicked through those society pages. That isn't the kind of life I can offer you here."

She pressed both her palms into his chest and flexed her fingers. "I walked away from that life willingly."

"But you're stepping back into it."

"Only to get Desmond out of it. I'm not going back to overpriced salads at the country club and dinners with pretentious people who smile to your face and lie about their wives' black eyes."

"I'm sure they weren't all like that."

"No. But they happily looked the other way when it was me. I don't know what I'm going to do with the money. Helen and I have a lot to talk about. But Vertex doesn't need its shareholders present to run. My dad is an expert shareholder but he doesn't know squat about running every company he has stock in."

"When did you get so smart?" he asked as he brushed hair that had fallen in her eyes.

"When I stopped being too scared to live," she told him.

"I'm never going to be able to compete with that life, Erin."

She placed the palm of her hand on his cheek. "I fell in love with you as a poor woman and I'll still love you as a rich one. Money didn't create us and it won't destroy us. And if at any time it is trying to do that, I'll walk away from all of it a second time."

Did she just say what . . . "Say that again."

"The poor woman bit?" she asked, smiling.

He lowered his hands to her hips, lifted her up, and set her on his favorite spot on her kitchen counter. "Again . . . this time with meaning."

She giggled. "I love you, Matthew Hudson."

He closed his eyes and soaked in her words. "Damn, that's sexy."

"Well, don't leave me hanging."

He lowered his lips to hers and kissed her until she was pliant in his arms. Only then did he whisper what she had to already know. "Come home to me and I'll tell you how much I love you every day and show you every night."

She wrapped her legs around his waist and scooted to the edge of the counter. "Let's start the showing part now, shall we?"

Matt lifted her off the counter and carried her into the bedroom.

~

At two in the morning his phone rang, waking him up.

It was his captain. "We need you. It's blowing up off the five in Castaic." Arwin told him where the command station had been set up and where to report.

Matt looked over at Erin, concern for her safety caught in his throat. "I'll be there as soon as I can."

Erin rolled over and flung her hand out across his chest. "What's going on?"

"There's a wildfire. I have to go."

She leaned up on her elbow and blinked several times. "I can make coffee."

Matt leaned over and kissed her. "No time. Go back to sleep. I'll call you as soon as I can, which might be a while. Don't worry."

She was already blinking heavy lids. "Please be careful. You have someone to come home to."

That was never going to get old.

"I'll set the alarm behind me. Go back to sleep."

He didn't need to tell her twice.

He fumbled around with minimal light and wished he'd insisted that Scout sleep down in the guesthouse with them. First thing Matt was going to do once this fire was out . . . go to the shelter and pick out a dog for Erin.

~

Everything in the main house was dark. The motion lights outside would pop on with every gust of wind, giving way too much light to the property. Using night scope binoculars he bought online, he watched lights go on and off inside Maci's house.

When her boy toy slipped out the front door and started up his truck, Desmond knew his plan was going to work. Simple people were so easy to manipulate. He just needed to take his time and not rush anything. Give time for Maci to fall back asleep and Fire Boy to make it to work, and he wouldn't be an issue for hours if not days.

Desmond patted himself on the back. He was actually pretty good at this. The only risk was the boyfriend not reporting to work. But if the fire was big enough, they'd all come in.

Thirty minutes slipped by in painstaking seconds. It took another ten to cut the power and the landlines that worked the alarm system to the house. The lack of emergency lights flickering on and off shot adrenaline down his spine.

Still he waited. No sign of activity in the main house . . . and everything was dark at Maci's. It was after three in the morning. It was time to end this.

He had a plane to catch.

~

A tree limb slapped against the side of the house with a continual beat. The minute Matt had closed the door behind him, Erin had dozed in and out of wakefulness. She managed about thirty solid minutes but the tree kept thudding. Finally things calmed down and the lights outside stopped flickering.

The next time she opened her eyes she realized her alarm clock had gone dark.

The tree outside stopped making noise, and the rush of wind died. Beside her bed, her phone lit up and vibrated. She glanced at the alert on the screen.

System offline.

She shook her head and sat up in bed. The power was out and the alarm was shooting a bad reading. Erin didn't need more than that. Even though she figured she was overreacting, she'd rather be safe than sorry.

She swung her feet off her bed and used the flashlight from her cell phone to locate her slippers and bathrobe with the intent of walking up to the main house.

Matt's discarded shirt from the night before lay in a crumpled heap on the floor. Picking it up, she brought it to her nose and sucked in a deep breath. "Be safe," she whispered to herself.

Not wanting to be mistaken for an intruder, Erin walked into her living room with her phone in her hand to call Parker and let her know she was walking in.

"Put the phone down."

The air swished from Erin's lungs and she backed up into the wall. Her heart jumped so fast and so hard she didn't think she would survive it.

There, in the shadows of a waxing crescent of moonlight flowing through the windows, was Desmond.

For one nightmarish moment she froze. Just like she always did.

He took a step toward her and his features came into focus.

"Get out!"

He laughed.

"Look who's standing up for herself."

She reached around the door where she thought she left the shotgun.

Nothing.

He took another step in her direction and she found her voice.

Her scream filled the small space of her home, and she tried to put distance between the two of them.

Desmond jumped across the room and slammed his hand over her mouth.

She didn't stop. Opening her mouth even wider, his finger slipped in and she bit down as hard as she could.

Outside the wind howled, and Desmond cussed and pulled his hand away.

Erin tasted blood. His.

And then it came. The blow she couldn't avoid since the wall was on her back.

So many memories surfaced as his hand reached for her throat. She stopped struggling when his words registered. "If they come down here, I will kill them."

Breathing hard, she tried to find her exit. The door was too far away.

Desmond held her tight, but wasn't putting enough pressure to crush her windpipe. He wanted something and whatever it was, it didn't include killing her with his fists . . . at least not yet.

"What do you want?"

"Now . . . that's what I like to hear." With his hand on her throat, he pushed her into her bedroom.

She battled panic. Not this . . . not again.

Desmond picked up her phone that had fallen on the floor. "You're going to call that lawyer of yours and leave a very convincing message."

Her eyes stuck to his. What she saw staring back was a man she hardly recognized. There was wildness there. The kind she once saw right before he would strike her and then flee. Only now it hovered just behind the iris and was highlighted by the way he didn't seem to blink.

Stay calm. "What do you want me to say?"

"Isn't this better? A nice conversation. You're going to tell her that I was right. That you're a liar and can't live with it anymore."

She jerked and he lost his sick smile.

He shoved her on the bed hard and covered her body with his. "We can do this easy, or we can do this hard." He pulled a bottle of pills from a pocket and rattled them in front of her eyes. "You're going to leave the message and then take a little nap. Or we're going to have a psychotic break and play murder-suicide with your new friends."

Did he really think he was going to get away with this?

The crazed depths of his eyes said he did.

Erin found her voice . . . Maci's voice. "Don't hurt them. Please."

"That's better."

He pressed the phone into her hand, and she dialed Renee's number. All the while she willed the woman to pick up, even though it was past three in the morning.

The phone rang once . . .

Twice . . .

On the third ring it went to voice mail.

Desmond kept a tight grip on her neck. "Make it good."

"Renee . . . it's me. I can't do this. Desmond was right. I'm sick. I'm sorry. I don't want to hurt anyone anymore."

Desmond pulled the phone away and ended the call.

"Perfect. Now let's go find that wine you love to drink."

CHAPTER THIRTY-ONE

Matt turned onto the street that would take him to the command post. Up ahead he could see emergency vehicles of all shapes and sizes.

The moment he put his car in park his cell phone rang. He didn't recognize the number and assumed it was someone at the post checking on his ETA.

He answered the phone with action. "I'm pulling in now."

"Matt?"

A woman. A frantic woman.

"Who is this?"

"It's Renee. I just woke up to a voice mail from Maci. Is she with you?"

He slammed on the brakes.

"No. What is it?"

"She said she was a liar and Desmond was right and that she couldn't live with herself. Matt, she didn't sound good."

Matt turned the wheel hard and hit the gas. "God damn it. Did you call the police?"

"I don't have an address, Matt."

He rattled off the address.

"Did you call her back?"

"And tip off Desmond? Doesn't she live with your family?"

"Son of a bitch. Call the police. I'm on my way." He hung up the phone, pressed Colin's number.

It rang.

And rang.

Matt slammed his hands on the steering wheel.

The call went to voice mail.

Thank God the road was deserted at this time in the morning. With one hand on the wheel, and the other on his phone, he shifted through the numbers until he found Parker's landline.

The call instantly said the line was out of service.

He pressed down on the gas and tried his brother's number again.

~

Desmond pulled her into the kitchen.

He blinked several times when he saw a shotgun lying on a table. How had he missed that?

Grabbing it, he tested the weight with one hand while shoving Maci into a chair with the other. "Well, this is convenient."

He dropped to his knees beside her and put the barrel to her chin and at the same time attempted to pull her hand down to reach the trigger.

Much as he pulled her arm, it just wouldn't stretch.

But the fear in her eyes was worth the exercise. "Looks like a nap it is."

He jumped to his feet and kept her in place by aiming the gun her way.

An open bottle sat in the door of her fridge. He grabbed it and then removed a wineglass from a cupboard. "No reason to go out like the lower class. My Maci always drank out of a proper glass. Isn't that right?"

He glanced back to see her looking around the room. He laughed and flopped into a chair opposite her. Placing the gun in his lap, he poured her a glass of wine and set it in front of her. "This will make these work a little bit faster."

"You don't have to do this, Desmond."

He pushed down on the cap and twisted it off. "When did you get so chatty?" He sat the bottle on the table and stared at her. "I really hate the short hair. Did you know that most women commit suicide with pills? I looked that up." Because he was a smart man. He handed her two pills.

She didn't take them from him.

"Open your mouth."

"What is it?"

He smiled now, shoved the bottle in front of her eyes to see. Not that she could in the moonlight. "One of the many you left behind. Look. It even has your name on it. Now open your mouth and stick out your tongue."

She did and he dropped two pills. No use getting bit twice.

He pushed the wineglass toward her. "C'mon."

Without argument, she brought the wine to her lips and swallowed.

He reached for her cell phone and turned on the flashlight. "Let me see."

Maci opened her mouth and lifted her tongue.

"Good girl. Now . . . two more." He watched her closely as she swallowed.

On the third go her eyes shifted to the gun in his lap and he dropped one hand on it. "Don't go getting any ideas."

"How are you going to get rid of me?" she asked.

He blinked a few times until her question registered. "You're just going to die."

"But you hit me. And my neck. There are bruises on my neck."

He lifted the phone and pointed the flashlight at her face.

Well, damn.

"Take two more."

With one hand, he poured the pills onto the table, then picked up two and placed them in her mouth. Slim fingers wrapped around the wineglass, and with only the light of the cell phone he noticed her fingerprints on the glass.

Desmond looked at his hands, then back to her neck.

Well, damn.

Several seconds ticked by.

"How are you going to do it? Is it too much to ask to know what you're going to do with my body?"

"Shut up and take the pills."

She reached for the wine and her hand slipped.

That's when he noticed her eyes losing focus. "Speed this up, Maci. I don't need you passing out before they're all in."

"You should have one of these. They feel pretty good," her voice slurred.

"Maybe next time." Right now he needed to figure out how to get rid of her body and wipe any fingerprints away.

Outside the wind howled. The same wind that kept her lover busy.

Of course.

Fire.

He wouldn't have to clean anything. A fire would destroy it all.

~

Erin lost count of how many pills she had actually swallowed. Most of them were tucked under her leg. Even the wine she was spitting back in the glass. Desmond had stopped checking her mouth with the flashlight. She could see his mind racing around for solutions, and he became more distracted. All of which made it easier to hide the fact that the pills were leaving the bottle but not going in her system.

Still, many had gone down. From the size and aftertaste of the pill, she assumed it was a painkiller. Narcotic. The kind that made her sick to her stomach. Already she could feel her body protesting and her head spinning.

Passing out was not an option. Matt was at work, and no one in the main house knew what was happening. Her only hope was that Renee had gotten the message and called someone.

Banking on that wasn't an option either.

~

Matt skidded to a stop behind three black-and-white squad cars that were parked outside the gates of The Sinclair Ranch. He jumped out of his truck.

"What the hell are we doing out here?"

Ty turned to him and lifted a phone in the air. "We just got confirmation that someone is in the house with her."

"How? Colin isn't picking up."

"Your dad called one of the kids."

Kids? "Austin?"

"Colin can see a flashlight and two people sitting at a table. We told him to back off. SWAT is on its way."

Matt pulled his hair with both hands. "Fuck, fuck, fuck."

"Calm down, Matt. Your brother's close and watching, and we have four uniforms inside the property now. Soon as he knows we're here, we have a hostage situation."

"How long is that?"

"Soon as we're in position, we'll let him know we're here."

Matt looked at his watch. "I've been gone just over an hour. The damage he could do in an hour . . ."

"Phone line and power was cut thirty minutes ago, and we've been here for ten. Colin's eyes have been on them almost the whole time we've been out here."

None of that made Matt feel any better.

Ty's radio went off. Someone on the line spouted codes that Matt couldn't follow.

Another car pulled up behind them. An officer Matt didn't know walked up. "The adjacent neighbors have been evacuated."

"Roll in and take position."

"Air support?" Ty asked into his radio.

"Negative. Weather is not giving us clearance."

Matt cussed.

"You stay here." Ty pointed at Matt.

"Really?" That was not going to happen.

Ty narrowed his eyes. "Stay where I can see you."

Another car joined the party, this one wasn't marked, and one of the detectives Matt and Erin had talked to got out. "Let's do this. SWAT is behind me."

Matt walked slowly behind Ty's squad car, crouched low with the officers flanking the side. With their lights off, they rolled in as quietly as they could. Matt found himself thankful the winds gusted every so often, deafening their sound.

They cleared the wash and stopped their car several yards away from the guesthouse and on the lawn. Another squad car crushed gravel under its tires as it went into the field to keep anyone from fleeing out the back. Not that there was a back door, but Erin did have windows.

His entire body was a tightly wrapped bow with an arrow ready to burst. *C'mon, baby . . . stay strong.*

How he wished Erin could hear him.

~

Something shiny outside the window caught Erin's eye. She rubbed her head and tried to see what it was.

Something ran by . . .

Someone.

Desmond caught her smile. "What the hell are you happy about?"

She forced herself to look away from the window. "I'm higher than a kite, Desmond. What do you expect?"

He picked up the empty bottle of pills and stared at her. "You are, aren't you? Finish the wine. I have to go."

A noise outside turned his attention away from her.

"Is there more?" she said a little too loudly. Erin picked up the half-empty glass and waved it in the air.

Desmond looked at her.

"No use in it going to waste. I know how much you hate wasting good things."

He actually took the bait.

With his back turned, she opened the blinds a little more so whoever was outside could see in.

With the bottle in one hand and the gun in the other, he poured the remainder of the wine in her glass and slapped the empty bottle on the table.

She reached for it, and he yelled, "Guzzle it."

Erin flinched, and the pills she'd shoved under her leg dropped to the floor.

Desmond leaned over and peered through the darkness.

Her heart and breath paused as his eyes moved to hers. "You bitch."

Next thing she knew, Desmond was shifting the gun in his hands, and she grabbed the first thing her hand came in contact with.

She threw the wine and the glass at him. Her other hand met the empty wine bottle, and she brought it up with as much force as she could, making contact with his chin.

Blood went everywhere.

The element of surprise would only last for a minute and then she'd be dead. Erin had one thought, and one thought only. *Get the gun.*

Lights outside blasted the inside all at once, blinding them both.

Erin shook the daze from her head and rushed.

Desmond's grip was loose.

Surprise, shock . . . she didn't know.

Erin grabbed the barrel and twisted.

Desmond grasped the air as she pulled it away.

Her legs came out from under her and she fell to the floor.

Someone outside was yelling into a bullhorn, but all she heard was Desmond calling her a bitch over and over.

Erin rolled over with the gun in her hands and the end pointing at him. Two loud clicks filled the room as she cocked the gun.

"You bitch."

He lunged.

And Erin squeezed the trigger.

~

"Shots fired! Shots fired!"

Matt's entire world came to a screaming halt with the sound of a shotgun blast. "Erin!" he yelled as he started to run.

Someone grabbed him and held him back.

Matt took a swing, made it three steps, and two men tackled him.

Men were yelling. Guns were level with the house.

Cops were swarming, covering, and moving closer to the door.

"Erin!"

A boot hit the door and flung it open.

No one charged out.

Three cops charged in.

Seconds ticked by and Matt's gut started to coil. "No, no . . ."

"We're clear. Someone get a medic."

The two men holding him back let go, and Matt ran.

Blood was everywhere.

Erin was curled up on the floor, her hands covering her face.

He dropped to his knees and touched her.

When her eyes came into focus, she reached for him.

"I thought I lost you. God, Erin. I thought I lost you."

Sobs racked her body until she pulled away. "I'm going to be sick."

EPILOGUE

Two days in the ICU, having your stomach pumped, and drinking activated charcoal was not Erin's definition of a good time.

There were hangovers that cured you from ever drinking tequila again, and then there was this. When it was all said and done, the doctors didn't think she'd have any significant organ damage from the overdose.

Matt had taken up residency in a pathetic attempt at an overnight family chair that lay flat beside her while a never-ending stream of visitors flowed through the room.

Renee made it in on the same flight as her father. Helen and her family showed up less than eight hours later. The entire Hudson family camped out in the waiting room, and Parker, Austin, and Mallory played host. Not that they could house any guests, since apparently the police weren't allowing anyone back in.

In truth, Erin couldn't really tell you what happened the first two days. She saw people coming and going, but she just couldn't deal.

On the third day, the fog cleared.

One of the nurses asked Parker, Matt, and Colin, the three guests allotted at a time, to leave the room so she could shower. Helen popped in to lend a hand. Considering what activated charcoal did to her GI tract, she was never so happy to take a proper shower. She emerged feeling like a new woman . . . albeit one dressed in a blue and white, open in the back, hospital gown. She opted for the chair and not the bed when someone offered her real food for the first time in days.

Only a few bites in and she was getting full.

"That's not enough," Helen chided.

Erin loved her sister's nagging. "It tastes like asphalt."

Helen stood. "Then I'll go grab some of the food in the waiting room. Your new firehouse family really knows how to cook."

"My what?" Erin didn't recall anyone from the fire station coming in.

"The wives from Matt's crew. Tamara, Kim, and Christina have been feeding everyone out there since you got here."

"I didn't realize. That's so kind of them. They barely know me."

"Yeah, well . . . they're a solid group. Loyal."

"Did they come into the room when I was out of it?"

Helen shook her head. "No. Kim said they'd leave off until you were out of the ICU. They wanted to make sure everyone else closest to you was taken care of."

The sentiment had Erin blinking back tears. "Thank them for me."

Helen leaned over, kissed her cheek. "I'll be back."

Voices drifted in from outside the door before a woman walked in the room wearing a skirt, blouse, and holding a notepad.

"Mrs. Brandt? Or do you prefer Fleming?"

Erin shook her head. "Fleming."

The woman pulled up a chair and sat in front of her. "I'm Dr. Reynolds. Your primary doctor asked for a psychiatric consultation."

Erin lost her appetite altogether.

"It's more protocol than anything. Overdoses call for my specialty."

That made her feel slightly better. "Oh."

"I read your file. You've been through quite the ordeal."

She didn't know what to say, how to act, or what to do. "I have."

"It wouldn't be uncommon for you to have some lingering effects after this week. How are you feeling?"

"Numb, I guess. But better today."

Dr. Reynolds nodded several times. "Good. You have an extensive support system out there."

Erin caught a smile sneaking through. "They're helping."

"I'm sure they are. Are you sleeping?"

"With nurses walking in every hour, no. But that isn't what you're really asking, is it?"

She shook her head. "No. I want to know how you're coping with the death of your husband."

Erin closed her eyes and saw everything in living color. When she opened them she saw Matt standing in the doorway.

"My boyfriend's father is a retired police officer, Dr. Reynolds. The first thing he said to me when he showed up at the hospital was that all trained officers were forced to talk to the '*head doctors*' after any shooting. And that I wasn't any different. Probably needed it more considering I had been married to the man. And since I want to recover from this, mind, body, and soul, I should probably get your number and make an appointment once they send me home."

Dr. Reynolds slowly started to smile. "I think that's a brilliant idea." The doctor stood and handed Erin her card. She hesitated next to Matt before leaving. "You must be the boyfriend."

"I am."

Dr. Reynolds reached out a hand. "Thank your father for me."

Matt walked in and took the chair the doctor had vacated. "That the shrink?"

"Yup."

"Good. Maybe my dad will shut up about that now."

It was nice that he cared that much.

"What's up with this?" Matt pointed at the food. "Is that all you're eating?"

"It's pretty nasty," she told him.

"I can sneak you an In-N-Out burger."

That sounded marginally better. But she shook her head. "I don't want to ruin the experience if it doesn't go well. I'll stick with hospital food until I stop burping up charcoal."

"Much better plan. They're talking about springing you free in the morning."

And for one fleeting moment she dreamt of her own bed. "Oh, God . . . Parker's guesthouse."

"About that. Your dad is throwing around some serious guilt money. The sheriffs finished up their investigation this morning, and your dad is insisting on bringing in a team of people to do whatever needs or wants to be done. No one is expecting you to move back in there."

She loved that little house. Even though it came fully furnished, she had made it her own. Erin wasn't naive enough to think she could just walk back in, clean or not, and not see *him* in every corner. Not until she and Dr. Reynolds knocked it over a few thousand times.

"What does Parker want?"

"This isn't about Parker, this is about you."

"It's her house."

"We're all here for you, Erin. You give us the green light and we'll take care of it for you, or let your dad deal with it."

She reached her hand over to his. "Let my father spend his money. It will get done faster, not cost Parker a dime, and make him feel better."

"Perfect. And Grace and Parker will bring your things over to my place."

"They're gonna what?"

Matt looked at the ceiling and then flashed that coy smile that always told her he was about to get his way. "My house. The one you're moving into. You know, so I can come home to you."

Her heart warmed. "Are you asking me to move in with you?"

Matt winced. "I hate to ask because you might say no. Can't we pretend we already did that and you said yes and it's a done deal?"

God, she loved this man. "Since I did promise to come home to you, I guess it would be okay to pretend we already had that conversation."

Matt did a little fist bump in the air. "Yes!"

"You're like a kid who just hit a home run on the Little League field."

"Yes . . . yes, I am." He leaned forward and kissed her. "I love you."

"I love you, too."

He stood. "I need to let some of the masses in before I put them to work." He started out the door and she stopped him.

"Matt?"

"Yeah?"

"Thank you. For giving me someone to come home to."

He blew her a kiss. "Every day that you'll have me."

ACKNOWLEDGMENTS

Every book takes a village. Now it's time for me to thank the townspeople.

Thank you, Amazon Publishing and Montlake, for encouraging me to write the books I want to share with the world. My editor, Holly Ingraham, for finding the pieces that don't work so I can fix them. Maria Gomez, my Amazon cheerleader. Thank you!

My agent, Jane Dystel, thank you for always being there. I'm super blessed to have you in my life.

Thanks to the firefighters everywhere for all the missed meals, holidays, and night's sleep while you're on the clock working to protect people you don't even know.

A special shout-out to my oldest son, Jeremy. My own personal firefighter, hotshot, and hero. You thrive on the chaos and adrenaline and never think twice about helping someone else before yourself. I love you.

Now, on to those women brave enough to share their stories. You—we—fall into one or all three of these categories. Victims. Survivors. Warriors.

To the victims that have yet to find the strength to break away from toxicity: Bruises are an easy identifier of abuse, but many times those scars are on the inside. Neglect and emotional abuse can be just as debilitating. Sadly it often comes from the people we love the most.

Breaking the cycle is the hardest part. But I'm here to tell you . . . it can be done and you will be stronger for it.

For the survivors that severed the link between the abuser and yourself: You've broken away and are trying to piece together the broken bits of your life. Every day you wake up and keep moving means you've survived. It isn't always easy. Working through all the emotions takes some serious dedication and often, outside help. Don't be afraid to ask for it.

And you . . . my warriors: You're no longer a victim and have left the past behind enough to stop classifying yourself as a survivor. No, you're a warrior. Strong on your own two feet without letting the past define you. You're an example to everyone.

There is a reason your windshield is larger than your rearview mirror.

It shows you where you're going, not what you left behind.

Blessings,
Catherine

ABOUT THE AUTHOR

Photo © 2015 Julianne Gentry

New York Times, Wall Street Journal, and *USA Today* bestselling author Catherine Bybee has written thirty-four books that have collectively sold more than eight million copies and have been translated into more than eighteen languages. Raised in Washington State, Bybee moved to Southern California in the hope of becoming a movie star. After growing bored with waiting tables, she returned to school and became a registered nurse, spending most of her career in urban emergency rooms. She now writes full-time and has penned the Not Quite series, the Weekday Brides series, the Most Likely To series, and the First Wives series. For more information on the author, visit www.catherinebybee.com.